AN ALIEN FOR THE FUTURE

A NEW HOME
BOOK THREE

AG WILDE

This book is dedicated to all those humans who've given up on finding that perfect someone.
This is for your future.

AN ALIEN FOR THE FUTURE

Donna

I've been burned too many times to believe in fairy tales. So when this golden-eyed alien, Tovan, shows up claiming I'm his destined mate, I'm not buying it. Sure, he's gorgeous and infuriatingly persistent, but I've got a farm to run and a life to live. I don't need some whirlwind romance complicating things. So, why does my heart race every time he's near?

Tovan

From the moment I saw her, I knew. Donna Johnson is my kahl, my destined mate. She's everything I've ever wanted: strong, passionate, and beautifully stubborn. But she denies our connection, pushes me away at every turn. I must prove to her that our love is real, that we belong together. For without her, my life, my existence, will never be complete.

BEFORE YOU READ!

Hi there!

While this book is intended to be a heartwarming journey, it does contain themes and situations that some readers may find sensitive:

Passionate encounters: This book does not shy away from depicting the fiery and sometimes primal nature of the characters' connection, including an intense mating ritual that involves power dynamics.

Past trauma: The main characters have both experienced significant trauma in their pasts, including abduction, war, the loss of loved ones, and past relationship trauma. These experiences are discussed and explored throughout the story as part of their healing journey.

Possessiveness and dominance: The male protagonist, Tovan, exhibits strong possessive and dominant tendencies, particularly during his mating rut. While these behaviors are ultimately consensual within the context of their bond, they might be triggering for some readers.

Injury: There is a scene involving an injury.
Animal distress: There are brief scenes of animal distress.

My goal is to create a safe and enjoyable reading experience for everyone. If you encounter any content that triggers you or that you believe should be added to this list, please don't hesitate to reach out to me on social media. I'm always open to learning and improving.

Till then,
Happy reading!
 AG

DONNA

Ma once said, "Life's like a game of dodgeball, sugar. Just when you think you've got it all figured out, here comes a curveball aimed straight at your pretty little head. You gotta duck, weave, or catch that ball and throw it right on back. Tough times don't last, sugar, but tough people sure do." She'd set a large slice of freshly made cornbread before me, still hot from the oven. Even now, I still remember how good it tasted.

I stare at the cornbread on the counter before me now. It's nothing like Ma's. For one, it's made from a pale blue grain called grushi, the flour just as blue as the grain itself. The texture's all wrong. Gritty and dense, nothing like the light, crumbly perfection Ma used to whip up. And the smell? Well, it's a strange mix of earthy and faintly sweet, like beetroot. Not the warm, buttery aroma I know so well.

I sigh, cutting a slice and turning it over in my palm. It's been years since I've tasted real cornbread. Sometimes I wonder if my memories of Ma's cooking are just getting sweeter with time and distance, like a faded photograph. All the sharp edges softened, the imperfections blurred away.

And, sometimes, I think maybe I'm too old to be missing my mother's cooking. A soft, resigned laugh huffs through my nose as I stare at the "bluebread" in my palm. Maybe this whole alien abduction thing has me going crazy. Missing things like the sound of rain on a tin roof and the taste of a strawberry milk-shake on a summer afternoon.

"Oh, Ma…" I whisper. "If you could see this now, you'd say I caught one hell of a curveball and ran with it." My gaze slides from the bread to the scene out my window. "I finally got my wish about seeing the world, but you wouldn't believe just how far out I've ended up."

Before me, my kitchen window gives a view of the Hudoian plains stretching into the distance, a sea of orange grass rippling under a pink sky. Soft golden clouds drift lazily towards the horizon. It's beautiful, serene, like a postcard from another world. Which, I suppose, it is.

Just not the one I ever expected to call home.

Lifting the slice of the bluebread, I take a bite, my eyes still on the view. The quiet of the plains grips me. Out there, through my window, not even the wind makes a sound. It's no wonder I'm reflecting on things from long ago, dredging up old memories, old worries. Seeking something…else. Only, I'm not sure what.

I knew I'd be alone in this wilderness, this farm out here in the doohickies, but I didn't quite understand just how…peaceful it would be. How *quiet*.

All I've got, apart from the animals and the soft sound of insects, is my big 'ole voice in my head. All I can do is *think*. And too much thinking has never gotten me anywhere good.

I grunt, chewing slowly as another sigh makes my shoulder rise and fall. My gaze shifts to the view of the road and I sigh again.

For a moment, I don't see anything there—which isn't surprising. No one comes this way. It's the reason the New

Horizons Initiative was so tempting. The whole reason I signed up. They promised peace and safety, and after waking up from something called "stasis" surrounded by aliens in an intergalactic war, peace and safety sounded real good.

I'm about to turn away from the window and dump the entire tin of bluebread when I notice movement on the road. Whoever is coming is still a far way off, but I spot the white fur anyway. My heart does a little thud. A little leap.

It's Xarion, the New Horizons representative who introduced me to this place. I never thought I'd be so happy to see an alien pulling up to my door, but Xarion's my only friend—apart from the two other humans I know who signed up for the initiative.

Plopping the bluebread back on the counter, I cut another slice and put it on a flat square I use as a saucer. I'm out the door and by the gate by the time Xarion pulls up.

"Well, look what the Hudoian wind blew in." I grin at the rabbit-like alien as he comes closer, the ooga he's riding making him sway with each step.

I don't want to admit it, but I'm a little excited to see his expressionless face, and that's saying something. I really am starved for company, aren't I?

"I can assure you, the wind was quite tame this journey," Xarion says. "It had zero effect on my speed of arrival."

I snort. "Mmhm." My gaze shifts over him. He's dressed like he usually is. In a dark suit that makes me wonder how he's not burning up in this warm weather. "What are you doing all the way out here, anyway? Come to check if the wilderness hasn't swallowed me whole yet?"

Xarion hops off the ooga with such grace I want to roll my eyes at him. His feet land on the dusty earth almost without a sound. "I am here on a welfare check." Those red eyes shift to me as he secures his ooga to my fence. "I trust your acclimation to Hudo III continues…smoothly?" He glances at the slice of bluebread in my hand, his nose twitching slightly.

"Oh, it's been a real hoot." I brandish the bread, thrusting it in his direction. "In fact, I was just about to declare this the best darn bluebread on the planet. Want a bite?"

It's hard to hold back my smirk as I hold the food out to him, knowing full well he won't touch it. Not Xarion, with his refined palate and access to the delicacies of a thousand worlds. He wouldn't be caught dead eating something as…rustic as my bluebread.

His nose twitches again. "I appreciate the offer, Donna Johnson, but I'm afraid I'm not particularly…" He pauses, I suppose, to search for the right word.

"Hungry?" I offer, unable now to hold back my grin. "Famished? On the verge of starvation?"

"All three."

I roll my eyes, following his gaze as it shifts down to my little farmhouse.

"You're doing well with the place. The New Horizons board will be pleased."

"Mmhm." I roll my eyes again, pushing off from where I was leaning on a fence post to start walking back down to the house, because I just know what he's going to say next. He's alluded to it many times before.

"They would be even more pleased if, like the other two humans—"

"Xarion, I don't want a man." I don't even glance behind me but I know he's following.

"It doesn't have to be a Kari mate like Eleanor Taylor and Catherine Richmond. Even a female acquaintance—"

I snort a laugh. "Experimented with that back in college, baby. Not my thing. I like cocks. I just don't like what they're attached to." I think that will shut him up. It doesn't. Surprising me, this cultured alien isn't even mildly fazed.

"And why is that, Donna Johnson? Scientifically, you are biologically suited for a variety of male shafts—"

"Xarion!" My mouth falls open as I gape at him. I can't believe he just said that. "Have some bluebread." I thrust the food in his direction again, intent on ignoring the heat rising in my cheeks. "And stop calling me 'Donna Johnson', like I'm in trouble or something. Just call me Donna."

"Right. Humans like when their names are butchered. I remember." Xarion blinks at me as I huff a laugh through my nose before his gaze shifts to the bluebread still in my hands. "Grushi grain?" he asks, and I nod.

"One bite won't kill you." His ears twitch and I try not to laugh again. "Probably."

With a sigh that could rival a deflating balloon, Xarion delicately picks up the slice and takes a tiny nibble. His whiskers twitch, and I swear I see his white fur pale even further.

"It's...quite unique," he manages, swallowing hard.

I snort. "That's a polite way of saying it tastes like dirt." But even knowing it, even expecting him not to like it, my shoulders sag a little. I need this recipe to work.

"Well," Xarion says, and I don't miss that he's discreetly trying to wipe his tongue, "perhaps your culinary skills might improve if you were to...expand your ingredient selection. Have you considered foraging for zimi berries in the pasture across from your farm? They are often used as a sweetening and flavoring ingredient in doughy meals like these."

My eyebrows lift, almost reaching the headscarf tied tight around my head. "What now?" My focus shifts to the pasture across from mine, even as I try to temper the little hope flaring in my chest. The pasture stretches so far, I don't know where it starts and where it ends. "Zimi berries?"

"Quite delectable little things. Though they must be handled with protective gear lest they stain your fur." His gaze shifts down me. "Or rather, your dark skin."

I stare at him for a few beats before I get an idea. "Wait here."

Picking up the long skirts flowing around me, I hurry back inside. There's a satchel I tied together using pieces of linen, one that serves as my grocery bag, and I hurry to take it from where I'd hung it in the kitchen. About a minute later, I'm shutting the front door and turning to face Xarion. Surprisingly, he's finished the rest of the bluebread and is looking at me with one ear high and the other folded.

I snort. "Thought you didn't like it."

"It could be better."

I roll my eyes again. "Come on, you're going to help me forage for these zimi berries."

I march towards the pasture, my satchel swinging at my side. Getting underneath the perimeter fence takes some acrobatics my hips don't like, but I make it. When I look behind me, Xarion is hesitating, his pristine suit a stark contrast to the wild orange grass.

"Donna Johnson—Donna, I'm not sure this is entirely necessary—"

"Oh, come on, cotton-tail." I turn, pushing through the tall grass. "You suggested it, now you're gonna help. Besides, aren't you curious to see how your little human experiment is surviving out here?"

Xarion sighs, a sound I'm becoming quite familiar with, and reluctantly follows. "I assure you, the New Horizons Initiative is not an 'experiment'. It's a carefully planned resettlement program."

"Uh-huh," I grunt, still pushing through the waist-high grass. "And I'm the Queen of England."

We trek further into the pasture, the orange grass giving way to patches of light brown shrubs. Xarion delicately picks his way through, trying (and failing) to keep his suit clean.

"You know," he says, stepping around a bunch of shrubs with burs on them, "the other human homesteaders have been quite proactive in building a community. Because your species is so rare and both of them have turned out to be mates fated to males who thought such impossible, Eleanor Taylor and Catherine Richmond have even started a weekly gathering—"

I whirl around, nearly causing Xarion to bump into me. I know exactly what he's doing. The same thing he's been trying to do from the start. Get me *integrated*. "Let me guess, a book club? Quilting circle? Alien crop appreciation society?"

Xarion's whiskers twitch. "Actually, it's a cultural exchange. Tensions are high among the Kari, so they've been teaching some of the males about Earthkind. Females."

"What does that have to do with me?" I ask, turning back to forge ahead. "They have Kari mates. What they're doing is only logical. I'm sure they're all having a grand old time, swapping stories and braiding each other's tentacles."

"Kari don't have tentacles." Xarion says. When I glance back at him, he's looking at me strangely before his gaze drops to my bum. "Do humans—"

"No, Xarion! I was joking."

His gaze lifts to my eyes. "I see."

I think that's the end of it so I keep on walking. Truth is, I would love it if he dropped it. I know Eleanor and Catherine are navigating this new life just fine. They've both got mates. Fated mates, apparently, if I dare believe such a thing is truly possible. It's great, what they've found. I've only just found peace, and this is supposed to be a new start. A new home for me where I can live the rest of my days in solitude without some man making my blood pressure skyrocket.

"Donna," Xarion's voice cuts through my thoughts and I stiffen a little. "I understand your desire for solitude, but isolation isn't healthy for humans. You need companionship, connection—"

I stop, this time to scan the bushes around us. "What I need is to find these damn berries you promised. Unless this is just some wild goose chase to get me socializing."

Xarion's ears droop slightly. "The zimi berries are quite real, I assure you. They should be on bushes with silver-tipped leaves."

As we continue our search, Xarion persists. "Have you considered joining one of the communal projects? The Kari are quite interested in Earth agricultural techniques."

I snort, pushing aside a thorny branch. "Sure. That's definitely what they're interested in. I'll just mosey on down to one of these meetings and show 'em how to grow corn in soil darker than a moonless night. Maybe I'll even throw in a lesson on how to make bread from blue grain that tastes like dirt."

"Your expertise could be valuable." That's the thing with Xarion. He doesn't react to my quips. He gets me. Gets that I'm not being prickly, just being me. Talking to him is like talking to one of my cousins. "The Initiative encourages cross-species collaboration," he continues, yelping as his suit catches on a thorn.

"Cross-species collaboration," I mutter. "Is that what they're calling it these days?"

Xarion blinks at me. "I don't understand your implication."

I sigh, pausing our trek. "Look, Xarion, I appreciate what you're trying to do. But I didn't come here to make friends or find a fabled 'mate'. I came here for peace and quiet." I frown at him. "Weren't you the one adamant on not letting Catherine go fulfill her matebond with a Kari? You were so scared it would kill her. Now you're here trying to convince me to get one."

Xarion's nose twitches. "Now that I have seen the positive effects of these bonds, we believe it might be in your best interest finding a Kari mate, after all."

I give him a dry look. "Mmhm."

"You do not have to become mates. Companionship is also good."

"Companionship. Right. You really think those males want to hang out in my kitchen exchanging stories and singing blues while I bake bluebread?" When he doesn't answer, I give him another dry look. "Don't think so. It all sounds like bullshit to me."

He doesn't argue and I'm glad. Nothing on that flyer New Horizons distributed said anything about getting a mate or socializing. This whole move is supposed to be about me. Healing Donna. This Initiative is for women divorced, widowed, or those who've basically had a shit dating life like me. Why would I, when I've finally found some peace in life, destroy all that by trying to find a man who will simply come in and destroy it?

For a moment, I think about the quiet nights, the endless alien sky, the memories of Earth that seem to grow more distant each day. But I shake it off. "I've got my animals, my farm, and occasionally, an annoying rabbit in a suit. What more could a girl want?"

Xarion opens his mouth to reply, but suddenly his eyes widen. "Ah! There!" He points to a bush just behind me, its leaves tipped with silver just like he said, small purple berries nestled among the foliage.

"Well, I'll be," I mutter, reaching for the berries.

"Wait!" Xarion is by my side in a split second, his furry hand grabbing my wrist. "Remember, protective gear. The extract stains quite permanently."

I look at his white fur against my dark skin and can't help but chuckle. "Somehow, I don't think that'll be much of a problem for me, cotton-tail."

As I start picking the berries, dropping them into my satchel, Xarion watches in silence.

"You know, Donna," he says softly, "it's okay to admit that you miss your home, your people. It doesn't make you weak."

I pause, a berry halfway to my bag. For a moment, I consider brushing him off with another sarcastic comment. But something in his tone, in those big red eyes, makes me hesitate. He's never spoken to me like this before. In the month or two that I've been here, he's always been his businesslike white-rabbit self.

The switch does something. Makes me pause. Raps on a door I've had closed for a long time.

"I do miss it," I whisper. "More than I thought I would. But this is my choice, my new start. I can't spend all my time looking back." I give him a soft smile. "Just playing dodgeball."

Xarion dips his head in a nod, even though he probably has no clue what I mean, but his ears perk up slightly. "That's a very positive outlook. But it would be good for you, for the Initiative, if you don't do it alone."

Back to the darn Initiative. I'd tell him to stuff it, but it's his job. It's the whole reason why we met. And truly, I know they have my best interests at heart.

"The more integration—" he continues.

"The more people the Initiative can sponsor. I get it." I roll my eyes, but there's less heat in it this time. "Fine, fine. Maybe I'll stop by one of those cultural exchange things. But I'm not promising anything."

" Wonderful!" There's a new pep in his voice as he whips out gloves from hidden pockets, slips them on his hands, and begins helping me harvest the berries.

I turn away, pretending to focus on picking berries, but it's really to hide my face. In my head, I'm asking the Lord to forgive me for this lie, but it'll keep him off my back for a while.

I have no intention of going to any cultural exchange, no matter how brightly Xarion smiles when I feign enthusiasm. But sometimes a little white lie makes life easier, especially when you're trying to maintain your solitude on an alien world. Or at least, that's what I tell myself as I pluck a handful of zimi berries, dropping them into the basket with a soft thud.

A wave of quiet settles over us as we work, the only sounds the rustle of leaves and the chirping of unseen insects. It's a peaceful sound, the kind that seeps into your bones and stills the constant chatter in your mind. And I'm reminded that the loneliness I felt earlier is also, in a way, a loneliness I'm protecting. It's confusing, wanting companionship but also wanting to be left alone. But this quiet, this type of quiet, where my heart isn't laden and worry, anxiety, and stress aren't constant, is a silence I'm fiercely protective of.

Xarion, bless his furry little heart, wouldn't understand. He thrives on connection, on bridging the gap between cultures. It's his job. I, on the other hand, am perfectly content to observe from a distance.

I see what Eleanor and Catherine have. Mates. Love. But with all that goodness is the little voice that reminds me, life doesn't play out the same for everyone. History has taught me that too many times.

So, I'll keep telling my little white lies, offering up silent apologies to God. Out here, in this vast alien wilderness, I've finally found the peace I've been searching for. And I'm not about to give that up for some forced social gathering where I might meet some alien promising the world, no matter how good-looking he might be.

2

DONNA

The berries are so good, I spend the next three days milking oogas—which turns out to be a very, very messy affair—and baking all sorts of crap with grushi flour and zimi berries. Turns out they're like blueberries, but ten times sweeter. A bit like a fruit that tastes like coconut milk infused with honey. It's absolutely delectable and before long, I've tried every recipe I can remember and I'm completely out of berries.

My oogas, the cow-hippo-like animals that live on my farm, now eye me with suspicion whenever I exit the cottage. Today I laugh when I spot my main milker, Gertrude, bustling down to the far side of the pasture as soon as I open the door.

"I'm not milking you today, Gertie!" I adjust my headscarf as my body shakes with withheld laughter. I swear, sometimes I think these animals are more intelligent than they appear. I'm probably not milking them right. Well, I'm pretty sure I'm not. I catch just about ten percent of the milk that comes from their teats, and that's because it's nothing like milking cows.

I huff another laugh as more of the milkers spot me and head in Gertrude's direction. "Hey, don't teach them to do that, now." I laugh. "I'm not that bad at it, am I?"

I swear one of them snorts, and that makes me chuckle. Gripping my grocery satchel, I look toward the pasture across from mine. Time to get more berries. I'm pretty sure I remember where Xarion and I found them. I just have to retrace my steps.

Five minutes later, I'm pushing my big ass through the fencing, cursing my hips again 'cause they don't want to bend, but then I'm straightening and continuing on.

A song hums in my throat as I push through the tall grass. Not one of Ma's old hymns, but one of my favorites; something with a little more sass and a lot more soul. Aretha. Always Aretha and her song *Respect*.

I belt it out, my voice echoing across the alien plains. I'm pretty sure Aretha never imagined her music reaching a planet like Hudo III, but hey, a girl's gotta have her anthems, no matter where she hangs her hat. The orange grass sways in time with my crooning, the pink sun beating down like a spotlight. It's a beautiful day, the kind that makes you want to shake your ass and forget your troubles, even if those troubles involve intergalactic relocation and a distinct lack of decent cornbread.

I lose myself in the rhythm of my footsteps, the gentle sway of the alien foliage, the clean fresh air. For a few glorious moments, I'm not a displaced Earthling, not a reluctant farmer, not a woman in her fifties with more regrets than recipes. My feet pick up the pace, turning into an unchoreographed dance, and my arms reach out to embrace this new world, a surge of pure, unadulterated happiness coursing through me.

I'm just a soul set free, carried on the wings of a song.

It doesn't take long for me to spot the silver-tipped leaves of the zimi berry bushes in the distance and I pick up the pace, song still loud on my lips because well, there's no one out here to hear me. As I get closer to my destination, however, I notice something odd. The bushes look...different. Picked over, almost. My brows furrow as I draw closer.

"Well, I'll be damned," I whisper, examining the nearest bush. It's been stripped clean, not a single purple berry in sight. I move to the next one, then the next. All of them are bare.

A prickle of unease runs down my spine. Did Xarion come back and harvest them all? No, that certainly doesn't make sense. He wouldn't do that without telling me. He hardly even wanted to get his suit dirty. Plus, these bushes look like they've been ravaged, not neatly picked in the way Xarion would most likely have done.

I stare at the bushes before my gaze shifts to the surrounding area. I often see some tall creatures that look like dinosaurs mated with giraffes out this way. Could it have been them?

No. I don't see any close by. Haven't seen any in a few days, at least.

Straightening, I'm suddenly aware of how quiet it is now that I'm no longer singing. The usual chittering of the insect-like creatures that inhabit this world is absent. Even the wind seems to have died down.

I freeze for a second, scanning my surroundings, ears straining for any sound that's out of place. My heartbeat feels too loud in the sudden stillness.

Something's off.

This is where, in the movies, some idiot would call out 'Hello? Is anyone there?' Well, I haven't survived five decades and a year by being a fool. I don't call out. I'm not about to advertise my presence. Instead, I step back slowly, eyes darting around, keeping my breath steady. Whatever's out here, it doesn't need to know I am, too.

Taking another step backward, I cringe, now feeling stupid for my reckless and loud singing. Whatever it is that ravaged the bushes probably already heard me. Dammit Aretha, girl. This is not how I intended to come meet you in the afterlife.

I've taken two steps backward, intent on making my way out

of the pasture and back to the safety of my homestead when I hear a sound. And not just any sound. Something that sounds like a dying animal. I freeze again.

"Lord, have mercy." The whisper is barely there as my eyes open wider, because that strange sound takes me straight back to those hot summer nights in Mississippi, sitting on my granny's porch, listening to her stories about haints and boohags. *"Child, when you hear a sound like that,"* she'd say, her voice low and sinister, *"you best turn around and run the other way."*

There's the sound again, loud enough that it sends a shiver down my spine because this time I can tell it's coming from behind the biggest zimi berry bush.

Yeaaa…no thank you.

I turn and hustle my ass out of there, pushing through the orange grass as fast as I can go. No more zimi berries for me. I sure as hell will just eat that tasteless cornbread, cakes and cupcakes I've been making without their addition. I can live with eating food that tastes like dirt. No more zimi berries. No sirree.

But as I push through the grass, the sound comes again, this time morphing into a voice that speaks actual words.

"Frakk me."

I pause.

That sounded like a man. Well, not a man. Men don't exist here. Not human men, at least.

The voice sounded male. Masculine. *Very* masculine.

My eyes narrow as I bite my lip. I can just see my cottage over the rise in the field. I could carry on, pretend I didn't hear anything. For all I know, this could be a demon trying to lure me with his voice. You know, pretending to be human. Well, not human, of course, but the equivalent.

My eyes narrow on the cottage some more and a defeated sigh makes my shoulders rise and fall as I turn away from it.

Leaning forward, I try to peer through the bushes without going closer. Because I might be cold, but I'm not heartless. I can't let someone suffer if I can help it.

That doesn't stop me from finding a large stone and gripping it tight in my hand as I take a step closer to the location of that sound.

"I rebuke you in the name of Jesus. If you're trying to trick me, you've got another thing coming." I say the words underneath my breath, just meant for my ears—you know, just in case this haint will take my words as a challenge.

Pushing through the foliage, my heart pounds a rhythm against my ribs that's got nothing to do with curiosity and everything to do with fear. The sound, that awful, pained moan, grows louder with each step, and my grip tightens on the stone in my palm.

I steel myself for whatever horror awaits, for whatever alien monstrosity might be lurking in the shadows.

But what I find is...a male.

He's sprawled on the ground, half-hidden by a tangle of the thicket, his body contorted in an unnatural position. He's not human, of course, but I know exactly what he is. I'm very acquainted with his kind, because his kind is the one that Xarion is pushing me to befriend. The same alien species Eleanor and Catherine are mated to. Before me is a Kari male.

His skin is a patchwork of shimmering iridescent scales, his features sharp, predatory, with eyes that gleam like molten gold. Thick, green hair is pulled back away from his face, the sides of which are shaved, only highlighting the strong structure of his brow and cheekbones. One ear has a small device tucked into it, like an earpiece maybe. That same ear is adorned with a single golden ring.

I find myself staring, not because of his undeniable beauty, but because this is the last thing I expected to see. I came out here to find zimi berries, not a Kari male.

One that's definitely hurt. Badly.

His chest rises and falls with each ragged breath, as those slitted pupils go narrow at the sight of me.

Something twists in my gut, a knot of... What is it? Pity? Fear? Or something else entirely?

I step closer, cautiously, the stone still clutched tight in my hand. *What am I doing?* This is madness. He could crush me with a flick of his wrist.

But he's hurt. Something's gone through his boot, I can see now, something sharp and unnatural, like a shard of dark glass. My eyes widen even more when I see the extent of the damage. I see no blood, but piercing one's foot, alien or not, can't be good.

For a moment, we stare at each other, both seemingly shocked to find the other here. Me, a lone human woman on an alien planet, armed with nothing but a rock and a prayer. Him, a creature of raw power judging by those muscles, brought low by...whatever that thing is sticking out of his boot.

When his lips curl into a wry smile, flashing just the tips of vicious fangs, and a low chuckle rumbles in his chest, I lose about fifty percent of my shock.

Now what the heck is going on here?

"Good sol," he says, before he glances down at his boot. "A slight miscalculation. I assure you, this is not how I usually make an entrance. Though, I must admit, your timing is...impeccable."

My spine straightens.

You know what else is impeccable? My aim.

I don't say it out loud, of course, but my hand tightens around the stone still gripped in my palm. Wouldn't want to spook the poor creature, even if he does look like he could wrestle Gertrude on her worst day and win.

I can already tell this male is a problem. It's that same feeling you get when you lock eyes with your best friend across a crowded room, the one that says, *Girl, this one's trouble with a capital T.*

And I'm the fool that is going to help him.

3

TOVAN

The signal screeches in my earpiece, a piercing whine that cuts through even my sound dampeners. Frakking crukks. It isn't just interference; it's a deliberate, rhythmic pulse, like someone is using a sonic disruptor to scramble my long-range scanner.

"Report," Arnak's voice crackles through the comms. "Your *impression* distorted just now, Tovan."

I'm sure he meant 'signal' not 'impression'.

My scanner is going haywire because of an unknown frequency *and* my translator chip is choosing this moment to act up. I give it a light tap where it's embedded behind my ear and there's a faint hum that tells me it's functional again. That should fix it. I've been meaning to get it looked at, but the occasional misinterpretations...well, let's just say they add a bit of humor to an otherwise humorless life.

"Aye." My brow tightens as I look down at my scanner. "Some kind of sudden interference."

"What is it?" I can hear Arnak moving around, trudging through the tall grass-feed. I tilt my head in his direction and I can barely make him out in the distance. Almost hidden in the pasture far away.

"I don't know what it is, but it's...erratic. Unnatural." My brow tightens some more as I glance down at my scanner again. "Almost like someone's playing a melody on it."

Arnak grunts. "Don't tempt fate. We've already had enough surprises on these surveys. For just one sol, I'd like to have an uneventful shift."

He's probably talking about the group of tilgrans that chased us across the plains in the last pastures we were surveying. Or maybe even the malfunctioning farming bot that almost took a few scales off him *and* me.

But this is different.

I can feel it.

"Maybe it's a beacon," Arnak's voice crackles over the comm. "You know, one left behind before the settlers moved away."

"Possible," I grunt, but I doubt it. The signal is too strong. Too sudden. It feels less like a dying gasp and more like a challenge.

"Just keep your scanner locked. Identify the source of that signal and determine what the frakk it is. And Tovan—"

"Yes, I know." I cut him off. "No engaging without backup."

The comm goes blank as I tuck it into my trouse. If there's another surveyor out here jamming my signal, it's likely sabotage. Some other being who is intent on deterring others from discovering the treasures lurking beneath these soils. He is no ally, but a foe.

I must tread carefully.

My scanner's beeping intensifies as I approach a cluster of zimi bushes, their fruits stripped from the branches as if raided by a herd of hungry tilgrans.

I'm about to push through when a sound stops me cold. Years of training take over; I drop low, my scales instinctively dulling to blend with the shadows of the zimi bushes. One claw finds the scanner's mute button without a thought, plunging me into sudden silence.

But the silence isn't complete.

There, carried on the soft wind, is a sound unlike anything I've encountered in my orbits of surveying. It's...a melody. *Music.*

My ears flatten against the sides of my head as I crouch low. Still hidden by the bush, I inch closer to investigate. The thumping grows clearer with each step, but instead of grating on my nerves as the scanner readings suggested it would, the rhythm vibrates right through me. A deep, rich melody that quickens my core-beat.

"Tovan?" the comm activates in my ear, but I can't answer Arnak. Not now. Because I'm frozen. There, just beyond the ravaged berry patch, is a sight that makes my breath catch in my throat.

A female. Of a species I can identify anywhere across Hudo. A *human.*

I must mutter the word, say something that gives Arnak a clue because his voice sounds in my ear again. "A *human?* One of the females that the brothers have mated? Frakk, Tovan. Those females are like gems. I'm coming your way."

"Don't you dare," I growl low, urging him to hush even as my eyes remain locked on the sight before me.

The female is picking her way through the grass-feed, completely oblivious to my presence. She's heading directly toward me, and for a moment, my core-beat does a frightened, stuttering thing.

She's...a goddess.

Her hair is wrapped in some kind of bright cloth, the same color as the grass-feed that stretches across the plains. A few dark tufts escape like thick clouds, framing a face that is dominated by gentle curves. Full lips move in sync with her song, and her eyes—by the gods, even from here I can see her eyes are like twin celestial bodies, dark and mysterious.

She sways and the star kisses her smooth skin. It's a rich, deep brown, like fertile soil after the heavens weep, and she moves with a grace that belies her curvaceous form, each step like a fluid dance through the tall grass.

At one moment, her flowing garments flare, lifted by the soft breeze, but even without that they do little to hide her generous curves. The tunic of blues and reds flows around her like a field of wildflowers in full bloom. Even the mud splattered on her garments seems to have taken on a vibrant hue. And as she moves, twirling to her song, I can see the sway of her hips, the fullness of her posterior...

No. Focus, Tovan.

Her voice must be what my scanner picked up. I can tell now, even without looking down at the readings flying across the screen, that the device is going erratic with the approach of this sonic frequency. Because hers is a voice that carries on the wind, a melody both foreign and captivating. The sound is... different; neither the harsh tones I'm used to nor the synthetic beats popular in the settlements. It's raw, emotional. Makes me listen as if it commands my attention.

Of all the beings I expected to be thwarting my survey, I didn't expect *her*.

This isn't my first encounter with her kind—I've met two before, the mates of the Korruk brothers. But those were brief meetings. Despite my interest in learning more about these females, the brothers are like vicious guards when it comes to their mates. Understandable, because since their mating, news has spread.

This female before me, singing and picking her way through the grass-feed, is from a species that has given mine hope. Hope that some of us can break the bonds of profound loneliness if our core-rhythms sing.

This female. She is a gem indeed. Does she even know how precious she is? Obviously not, because here she is, walking without a care in the world, completely oblivious to my presence or the potential dangers, though few, that could befall her out here.

I should alert Arnak immediately. Tell him there's no need to converge at my location. But something holds me back. Perhaps it's the peaceful scene before me, so at odds with the tension we've been existing under. Or maybe it's simply the spell of her voice, making me hesitate to shatter this moment.

As she nears the first zimi bush, her song cuts off in her throat, reduced to a mere hum as her brows furrow. She mutters something underneath her breath before walking slowly around to the other bush, and then the next. It appears she'd come here to forage but creatures have already taken their fill and left nothing behind. Her brow furrows deeper before she suddenly goes still, her head lifting as she looks around.

I go still, too. Does she sense me?

I, like all other Kari who heard the news about the Korruk brothers finding their *kahls*, scoured the archives for information about this new species. Nothing in the sparse records on humans mentioned them possessing auditory or olfactory perception that rivaled, or even surpassed, our own.

Though, that might well be the case. Because the female is standing at alert now, her spine stiff, that furrow still on her brow and her eyes searching around. She must know I'm here and I'll be discovered soon. She'll search the bushes and find this large Kari male hidden, watching her. Not exactly the way I'd like to introduce myself. I should reveal my presence before—

But, the female doesn't come closer. Instead, she backs away. Stupidly, I follow.

As if drawn by some invisible thread, I creep behind the cover of the bush, tracking her retreat. My gaze remains fixed on her, drinking in the sight of her: the way the light catches the richness of her scaleless skin, the determined set of her shoulders, the gentle sway of her hips underneath those flowing garments as she walks. It's…mesmerizing. *She's* mesmerizing.

Perhaps I should approach her. If she's here, there's no doubt her lodge is somewhere close. I'd heard that some branch of the Hudoian council was conducting a program to settle these females. I just hadn't known it had been out in these plains. But now that I do, I can find her lodge. Maybe pretend to be a lost, weary traveler and introduce myself. Maybe she'll want assistance with something on her farm.

The plan hatches in my mind. Yes, I could do that. Stumble upon her farm and offer my services tilling the soil or something else. That would give me reason to be in her presence. Speak to her. It's a good plan and I'm settling into it when a sharp, searing pain shoots through my foot. It's a sensation so unexpected, so at odds to my usual awareness, that it takes me a moment to even register what's happened.

What in the ten worlds…?

I look down, my core-beat sinking as I spot a wicked shard of black metal that's embedded deep in my boot—and, in extension, my foot. I can already feel the lifeblood soaking the interior and the hard thrum of veins that have been punctured.

Frakk. This was not part of the plan.

I collapse with a groan, but all hopes of keeping myself hidden are already shattered. The female has no doubt heard me now.

"Tovan?" I forgot Arnak was still connected via comm. His voice is etched with concern. "What's going on? Stay there, I'm on my way."

Gods. This can't get worse. "No. Whatever you do, don't come. I'll be fine." Because if he comes then he'll also encounter the female and…well…I don't want him to. Something I can't quite name is adamant that *I* be the one to speak to her first. "It's nothing," I lie. " Stay where you are."

I try to keep my voice low even as pain lances through my leg. Qeffing qrak. Which careless fool left this trap out here? From the looks of it, it's been lying underneath these bushes for eons. Probably left by the last settler who owned this pasture; a deterrent to wild tilgrans that would feast on this berry bush.

Trying to pull the metal from my boot, and in essence my flesh, fails on the first try. Stupid, archaic traps. I try again, a low groan rumbling in my throat as I adjust my leg and try to dislodge it from the spiked trap. It's a no-go. I'll have to stand to free myself, but the pain is too fresh, too strong.

Frakk. I might need Arnak to come after all. So much for an uneventful sol. And the female—gods, the female!

As I attempt to pull myself up, movement catches my eye and I look up to see deep brown ones locked with mine.

I freeze. It's the female. And...gods...she's *beautiful.*

The words lodge in my brain, scattering all coherent thought.

What now? Thank the gods Arnak is far away. He would never let me live down the fact that a tactical specialist like me, one who fought and faced the war, is completely out of my depth at the sight of the small female before me. My courage, my bravery, has deserted me, leaving me as awkward as a hatchling trying to fly for the first time.

She's here. Peering at me through the leaves of the bush between us. And I...what do I do? How do I salvage this?

I am at once startled by the fact we're facing each other and the fact she actually came to investigate the noise I made. Like a fool, I am frozen, watching as her gaze skips down my frame before landing on my boot and the offending piece of metal still lodged there, quite obviously piercing through.

"Good sol," I say. Those brown eyes shift back to my face and my words hang in the air, like a thin veil failing to hide my embarrassment.

I've come upon a human—a rare gem to us Kari, and I've just revealed myself in the most undignified manner possible. This isn't just a bad first impression; it's a spectacularly awful one. As her eyes shift over me, I can feel my scales burning with shame. By the gods, I've dreamed of encountering one of these unmated human settlers, dreamed of one making my core-rhythm sing, and this is how it happens? Caught in a bush like a clumsy chit? Arnak will never let me live this down.

"A slight miscalculation." I try to sound nonchalant, as if my lifeblood isn't flooding the earth between me. "I assure you, this is not how I usually make an entrance." The female stiffens at the sound of my voice and I curse myself further.

I think she will run away. Protect herself from this strange situation. But she doesn't. Instead, something changes in her face and those eyes swallow me whole.

The female lifts one side of her brow before placing a fist against her hip, making her elbow jut away from her. "Miscalculation?"

Ohhh. Oh gods. Her voice is just as rich as when she'd been belting that melody.

"Honey, it looks like you tried to tap-dance on a rusty sawblade and lost the rhythm."

Honey? My head tilts slightly, pain and embarrassment forgotten as my gaze heightens on her. That word translates to something sweet. Something to be devoured.

I reach up and give my translator a tap, sure it's gone haywire again. The faint hum that usually signals rebooted and fixed the error remains stubbornly absent. It's...working. But that can't be. That means the female really just said I look edible?

I—how do I respond? She wants to devour me? Usually, the thought of any creature wanting to consume me would bring discomfort. But I can see her blunt teeth. They most certainly can do me no damage, and the thought of them along with those full lips pressing against my scales has the opposite effect. Instead of disgust, a jolt of heat courses through me, going right to the center of my trouse and leaving a tingling trail in its wake.

"You must be in so much pain." Dried leaves and small twigs crack underneath her boot as she takes a step forward. "That there is a stroke of bad luck if I ever saw one." She gestures toward my boot with a jut of her small chin.

Bad luck? I almost chuckle. If she only knew... This "bad luck" might be the most fortunate event in my otherwise predictable existence.

"Something like that." I try to keep my voice neutral and fail. It comes out as a low growl. Thankfully, that doesn't deter the female.

"Looks like you need some help," she mutters, pushing the bushes out of the way as she comes closer. At the same time, Arnak's voice comes through my earpiece.

"Tovan? What's that sound? Is the female there?" It sounds like he's running, which means he's still heading my way. And I don't want him to. I resort to speaking to him in the old tongue.

"Gameshla friardi." In other words, "*Arnak, if you value your mating prospects, turn around and walk—no, run—in the opposite direction. And take your curiosity with you.*" Thankfully, the female doesn't understand a word I just said. Probably thinks I'm cursing the gods for my misfortune.

"Did you trip over a piece of space junk or somethin'?" She's close enough now that I catch her scent on the air. Grushi flour and something sweet. I can already tell without going nearer that the sweet scent is coming from her skin. Her direct essence. Would it be too obvious if I took a deep breath?

"It appears to be a primitive...snare," I reply. *And I managed to get caught on it.* "Highly effective, I must admit."

She raises her brow once more, deep brown eyes flicking to me before a soft, unexpected laugh makes her grunt. "A snare? Those are for catching rabbits, not…whatever you are."

I'm caught off guard by her laugh, but it's the fact that she's pretending not to know what I am that has me curious. I get the sense she knows *exactly* what I am. This isn't a demure, shrinking female, that's fearful in the presence of a large male she knows absolutely nothing about. There's a sharpness in her gaze, an intelligence that both intrigues and challenges me. And that voice… I wish for her to continue speaking. Would impale my other foot and both my claws if it meant more conversation.

"I'm a Kari," I venture anyway, more to keep her talking than for any other reason. "Homeworld Karicek minor. They call me Tovan. Tovan of the line Kamesh."

She's studying me and I'm not sure how to read those eyes. "Well, Tovan of the line Kamesh. Looks like you need a hand, yeah?" She frowns before looking behind her in the direction she came from.

"A hand?" Is my translator acting up or is she referring to her claws? I glance down at mine. I already have two. I don't need another one.

For a moment, I'm caught between horror and fascination. Do humans possess the ability to detach and regrow their limbs? I know some chitinous species are capable of such feats, but surely not humans. And even if they could, how would possessing a human claw assist me in any way? She means for me to use it to replace the foot I've impaled? The logic doesn't make sense. I would be…a sight. That is sure.

I find myself tilting my head, studying her arm with newfound curiosity. "I… appreciate the offer, but I'm not certain how that would help my current situation. And wouldn't the loss of a limb be…inconvenient for you?"

Her head snaps back in my direction, and I realize she'd still been looking off in the distance in the direction she'd come from. The frown on her brow disappears in a single instant as she snorts, her eyes widening on me. Have I offended her? Possibly it would have been wiser to thank her for the thought while convincing her there is no need for such a sacrifice.

I open my mouth to do this when, suddenly, the female bursts into laughter.

It's a warm, rich sound that fills the air around us. Her whole body shakes with it; the large mounds on her chest, even the swell of her thighs.

Gods… My throat goes dry. That heat that sparked within me heightens. I have never seen anything more—

She stops laughing to stare at me open-mouthed and eyes wide. "You thought I was going to…to *give* you my actual hand?"

I blink at her. "Weren't you?"

This sets off another fit of bubbling laughter.

Heat creeps up my scales, a wave of embarrassment so intense I swear I can feel the color shifting beneath my skin. But I can't help but be captivated by her laughter. It's like a melody, swelling up from somewhere deep inside her, a sound so full of life that it makes my chest ache with a longing I don't understand.

"It's just an expression," she finally says, but she's still laughing, though more subtly than before. "It means I'm going to help you. I won't be detaching any limbs." She sobers some more. "That's not something I'd willfully do."

"Noted." I dip my head slightly even as I store away every single bit of this interaction. Her way of saying things is colorful. Like her.

Her gaze falls back to my boot and she crouches, tilting her head as she looks at it. "Not sure if I have anything that can cut through that thing there." She glances up at me before pointing a digit at my boot. "Looks like it could've done some real damage. I don't suppose you can simply free yourself with a tug?" She pauses. "How long have you been stuck here?"

Oh frakk. She'll know I'd been creeping about watching her now. "Not...not long."

"Hmm," she hums a tone in her throat. "Doubt I can help you off that thing." Her gaze skips over me. "You're a big fella. Best to call for help."

I stiffen. No. Not only will that mean more spectators to this shameful injury, but more beings here will only mean I'll leave this little bubble sooner. The one where it's just me and a human female and no one else for leagues—well, except Arnak, but if he listens he'll stay away.

"Just let me—" She reaches into her flowing garments and takes out a communicator.

"No need." With a deep grunt, I stand, bracing on my good leg as I pull my other foot upward, dislodging it from the long shard. Frakk. Me. A deep groan of pain threatens, only held back because the female is looking at me. Can't go wailing like a chit that's lost its mor now. There's a beautiful female in my presence. By the gods, whatever you do, Tovan, do *not* show weakness.

So I don't. I keep that grunt of pain at bay, watching as the female's eyes widen, a mixture of shock and...is that admiration? in their depths. I can't be sure, but it's enough to make me stand taller, my chest puffing up a little.

"Holy hell," she breathes, clawless digits still frozen on her communicator. "You just...pulled yourself off that thing?"

I manage to jerk my chin in affirmation, but frakk, this qeffing hurts. "It seemed...the most efficient solution." Really, it was a distraction. One that's working better than I thought it would. Now she doesn't have a reason to call anyone.

The female shakes her head, one brow lifting while the other descends. She's giving me a strange look. One I can't decipher.

"Efficient? You're bleeding all over the ground, you know that?" Then her brows dive, her gaze falling no doubt to my boot. I don't even look. I can only remain focused on her. "Lord, forgive me. That looks nasty."

Is that...concern? Is she worried about me? A stranger to her?

"That's...a lot of blood." The female's brows furrow some more and when she looks up at me this time, I am transported to another realm where the world around us disappears. "A graze shouldn't do that. Must have taken off quite a bit of flesh."

A graze? Oh, she has no idea. I glance down at my boot only because staring at her for too long will no doubt spook her. Sure enough, thick dark liquid is seeping through the sole. Now this is going to take a few sols to heal.

"I suppose," I start, trying to keep my voice light, "I suppose this puts a damper on my plans of winning any ground races today."

She snorts, a sound I'm beginning to find oddly endearing. "Well, at least your sense of humor's intact. Can't say the same for your foot, though." She takes a step closer. "You need medical attention, Tovan of the line Kamesh. That's not a scratch you can just walk off."

Her concern is sending a flow of warmth through me. Maybe it's the reason I don't tell her I'll heal without medical attention. That I've had worse injuries than this and survived. Setting the foot down, I take a step. "It's not as bad as it looks. I am quite capable—"

My words are cut short as I stumble, my injured foot unable to bear my weight.

The female moves faster than I would have thought possible, her arm suddenly around my midsection. She's *supporting* me, her soft body braced underneath mine. My core-beat stutters as the contact sends a jolt through my system that has nothing to do with pain.

"Mmhm, you're *real* capable," she mutters. But the way she says it tells me she thinks I'm nothing of the sort. Usually, this would wound my ego. But right now, she could call me every deprecating thing she can think of if she just remains pressed up underneath me like this. "Hold on." She drops a rock I didn't realize she'd been gripping and grabs my claw. Forcing me to brace on her shoulder for support, she removes the bright headpiece from where it's wrapped around her head. Thick, dark coils are revealed, forming a mane that is quite unlike my own.

I'm entranced by it. My focus pulled to her beauty and then in a separate direction—to the sensation of her softness beneath my claw.

It takes all my willpower not to flex that claw. Not to probe the soft flesh I can feel just underneath my palm. Gods, this is hard.

"What are you—" I begin, but she cuts me off with a sharp look.

"I'm trying to help you."

Before I can process her words, she's crouching low beside my injured leg. With deft movements, she begins to wrap her head covering tightly around my leg. Her actions are swift and purposeful, betraying a level of practical knowledge that surprises me. Despite her earlier amusement at my expense, there's no hint of mockery in her movements now—only a focused determination.

I hiss involuntarily, more out of shock than anything else.

"Sorry," she apologizes, but she doesn't slow her actions. "But we need to stem this bleeding."

I go silent. I can only watch in fascination as she works, her small clawless digits moving with surprising strength and skill. The bright fabric is wrapped and secured tight and the gush of pulsing lifeblood slows in my boot.

"There," she says after a few moments, straightening. "That should hold for now."

I flex my leg. "Your skills are…impressive."

She shrugs, but I catch a hint of pride in her eyes. "Just basic first aid, darling. Nothing fancy."

Darling? My translator chip doesn't usually cut out so frequently. It certainly must be now because it's telling me the female just called me a term of endearment. That can't be the case. The archives said this is a prey species that is soft and easily frightened. The female before me is neither of those. This is…perplexing.

"You know, most females would feel unsafe at the sight of a strange Kari."

She raises an eyebrow at me as she adjusts herself beneath my arm once more. Another snort as her gaze sweeps over me, slow and deliberate. "I'm not scared of you."

I'm not sure whether to be offended or amused by that statement. Before I can decide, she's speaking again.

"Come on, tough guy. My place isn't far from here. We can at least get that foot cleaned up before you bleed out trying to prove how 'capable' you are."

I want to protest, to insist that I can manage on my own. I don't want her to believe I'm some weakling. But pretending means I can stay in her presence a little longer, and the warmth of her body against mine, the strength in her arm as she supports me…it's oddly comforting. If I'm being honest, the prospect of spending more time with this intriguing human is far from unpleasant.

"Frakk, Tovan. It sounds serious. I should come." I stiffen. I'd once again forgotten Arnak is still live on comm, listening to *everything*. His voice, sounding in my earpiece, is beginning to be a nuisance. I only manage a growl. Hopefully, it's enough for him to get my meaning. *Stay the frakk away.*

"Very well, female," I say this as if reluctant. Can't let her know that if I had a choice, I would follow her across the plains, injury or not.

The first step makes us sway and her skin, softer than I

could have imagined, sends tingles through my scales. No longer dulled, my scales are a riot of purple, pink, and blue that are doing a horrible job of hiding my excitement.

As we begin our slow, awkward journey from behind the zimi bush, the female uses one hand to ward away the branches till we reach the tall orange grass-feed once more. There, we pick our way across the plain, silence enveloping us. I find myself filling it with soft grunts as if to convince her I'm still hurt because I can tell she's deep in thought. Probably sorry she came out to forage now. Instead of the berries she sought, she's taking back a burden.

Putting most of my weight on my good leg, I test out a few steps with the other, ever mindful of the soft body pressed against mine. It becomes evident a few clicks into the journey that I don't need her assistance at all. Yes, there's no doubt there's a hole in my foot, but I can manage.

Will I tell her to let me go? I almost scoff. Shameless male that I am, I continue to pretend that I need her bracing against me as we make our way.

"What the frakk are you doing?" The voice is a whisper in my ear and I turn to look over my shoulder as we go. I can see Arnak now, just a few leagues off but completely visible. He's watching us.

I glare at him, using my free claw hidden behind the female to gesture that he should keep the frakk away.

He's a stubborn qeffer. I'm not surprised that he simply stands there. I watch as he rests his scanner, leans on it as he watches us go and I remember now that I left mine lying in the bush. Perhaps it's for the best. It would only make her ask questions about my purpose in that pasture, the answer to which I might not be able to provide.

"Almost there, now," the female says at my side. She glances up at me, those deep brown eyes catching the light. "It's just over that rise."

I stare at her, probably for too long because her brows furrow slightly.

"Thank you, female. For your help. It is more appreciated than I have words to say."

She studies me for a moment more before she jerks her chin. "Sure thing. I couldn't just leave you out there to suffer. We humans have big hearts. We do the right thing. We help each other."

My lips twist slightly. "I'm not human."

"Oh, I'm aware."

What's that supposed to mean? Is it a good thing? I can't quite tell.

"But you helped me anyway."

"I helped you anyway."

She stops so suddenly that we almost topple. When she looks up at me, there's a hardness in her eyes that makes me briefly aware of everything between us, even every breath she takes. "Now, look here. I'm helping you because that's what decent folks do when they find someone hurt." Her gaze never wavers from mine. "I'm going to get you patched up because I can't in good conscience leave you bleeding out here. But don't mistake my kindness for weakness."

The steel in her voice leaves no room for argument. She's warning me. Making it clear that despite her help, she doesn't see me as an ally. I jerk my chin slowly, a mix of admiration and wariness coursing through me. This human is far more perceptive and formidable than I initially gave her credit for.

"I understand," I reply. "You have my word, female."

She studies me for a moment longer, as if trying to gauge the sincerity of my words. Then, seemingly satisfied, she nods. "Good. Now let's get moving before you pass out and I have to drag your scaly behind all the way to my cottage."

I grunt a laugh, humor that never used to come easily

flooding through me, as if I hadn't forgotten how to laugh orbits ago. It's… unsettling. Pleasant, but unsettling.

As we resume our slow progress, a newfound respect rises for this human. She's compassionate enough to help a stranger in need, yet cautious and strong-willed enough to set clear boundaries. It's a combination that I find unexpectedly appealing.

For the first time in cycles, my sol isn't going exactly as I intended. It's a strange new feeling. One that sends a skitter through me. A ripple of unease.

One that makes me wonder if perhaps… I've stumbled upon something far more valuable than any rare ore, something that could change the course of my existence forever.

DONNA

This motherfucker is huge.

Even though I'm sure he's still shifting most of his weight on his own, I can feel his bulk. He could fold himself around me and I'm sure I'd disappear.

I'm not a small woman. Never have been. Ma used to say I was built for comfort, not speed, and she wasn't wrong. But this guy, this male, god, he's big.

I focus on picking my way through the tall grass, sweat tickling my brow as the sun gets higher in the sky and the heat of this alien's scales seems to burn straight through my clothes and seep into my skin.

When we get to the road and my farm becomes visible, I try to push back the thread of nervousness that shoots through me. I'm all alone out here. And now there's a big alien male in my presence.

My gaze shifts to him as discreetly as I can as we hobble across the road. He's not looking at me. His eyes are on the farm, and I get another prickle of awareness. I'll send a message to Catherine as soon as we arrive. Just, you know, as backup.

Because I can feel my heart rate picking up. It's not just from the exertion of supporting this massive alien. There's a growing tension in my gut, a mixture of excitement and apprehension that I can't quite shake.

I'll be fine, I tell myself. If he tries anything, I'll stuff a piece of bluebread down his throat and hope he chokes to death. Of course, that really isn't a plan; it's not even half of a plan. But I remind myself that Xarion said it's safe out here, and even though I haven't known him for too long, I trust the big white rabbit. Xarion said it's safe, New Horizons promised it, and Eleanor and Catherine are safe—have been safe.

But they're not you, Donna. They have big alien mates and you're all alone. I push the intrusive thought away, because being alone certainly doesn't mean I can't protect myself. I have a slew of butcher knives in my kitchen and I know how to use them. They can do more than slice beef for stew.

"Almost there," I say, more to myself than to him. The cottage looms ahead, and I can't help but think that maybe that eye-searing bright blue paint job wasn't my best design choice. It practically screams, "Hey, look at me!" It's not that easy to forget. But I've never been so glad to see its weathered boards and slightly crooked porch.

Tovan grunts in acknowledgment, those yellow eyes of his still fixed on the farm. I can't read his expression—do aliens even have the same facial expressions as humans?—but there's an intensity to his gaze that makes me nervous.

"So..." I start. "You've probably never seen a human before, huh?" I try to keep my tone light, casual, as if having a hulking alien leaning on me is an everyday occurrence.

He turns those piercing eyes to me, and for a moment, I forget how to breathe. "I...have," he rumbles, his voice sending vibrations through my body where we're pressed together.

My eyebrows rise. "You have?"

His gaze shifts from mine. "The Korruk brothers. They have human mates."

Ah, so he knows Eleanor and Catherine's husbands. "Friend of theirs?"

He grunts and I wonder if it's because of the pain or if it's a laugh he's holding back. "We're not allies."

My brows twist again and, as if he can tell that I will definitely distance myself if he's an enemy of my friends, he continues. "We are acquaintances. Neither ally nor foe. We arrived on Hudo a long time ago on the same ship. But I did not know the brothers before then. Since living here, we have merely passed by each other and exchanged greetings within the settlement."

I turn his words over in my mind and as I look up, I catch him watching me now. Those strange eyes skip over my face. As if to soothe my fears, he continues. "We Kari, we're a bit solitary."

My eyes narrow slightly. "Mmhmmm. Well, this is my place." I jerk my chin at the cottage before us. We're down in the yard, just by the porch now and I use one hand to brace on the wooden column. "Let's get you settled, and then I'll take a look at that foot. Think you can step up here?"

It's just one step, but if he can't put any weight on his bad leg then—

With a grunt, the alien hops up onto the porch and we do an awkward kind of stagger as I lead him to the single chair I have sitting there. It looks like a toy and he settles into it.

As I release him and his heat disappears from my skin, I take a deep breath and step back.

Tovan's eyes shift from me to skip around, taking in the blue walls with their orange trim, the flowers I hung in baskets on either side of the door, and even the little paper origami rooster I have perched inside on my windowsill.

"It's...quaint."

"Thank you. It's growing on me." If he were a human, I'd probably take offense to his "quaint" remark. But there's nothing malicious in his gaze. He seems in awe, drinking in every detail of the cottage.

Or maybe he's just scoping you out.

I can't stop my spine from stiffening. "Right," I say, clapping my hands together. "Let's see about getting you patched up, shall we? I'll go get the first aid kit."

I step inside and close the door behind me with a soft click. The familiar surroundings of my cottage do little to calm my racing thoughts.

Okay, Donna. You've got a giant alien on your porch. No big deal. Just your average Tuesday in Tennessee, right? Except even those tornado sirens never brought anything this strange to my doorstep. And this ain't Tennessee.

I shake my head, trying to clear it as I head for the bathroom where I keep the first aid kit. My eyes dart to the kitchen, where my trusty butcher knives gleam right where I left them.

Maybe I should grab one. You know, just in case he decides human flesh is the perfect dessert after bluebread.

I snort at my own ridiculous thought. Still, I can't shake the unease entirely. As I rummage through the storage boxes for the first aid kit, my mind conjures increasingly absurd scenarios.

What if he's engineered all this just so he could scope my farm out? A wave of weariness washes over me. It wouldn't be the first time I've fallen for a sob story, a charming smile hiding a less than honorable agenda. Fool me once, shame on you. Fool me twice...well, shame on me. It's not like I've got a track record of attracting the most...trustworthy...of men.

Brows still furrowed, I give the first-aid kit a yank the moment my fingers close around it. With the kit now clutched to my chest, I turn, worry still etched in my brow as I head out of the bathroom before I pause. Reaching into my pocket, I get my comm device. Better safe than sorry.

I quickly punch in Catherine's contact and wait, drumming my fingers nervously against the first-aid kit.

"Donna?" Catherine's voice comes through, sounding surprised. "Everything okay?" In the background, I hear a deep rumble and just know it's her mate, Varek. I wouldn't be surprised if they're in bed, *in the middle of the day.*

No, I'm not jealous. I'm—I'm just...ok, fuck it. Maybe I'm just a little bit jealous.

I release a sigh, shaking my head again to clear my thoughts.

"Hey, Cath." It's an effort to keep my voice casual with my thoughts getting increasingly troubled by the second. "So, funny story. I've got a, uh, visitor. Big guy. Scales. Says he knows the Korruk brothers?"

There's a pause. "Wait, are you saying there's a Kari at your farm?"

"Yep. He's hurt his foot. I'm about to put on my scrubs again and play nurse. Just thought you should know, you know, in case I don't check in later and you need to come rescue me."

Catherine's laugh is both relieved and exasperated. But she's laughing. So very different from the first time I met her. She'd been more reserved then. A lingering sort of sadness I knew too well etched in her features. Now, it's like she's been given the gift of a second life. "Oh, Donna. I'm sure you're fine. They may look big and scary, but the Kari are generally peaceful." She lets out a yelp and a giggle and I hear the distinct growl of her mate. "S-sorry about that. It's Varek. He's—" She clears her throat, sobering. "I appreciate you letting me know. Want me to come over?"

I consider it for a moment, then shake my head even though she can't see me. "Nah, I think I've got this. I'll patch his foot and send him on his way. But maybe check in on me in a couple of hours?"

"Will do. And Donna? Try not to overthink this. Not all aliens are out to get you."

Her words make me go silent. I know why she's said it. Like me, she also woke up on another planet, surrounded by aliens who'd saved us from going into sure slavery. The ones that had taken us from Earth, the Tasqals, they were horrible beings. We were lucky the Restitution found us, kept us safe. Lucky New Horizons exists.

"Right," I whisper. "Darling, I know you're right. I just have an overactive imagination." That and a past that's taught me not to trust. "Thanks, Cath. I'll talk to you later. Tell Varek hello for me."

I end the call, feeling slightly better. At least someone knows about my unexpected guest.

Taking a deep breath, I head to the door. Time to face the music...or the alien, as it were.

"Alright, big guy," I say as I step back onto the porch, but my next words die on my lips. He's got his boot off and is peering down at a wound that makes my eyes bug out. "Oh, my gosh!"

I rush forward, first aid kit already opening as I grab a set of sterile gloves and tug them on, all thoughts of potential danger momentarily forgotten. The sight of the alien's injury overrides my caution and the registered nurse in me wakes up and takes charge as if I hadn't had a break from the ward.

"That looks...Oh God, that looks bad." The word doesn't do it justice. The wound is massive—a deep, jagged gash that's gone through the center of his foot. Now that I can see it clearly without the boot, it looks even worse than I imagined. I suppose I expected that the shard actually missed his foot and only grazed the side of it or something. The low grunts of pain I heard him utter had been so...restrained, almost casual. I wouldn't have been caught dead being that calm with a hole straight through my *foot*!

I drop to my knees beside him, heart beating hard as I rifle through the first-aid kit.

"You're awfully calm for a man with a hole in his foot." I lift his foot in my hands, noting the sudden wince that seems to move like a wave through his entire being. "Oh honey, you should have said something." All I get is a low groan, but I don't look up. My focus is on the horrible wound. With one hand, I balance his foot on my knee as I use the other to pry open the first aid kit.

His foot is surprisingly similar to mine. Larger, of course. Wicked claws for nails, too. A bit thicker than a human's. But it isn't grotesque, at least.

"I'm gonna need some leverage with this. Gonna need both my hands." My gaze shifts to my door. With a nod of resolution, I gently place his foot back down before I rise and head back inside. Two seconds later, I'm returning with an empty supply box, the surface hard and firm. I set it down. Gesturing to his foot, I help him lift it onto the box.

My brows twist. This really is very bad. "I can't believe I made you hobble on this and you managed to bear the pain," I murmur, more to myself than to him. The jagged metal of that trap really did a number on him.

Tovan's yellow eyes meet mine. Unreadable. "Kari are… resilient," he says.

I roll my eyes. "You're probably right. Most folks would be hollerin' like a banshee by now."

"Ban…she?" He tilts his head.

"Something from Earth." I wave my hand in dismissal. "A…a screeching spirit." I take out a pack of gauze from the kit. "The kind that haunts graveyards and drives folks crazy with their wailing." I mime a scream, contorting my face into a theatrical mask of terror. "Wooooooooo!"

His lips twitch, and for a moment, I think he's going to make another joke. But then, his gaze turns serious, those yellow eyes boring into mine.

"Ah." Is all he says. So much for my distraction efforts, so I focus on his wound instead.

His scales gradually diminish in size as they approach his foot, fading into dark purple skin that looks surprisingly soft.

The gash runs right through the center, an angry red line against the purple. And it's still bleeding.

Reaching for the antiseptic, I put a generous amount into a piece of gauze and pause, gaze shifting to his. "This is probably going to hurt. Maybe you should bite down on something?"

To my surprise, he lets out a rumbling chuckle that does something to the hairs all along my arms. "I assure you, female, I can handle a little sting. I once wrestled ten Hedgeruds with my claws alone." Hedgeruds. He means those brutes that worked for the Tasqals that stole us from Earth. Nice to know they're generally just scum.

"Mmhm. Well, this ain't no wrestling match. You've got a hole in your foot the size of Mars." I frown. "Hold steady."

He grunts. "Are you scolding me, female?"

My brows dive and I meet his gaze, not backing down. "You've got that right. You've got a serious injury here, and playing tough isn't going to help it heal any faster." For a moment, it feels like I'm back in the hospital doing rounds. "So yeah, I'm scolding you. Got a problem with that?"

For a moment, this Tovan's eyes flash with something—surprise, maybe even a hint of respect. It's gone almost as quickly as it appeared, replaced by a look I can't quite decipher. His posture shifts slightly, the set of his shoulders changing in a subtle way that makes me feel like he's suddenly paying even more attention to me now than he was before.

"Apologies, female," he says, his voice low and rumbling. "You are correct. This injury is not to be taken lightly."

I nod, satisfied with his response, but there's a new tension in the air, not necessarily unpleasant, but definitely palpable.

"Good," I say, turning my attention back to his foot. "Now, let me finish cleaning this out. And no more tough guy act, alright? If it hurts, you tell me."

He doesn't even flinch, just sits there, his gaze fixed on me, a strange intensity burning in those yellow eyes even as I press the gauze to the wound. I work in silence for a few minutes, carefully removing bits of debris and applying antiseptic. The gauze soaks up some of the blood so I can see what I'm working with more clearly and it's nasty. He's either got so much adrenaline coursing through him that he can't feel the pain, or he's the toughest creature I've ever met. Maybe both. The shard went deep, right through the metatarsals—those long bones that connect your ankle to your toes. There's no way it doesn't hurt like hell.

I swallow hard, forcing myself to focus so I can help him as best as I can. "Okay, this is gonna sting a bit," I warn, reaching for a small tool in the kit that resembles tweezers. "You might want to...I don't know, roar or something. Let it out."

The alien's eyes narrow slightly, and I'm sure I see a hint of amusement flicker in their depths. "I don't usually...vocalize during intense sensations."

My eyebrows rise and I have to push past a mind laden over years of reading too many smut-filled books. Alien speak isn't the same as human speak, Donna. Aliens don't usually speak in innuendo.

Just to be sure, my gaze flicks up to his face, searching for any sign of a double meaning. A leery grin, maybe, or a glint of something predatory. But those yellow eyes are steady, focused on mine with an intensity that makes my breath catch in my throat. And his jaw, that sharp, chiseled jaw, is clenched tight.

"Alright then," I say, trying to sound nonchalant. Truth is, I'm unsettled and that's not normal. "Just...let me know if you need a break. Or, you know, a song to soothe your savage alien soul."

I'm okay with the fact he doesn't answer. It allows me to focus. But as I continue treating his wound, I can feel the alien's eyes on me. I try to concentrate, but I can't help wondering what's going through his mind. When I glance at him at different intervals, he's completely focused on me. Not wincing.

Not peering at what I'm doing. Not looking at the hole in his foot.

Focused. Focused on me only.

"What on earth were you doing out in that pasture anyway? You live around here?" I glance up and find those intense eyes locked on me still as if he hasn't even blinked. The realization sends a wave of *something* through me that makes the hairs at the back of my neck rise in a way that has nothing to do with fear but some other feeling. I should be afraid, shouldn't I? Those eyes don't exactly breed natural trust. And yet, I'm not afraid. I wasn't lying when I said I wasn't scared of him.

I'm something else.

I'm aware.

Completely aware of myself.

"No, not around here," he says, gaze shifting to my hand as I set the tweezers down and stare at the wound, thinking of my next best bet at helping this male.

"Well, you're a long way from home, then." I rifle through the first-aid kit, my fingers brushing against bandages, antiseptic wipes, and tubes of alien goo that promise to heal everything from a paper cut to a broken bone. I'd had Xarion help me relabel the items in English but even then, some of the things make no sense to me. What I need is a suture kit, and maybe a shot of something strong for both of us. "What brings you to this neck of the woods, then? You lost or somethin'?"

He chuckles, a low rumble that vibrates through the floorboards, and the sound does strange things to my insides. Strange things that make me even more aware of myself and the fact that this is a *male* and I am *female*.

"Not exactly lost," he replies, his gaze flicking back to mine, a spark of something unreadable there in those eyes. "More like...drawn in."

"Drawn in?" I echo, trying to ignore the way my heart does

something strange at his words. "By what? The scenery? The smell of ooga dung?"

He smiles then, a slow, predatory curve of his lips that sends a shiver down my spine. "Something like that," he says, his voice a low purr. "Something...unique."

I glance up at him, dividing my focus as I continue working on his foot. Is he...flirting with me?

There's a part of me, a small, foolish part, that wonders if he sees me the same way Catherine and Eleanor's mates saw them —as a potential mate, a solution to his loneliness. But that path...it leads to a place I've sworn never to go again. If he thinks sweet talkin' is going to get me rattled, he's setting himself up for a whole heap of disappointment. I might not have much, but this girl's got a PhD in deciphering male BS. Years of bad dates, broken promises, and enough smooth-talking heartbreakers to fill a galaxy have taught me one valuable lesson: trust your gut, not their honeyed words.

"Isn't it all just the same thing out here?" I peer at his foot. "Tall orange grass, pink sky, and silence? What's there that's unique?"

He grunts. "There is much." I glance at him and he continues.

"Truth is, human, I was surveying the terrain before you found me wounded in that zimi bush."

"Surveying?" I echo. "Are you some kind of real estate agent? Looking for a prime piece of property?"

His lips twitch, and for a split second, I think he's going to smile. But then it all closes off, as if he's retreated to some far-off corner of his mind.

"Something like that," he murmurs, his attention for the first time shifting to the wound I'm treating. Silence envelops us and soon I can feel those eyes on me again, watching, assessing.

And that's when I realize...I'm not just patching up a wounded alien. I'm being...studied.

Donna dear, what have you gotten yourself into?

I try to ignore it. *Just patch him up and send him on his way, Donna.* So I focus on cleaning out the wound. I have a stack of bloody gauze by my side that would make any normal citizen queasy, but the bleeding has finally slowed down.

"You're lucky it missed any major tendons," I say, my voice taking on its professional tone as I pack the wound with more gauze. "But it's gonna need stitches. A lot of stitches." I meet his gaze. "And I don't have the equipment for that out here. So, unless you've got some kind of magical alien healing mojo up your sleeve, we need to get you to a real doctor."

"No!" It's not a shout, more like a sudden utterance, one that has me pausing, going still as I blink at him. "No medics," he says.

The force of his denial vibrates through the air, a stark contrast to his previous playfulness. A stronger wave of unease washes over me, cold against the day's warmth.

"No medics," he repeats, softer this time, his gaze dropping to where I'm holding the antiseptic gauze. "Please."

I swallow, my hand hovering over his foot. "Okay," I say slowly, really darn happy my voice is steady because my heart ain't. "No medics."

But he's observant, or, at the very least, he can read my apprehension.

"It's...complicated," he says finally, so low I almost don't hear it.

Complicated. Mmhm.

He's a fugitive, isn't he.

A criminal.

I wouldn't be frickin' surprised. I found him *hiding in a bush.* I'm suddenly three times happy that I called Catherine and told her of his arrival.

There's a lump in my throat as I continue working, feigning control even as my mind races.

If he is a criminal, I sure as hell need him to leave. Maybe I need to set Gertrude on him, have the oogas chase him from my land.

With a sigh, I say, "Alright." I'm not going to push for information I might not need to know. When the alien FBI scours down this place I can say I'm just an innocent bystander. "I'll wrap the wound, but you'll still need to see someone who can patch it up properly."

I don't meet his gaze now, because I'm sure he'll see everything I'm thinking in my eyes. The air surrounding us seems to have changed too. Filled with uncertainty and potential danger.

"It isn't what you think," he suddenly says, shifting in the chair and leaning forward the moment I remove the gauze from the wound and wrap his foot tight. He's close enough now that I can see the slight shimmer in his scales.

"Hmm?" I glance at him, feigning ignorance. My acting skills are totally up to par for when the authorities come knocking. "What's that?"

He grunts, a soft laugh brushing through his nose. So... maybe my acting *isn't* really that great. "It isn't what you think," he says again.

"What do you mean? What isn't what I think?" I don't know what he's talking about, remember?

"To call a medic all the way out here will waste a hefty block of credits."

My gaze shifts to him now.

Is he...broke? Is that it? Has this warrior, this proud alien, fallen on hard times? The thought, as unexpected as it is unsettling, stirs a strange mix of sympathy and apprehension within me. To not want to spend money, even when there's a massive hole in your foot, must be some kind of sacrifice.

I almost do a Hail Mary. May such hard times never find me.

Especially not on a planet where I probably have no employable skills. Lord knows I haven't earned one credit yet that could buy a decent cup of coffee, let alone afford alien healthcare. I've been living off the funds New Horizons gifted me. I shudder, picturing myself bartering bluebread for a tetanus shot. No, ma'am, not gonna happen. This alien's just proof I have to get this farm up and bringing money in soon. Financial stability is a must-have, not a nice-to-have.

But it's not like I don't understand. If healthcare here is anything like it was back home, without a solid insurance plan things can get tough. So, I nod, setting the alien's foot down on the box as I stand. I've done about all I can do to help him now. I can only leave him with a prayer and hope he accepts the debt and actually goes to a medic on his own time.

"Well, that's all done now," I say, gathering up the scattered supplies. I avoid his gaze, focusing on the task, suddenly hyper-aware of the quiet intimacy of my little cottage, the scent of antiseptic mingling with the earthy aroma of freshly cut grass.

"I don't know how you'll manage to get to the town on it," I continue, annoyed that my voice has gone a bit breathless, "but you're welcome to rest here for a few hours until you can call a friend or someone to pick you up."

Silence hangs heavy in the air, broken only by an ooga baying in the field. I glance at him, expecting a grateful nod, a plan of action. Instead, I find him watching me, his gaze intense, those yellow eyes boring into me like they can see right through my skin, my bones, into the very heart of me.

I busy myself cleaning up the mess, my movements a bit too brisk now, a bit too frantic. I need space. Need to breathe. Need to process this whole bizarre encounter before it turns my carefully ordered world upside down.

Turning to head back inside, I'm suddenly eager to put some distance between us, to escape the intensity of his gaze, the unsettling questions swirling in my mind. But just as I reach the door, he speaks, his voice a low rumble that seems to stop time itself.

"Thank you." I don't know why those two words hold me

frozen. Why I can't move. "For everything. You did not need to help me...but you did. You saw me...not as *other* but as a being in need."

My hand freezes on the doorknob and I turn slowly, my heart pounding a frantic rhythm against my ribs.

His words strike a chord within me, a chord that resonates with the echoes of my own past, my own experiences of being judged, of being dismissed for simple things like the color of my skin or the kinks in my hair. And then to be taken from the only world I knew simply for the purpose of being used, abused, thrown away. As if I wasn't a person, a being, but a *thing*.

I swallow the lump that rises in my throat, the urge to confess, to tell him that I, too, know what it's like to be seen as "other," to be feared for what I am, not who I am. But the words remain trapped behind my lips.

"It's...no big deal," I manage, forcing a lightness I don't feel. "Like I said, we humans...we tend to look out for each other."

I say that even though he's not one of my kind, hoping he understands it extends to other beings, not just us. But it's a lie, of course. I'd been alone on Earth for far too long to believe in the inherent goodness of humanity. Seen too much. Saw the results of some of the worst parts of humanity back in the emergency room. But something about this alien, this wounded warrior with a heart that beats beneath those iridescent scales... makes me want to hang on to the ideal.

I give him a ghost of a smile as I open the door and step into my cottage. Closing it behind me, I lean against it and release a slow breath, the weight of his presence, his words, settling over me like a storm cloud gathering on the horizon.

My hand trembles as I slide the bolt home, a flimsy barrier against the unknown. He's out there, on my porch, wounded, alone.

I close my eyes, pressing my forehead into my palm. For a moment, the scent of the sweet blossoms by my door fills the air and there's a sudden, unexpected ache for a garden a million light-years away.

But then, a low groan, muffled by the thin walls, brings me back to the present, to the alien warrior on my porch, to the storm that's gathering on the horizon. And as I turn towards the sound, a sense of inevitability settles over me, a certainty that this day, this encounter, is about to change everything.

5

TOVAN

I didn't lie to her...but I wasn't forthcoming with the truth, either.

Yes, calling a medic to the plains will only waste credits. But it's not that I'm trying to save after orbits of having nothing to spend on. I just...really don't need to call a medic.

I pop out my comm anyway, sending a quick note to Arnak to let him know that all is well.

'Situation under control. No need for extraction.'

A beat of silence, then Arnak's reply flashes across the screen.

'Under control? I can scent your lifeblood from here. You're bleeding out in a human's dwelling? Should I bring the emergency life-pack?'

'Negative, Arnak. She has taken care of the wound and her methods are...effective. You can return to town without me. I will get my grav bike later.'

For a few moments, there is nothing on the screen and I'm a bit surprised he's dropped the matter so quickly. Arnak is usually far more...persistent. I'm about to put the device away when it suddenly lights up again.

'Just out of curiosity, brother...this human female...does she have a mate?'

Even during a crisis, his priorities remain predictable.

'I do not believe she does.' But I know why he asks. He's as interested in her as I am. *'Focus on your surveying, Arnak.'*

His next message appears quickly.

'Tread carefully, brother. They will soon pass a law that we Kari are harassing these poor females. Coercing them to stay in our presence. You have no reason to be there.'

He's right, of course. I have no reason to be here. And yet, I remain.

'I will leave soon.'

With that, I switch my comm off. Tucking the device away, I glance at the closed door of the human's dwelling. I don't even know her name. That curious, intriguing, *lira'an*. The word comes naturally, probably because it suits her so much. As if she was sculpted by the very star itself.

A slow grin comes to my lips as my gaze moves around her farm. She's put fresh wall varnish on the main dwelling. It's a vibrant blue that makes the lodge stand out rather than blend in. A splash of audacity that tells me this female has a profound misunderstanding of the concept of camouflage.

My grin widens as I grunt.

She...captivates me. The way she tended to my wound without hesitation, her touch gentle, so at odds with the hardness in her tone as she scolded me. It's been a long time since anyone dared to speak to me that way. Longer still since I allowed it. But from her, it was unexpected. Refreshing.

I flex my foot now, testing it out. The lifeblood has ceased seeping. In a few sols, it will be like this accident never occurred. But the female doesn't know that.

Maybe I should knock on her door. Tell her the truth. That she wasted her supplies helping me. That I'm a brute who couldn't stop himself from accepting her assistance. That I am utterly shameless. And that I will leave now. Make my way off her land.

Only...I don't.

I can already feel the slight change in the air, the way the clouds above seem to be rumbling and congealing together. The plains will get a shower soon and piloting a grav bike through the torrent will be less than pleasurable. Yet still, the thought of leaving, of bringing this meeting to an end, feels instinctively wrong.

My brow tightens as I stare at the sky for a few moments before my gaze sweeps over the lush fields surrounding this female's small farm. It is peaceful out here, far from the chaos and soullessness of the town.

When the torrent comes, the female will be safe. In her lodge, it will be like surrounding herself with a cocoon, locking out the outside world. For that alone, it's clear why her kind has chosen to come to live out in these plains. Whenever I and Arnak venture out here for the surveys, I've always noticed it. The peace. The sort of peace I crave, but one that always remains just out of reach. Because even with the calmness around me, there will always be that one part deep inside that is still trapped with the greatest wound for my kind.

The ache of a species designed for a bond so profound, so rare, that most of us live and die without ever experiencing it.

And maybe that's why my thoughts shift back to the female. To the compassion in her eyes, the strength in her soft claws. To the way she looked at me simply as a being who needed her help.

That compassion was a reflex. As if she's spent a lifetime tending to wounds, both physical and unseen.

As if she could tend to mine.

Foolish thought. Helping me meant nothing, not to her, I'm sure. But it's been a long time since anyone looked at me the way she did. Touched me, the way she did. *Cared* for me, the way she did—even if it was fleeting.

I close my eyes, letting the cool breeze wash over me. I'll have to leave soon. Despite that I'm sure she'd deny it, she's probably hidden away because I'm unsettling. Even Kari females find my size disturbing. If I were a smaller male, she might have spent more time with me. Tarried a little longer. Now she's gone in, her sweet scent and presence missing, and I can't even hear a sound inside.

I am aware, however, that she might be watching.

The thought sends an unexpected thrill through me, one that I quickly suppress. I am not here for...whatever this is. I have a job to do, one that extends far beyond this small farm and its intriguing inhabitant.

Plus, there's the other matter entirely. That within me lies a silent song. The one thing that's supposed to let me know when I've found my mate is painfully absent. My core-rhythm doesn't exist. For all I know, this female might belong to another of my kind. To Arnak even.

A particularly chilly gust blows across the porch. Everything within me stills. If she belongs to another Kari, to Arnak of all males, it should bring me joy. It would mean she will be protected, cared for. But the idea is like a misaligned scale. Wrong. Uncomfortable.

Frakk. This is why I should leave. I'd thought the others of my kind, the males that have flocked our town searching for these females, were hoping for too much.

That the insanity was driving them. But they aren't insane. Because that insanity is the same thing driving me now. The same reason why I'm seated at this female's cottage, feigning a serious injury, and hoping for even a few more moments in her presence.

But...she did nothing to indicate she was in the least bit

interested in me. I am not some juvenile pining after the first female to show him kindness.

I should leave...

Instead, shifting on the seat, I angle my body slightly towards the human's door. Just in case she does emerge. Just in case she decides to grace me with her presence once more. It's foolish. Dangerous, even. But I can't seem to help myself.

She wanted to devour me at one point... That could have been a sign...

Or maybe it's just a sign I should stop being stubborn and get my translator updated. It's an easy process enough. I know a male, a bounty hunter, that could get me the latest unreleased version of languages. I just have to give him something he wants in return.

Go, Tovan. You must leave. You have tarried too long. Want to be soaked in the torrent, half-blinded by the intensity of the showers on your way back to town? No? Then you should go now.

I tarry. My gaze drifting back to the door. My ears straining to catch even the faintest sound of movement within. But there's nothing. Just the whisper of the rising wind through the grass-feed and the distant call of grazing oogas.

It is not till the sun begins to pass its midpoint in the sky, it s light fading behind the converging clouds that I finally accept that I must leave. I've lingered far too long, indulging in juvenile fantasies and dangerous hopes. It's time to go, to return to my duties and the reality of my predictable existence.

I rise from the seat. Glancing at the door, I try not to peer through her windows. That would make me certainly look like someone she doesn't want inside. Instead, I dip my head and rummage in my pockets for credits. I will get her name some-how. Pay her properly, but I hope this can settle my debt for now.

Lifting a fist, I'm ready to rap against her door, when I pause. She obviously does not want to speak to me again. Why else would she have not come back outside after so long? So, lump in my throat, I leave a hundred credits at her door before lifting my voice.

"I'm off now." I pause, waiting, listening. There's only silence. "Thank you again, female, for your…" For her presence? For the fact she's suddenly lit a spark within me that's making me hope again? "For your assistance."

It seems woefully inadequate.

With a sigh, I turn, ready to leave. I don't even know if I will ever see her again. Short of positioning myself outside her door another sol, how would we cross paths?

The thought turns over in my head as I make my way off her porch. For a moment, I consider simply walking away normally, but then a ridiculous thought strikes me. What if she's watching? What if she sees me leave with barely a sign of the injury she so carefully tended to?

Before I can talk myself out of it, I hobble dramatically towards the transit path. It's a pitiful display, really. A Kari warrior, limping like a wounded animal. But some irrational part of me hopes it will show her that her efforts weren't in vain, that she truly helped me.

I'm halfway across her yard when I hear the door open behind me. My core-beat stutters in my chest, but I force myself to maintain the charade, continuing my exaggerated limp.

"Hold on now…" Her voice floats out, a mix of concern and something else I can't quite place. "You better—" I turn, trying to keep the surprise and joy off my face. Her voice muffles and I find her bustling back into the lodge. She appears again a second later, slipping her feet into her boots. "This alien is gonna be the death of me." It's muttered under her breath, but I hear it anyway.

She thinks I'm going to cause her demise? That is *not* what I intended. But when her gaze meets mine, it isn't worry I see there. Well, at least, not for herself, I don't think.

She's worried about *me*. The thought is so unexpected, it sends a jolt of warmth right through me. But before I can savor it, she's at my side, her clawless digits on my arm, a touch that sends another jolt through me. This time, raw, powerful electricity shoots down my spine.

"You're crazy if you think I'm letting you hobble off into the sunset like that," she says. And then I realize how ridiculous I must look—a towering Kari male, pretending to be crippled by an injury that will most certainly heal without delay.

Shame washes over me. What am I doing? This isn't who I am. This isn't how a warrior behaves.

Her touch, light yet insistent, guides me towards the remains of a tree.

"Here," she says, steering me toward the stump. "Lean on this for a minute. I'll be right back."

"I—"

"No buts, Mr. Tovan." Her tone. It's laced with that same authority that I'm finding surprisingly...endearing. "Now, lean here on this rotten tree while I fetch you something."

Before I can even process the whirlwind of sensations her touch has unleashed, she's gone, her retreating form a blur of blues and reds.

I lean against the tree, my willpower not as strong as I thought. This whole charade is getting more complicated with each moment.

A few clicks later, the human reappears, carrying a thick, sturdy branch, stripped of its leaves and smoothed at the top. I'm not sure what she intends to do with it till she reaches my side and plants it into the earth at our feet.

"Here," she says, thrusting the upper end toward me. "This should help you keep the weight off that leg. Now, did you manage to call someone while you were waiting?"

Her gaze is sharp, assessing, and I know she's not just asking about transportation. She's watching me, testing me, trying to decipher the truth behind my next words.

"I have transportation." I dip my head slightly in respect to her and to communicate my gratitude. Because she has brought me a walking staff. I might not need it, but her care and attention strike me deep anyway. It's a small gesture, this crude walking stick, yet it means more than she knows.

I take the staff from her, feeling its weight in my claw. It's a simple thing, but sturdy and well-crafted. *Just like her.* My gaze heats before I can stop myself.

"Thank you." My voice ends up a bit more gruff than I want. "I am forever in your debt."

"Oh, don't be silly." But she nods, a small smile playing at the corners of her mouth. "Can't have you stumbling around out there, now can we? It will make me look bad. Now, about that ride..."

I would laugh at her joke but something else swells in my throat. A ball of tension. I'm suddenly aware of how close she's standing. Her scent envelops me, an intoxicating mix of that sweet trace and something more.

"It's just...that way." I gesture vaguely toward the transit route.

"Oh, alright." Her brows furrow now in a way I'm beginning to realize is skepticism. "I'll walk you to the road, at least. Make sure you don't fall into a ditch or something."

Before I can protest, she's moving, her stride purposeful. I have no choice but to follow, leaning on the staff more for show than actual need.

We walk in companionable silence, the shadows creeping across the sky and settling around us like a blanket. I'm acutely aware of her presence beside me, of the way she occasionally glances up at me, her eyes unreadable brown pits that have me desperate to know what she's thinking. Because although I'm ecstatic that she graced me with her presence again, I'm more than aware that it is only for a brief moment. As soon as we get to the transit route, we will part ways and she will be gone again.

But as we near the transit route, I can see the confusion growing on her face. There's no vehicle in sight, no sign of any being waiting for me.

"I thought you said your ride was here." She's staring at me now, but it isn't full-fledged. It's a sideways look as her eyes narrow.

That hard thing in my throat swells. I've backed myself into a corner. "It's...across there." I admit, gesturing to the pasture beyond.

Her eyes widen immediately. "Across the road? In that pasture? That's...that's miles of open field!"

"Yes. I...left it there before our encounter." I'm full of shame. So much so, I'm unable to meet her gaze now. I can feel her staring at me for a long moment. Then, to my surprise, she lets out a soft laugh.

"You know what? I don't even want to know," she says, shaking her head. "But you can't trek across that field in your condition. And I don't have the resources to escort you there and back. Not with that storm coming in."

Storm?

I lift my head then, gaze flicking to the sky above. She's right. Those clouds have finally converged. Heavy and threatening, they're quickly blocking the star's light as they swell with warning for a torrent that will soon come. Frakk. If I'd been paying better attention, I would have noticed that fact.

Only, it wouldn't have forced me to leave any sooner.

"Right, the storm."

She sighs, running a claw across her head, and her tight coils spring back into place, dark spirals that seem to defy gravity. "Look, I've got a barn. It's not much, but it's dry and warm. You can stay there till the storm passes, rest that leg properly. Then in the morning, if you're still set on crossing that field, well...I won't stop you."

Words fail me. "I...I couldn't impose..."

Gods, please let her make me impose.

"It's not an imposition," she says, voice still firm.

Gratitude, god of the moon. I will worship you harder from now on.

I don't understand this female at all. But I desperately want to. She locked herself away and I believed her to be done with my presence. But here she is offering me more assistance.

"It's common sense," the female continues, frowning up at the darkening sky. "Now come on, let's get you settled before the rain starts."

She turns, clearly expecting me to follow. And despite logic telling me I shouldn't, I find myself hobbling back towards her homestead.

This is...a strange turn of events. This human female, barely half my size, taking charge, offering shelter to a Kari warrior she barely knows. It's unexpected, unprecedented, and yet... completely and utterly what I want.

I really am shameless. I don't even have the shame to care.

I glance at her profile, bathed in the dying light, and something stirs within me. Something I thought long dead. Need, perhaps.

Or perhaps something even more dangerous.

Hope.

6

DONNA

Please, Lord. Don't let this be a mistake. I don't want Catherine calling only to find my farm ransacked and my body lying underneath the hay. I've binged on enough CSI to know I might die because of a heart that's too big.

Being kind doesn't always make you friends. Sometimes, it just makes you a target.

As I steal glances at the large alien hobbling beside me, I want to believe this isn't a mistake. At least, I hope it isn't.

"Watch yourself," I warn as we reach the barn doors and I open one side. The other side is stuck and I haven't had a clue how to fix it myself. He doesn't seem to mind. Hobbles in sideways, although his massive frame barely squeezes through the entrance. Inside, his scent displaces the musty air filled with traces of hay and old wood.

"As I said, it's not much." I'm suddenly self-conscious of the humble space as I look around it. I got the Raki workers to fix the roof and some parts of the wall, but it's a mess in here. Hay scattered everywhere and stalls that I've promised Gertrude I'll muck out this week. "A bit cramped, I suppose. But it'll keep you dry."

I look up to find the alien's gaze sweeping the barn, taking in every detail. "It's more than sufficient. Thank you, lira'an."

His voice. It resonates in this enclosed space, sending tingles across my skin. "Leera an?"

My question makes him pause. Visibly so. And I swear his scales darken.

After a beat, he makes a sound in his throat. "Your designation…" He turns to face me. "I do not know it."

Only then do I realize that after all this time, I haven't yet introduced myself.

"I am Tovan of the line Kamesh." He does a dip of his head, bracing on the staff for support.

"Yes. You said," I murmur, a small smile tugging at my lips as I watch him straighten once more. He's being awfully polite. And…I like it. A thief and murderer wouldn't be so polite, would they? I guess it won't hurt if he knows my name. If he came here to rob me, what would he do, steal my name and ride off in the wind with it, too? So I push my caution aside and perform the best curtsy I can.

"Donna," I say. "Donna of the line Johnson." I rise and stretch my hand toward him for a handshake.

Tovan's gaze shifts to my outstretched hand and before I can react, he's grasping it in his much larger one. His palm is rough, calloused, making mine feel dainty and soft. But it isn't his gentle touch that suddenly has my heart flying in my throat.

It's when he dips, almost bowing before me, his face pressing against the back of my hand that I startle. There's a deep inhalation, his nose brushing against my skin in a way that sends a bolt of shock right through me. One that culminates right at the center of my thighs.

It's so sudden—the slight brush of his breath against my skin, the sensation that shoots straight to my core, that I gasp. I can't help it. My hand trembles in his grasp and my tongue gets stuck in my throat. And he doesn't let go.

"Sweet," he rumbles.

I know my eyes are like two big dumplings in my head, but I can't school my features. It's very clear handshakes aren't the same thing to him as they are to me, and I realize I've never tried to shake Eleanor or Catherine's mate's hands. Even then, something tells me they wouldn't react in the same way as Tovan is reacting now.

He inhales again, so unashamedly that I can hear the very breath filling his lungs. When he releases my hand, almost reluctantly, I, a woman who has always been quick with her tongue, am speechless.

I turn away, desperate to focus on anything else but the sudden shiver that went through me, rattling even the blood in my veins. With one arm, I gesture to the barn.

"There's a pipe at the back if you'd like to wash off, though I'm pretty sure you'll just want to lie down, rest that leg." I clear my throat, my brows furrowing not at the state of the barn but at the fact that my heart's beating a little harder. A little faster. Enough for me to notice it.

"Gratitude...Donna of the line Johnson."

I push past that lump that won't clear in my throat, forcing myself to focus on what I should do next. "Just Donna is fine."

"Donna."

Oh, no. No no. We're not going to focus on that. I busy myself with nudging hay bales together to make a bed while trying to ignore the way my heart quickens at the sound of my name on this alien's lips.

Something's wrong. That simple touch, that unexpected gesture, has left me more flustered than I've been in years. A brief touch shouldn't have me feeling a single thing.

As I push the last hay bale into place, I purposefully ignore the alien in my midst and head to the back of the barn where I have some tools leaning against the wall. I'm equal parts ashamed of myself and horrified I reacted at something so simple and so easily.

I'm better than this. Stronger than this. Hurt enough times that such foolish instinct should be dead in me.

Despite myself, memories I'd rather forget rise in my brain as if summoned just like the incoming storm. Memories of men I'd rather forget. Reasons why a simple touch should have zero effect on me. I push back at these reminders, but they flood my mind anyway.

The first one, a piece of shit called Damian, had laughed when I told him about my dreams of becoming a singer. *"You're going to be a nurse,"* he'd said. *"Now why would you go chasing after some silly dream when nursing's a stable job?"* He'd laughed then. *"Now, you see, this is why I say you women should leave the business and planning to us men. That's our language."*

I'd shown him the door that very night. Turns out 'single and thriving' is a language I speak fluently.

I roll my eyes, pushing a bucket out the way with my foot as I scan the wall for the thing that looks like a rake.

But back then, and even now, Damian's words stung. I'd dropped my dreams of singing and worked as a nurse for over two decades, pouring my heart and soul into caring for others. It was rewarding work, but draining. And through it all, I'd struggled to find a connection, a partner who could understand and support me.

After Damian, there was Mark, the charming doctor who turned out to be married—with kids and a pregnant wife. He was a royal piece of shit. Then there was David, who was all about grand gestures and whirlwind romance, showering me with flowers and whisking me away on mini breaks. But the minute I mentioned moving in together, he backpedaled faster than a crawfish in hot water. Apparently, he needed his "space" and he "wasn't ready for commitment".

And who could forget Tyler. He was a project, a fixer-upper

I thought I could, you know, *fix*. He was lost, confused, and I thought my love, my support, could somehow magically heal his wounds. But a therapist I am not. And trying to change a man is like trying to herd a bunch of cats—frustrating, exhausting, and ultimately pointless.

There were more, of course. At some point, I'd started to wonder if there was something wrong with me. I'd entered my twenties being hopeful, thinking I'd be married with kids by twenty-five. Then twenty-five came and went and before I knew it I was thirty, a nurse, and the years started going by even more quickly.

Two more decades passed and here I am, on a world far far away from all that I ever knew, and I'm still alone. Indefinitely now, perhaps.

I've accepted it. Accepted it a long, long time ago. The love of my life? Not gonna happen. The kids? Not gonna happen. But what did happen, what surely did occur, was that I got wiser.

Which is why my heart shouldn't be fluttering over an alien's touch like I'm some lovestruck teenager. I should know better. After all the disappointments, all the times I'd picked myself up and carried on alone, I should be immune to something as simple as a mere touch.

"A pretty face is just a distraction, honey." Because he *is* pretty, this Tovan. Well, not *pretty* per se, far too rugged to be simply called 'pretty'. He's handsome. Tall, bulky, and attractive in the exact sort of way that would have me fanning myself and appreciating what God gave him if I let myself. But I won't let myself. "I'm Donna Johnson, damn it, and I built my own damn castle. I don't need no knight in shining armor, especially not one with scales."

"A castle?"

I almost jump out of my skin. The rake I'd just grabbed off the wall goes clattering to the ground as I jerk at the voice *right* behind me. The shock makes me almost stumble, but a strong arm snakes around my waist with such ease it's like he's done this a million times.

For a moment, I'm suspended, my eyes wide as I look up into the stranger's face.

Just how long had he been standing there? And why didn't I hear him approach? Was I so much in my head that I didn't hear this giant of a male hobble across my barn floor to stand right behind me?

"Goodness," I breathe, my hand coming up to clutch my throat. "Good heavens."

"I startled you, didn't I." A statement, not a question, and I can almost see the regret in those yellow pits.

"You didn't." I swallow hard, because everything I was thinking is coming right back and with it is another heavy dose of shame. Because it's not gone yet. That rattle in some central part of me. I know it isn't gone, because the sensation of this male's arm around me is being seared into my very consciousness.

He holds me so effortlessly; I feel...I feel like a woman again. "I mean, you—you *did*, but it's fine." I clear my throat. "You shouldn't be walking around. We don't want you to start bleeding again."

Maybe *I'm* bleeding. Internally. In my brain.

"I heard you talking. Thought you were speaking to me." His intense gaze moves over my face so slowly I'm immediately brought back to reality. To the fact I'm still in his arms, my body pressed against his solid form. Regaining my balance forces him to let me go. But now there's the wall behind me and an alien in front. I'm trapped.

"You heard me talking?" I can already feel my cheeks heating. Just how much did he hear? Living on my own for so long, I suppose I've gotten used to speaking my thoughts out loud—to the animals, the flowers in my garden, to even the flies on the wall. But now, this alien just heard my private musings. Without realizing, I've shown him a part of me I keep hidden, tucked away behind the Donna I show the world; the one everyone else knows.

"About building castles." The way he says it, his bass a soft rumble that makes the word almost...intimate, makes a tingle go down my spine.

My gaze snaps up to his, searching for a hint of mockery, of judgment, but all I find is...curiosity. Genuine, unadulterated curiosity. It's disarming. His unassuming interest catches me off guard.

I don't know how to answer him. How do I explain without explaining that I was talking about a heart patched up over years of disappointment. That the past has been a great teacher, telling me not to hope too much for the future and that those castles? Those grand, impossible dreams, were more about finding a place to hide than a place to call home?

The realization is all so sudden, so raw, that I can't say a thing. Instead, I do what I do best: I deflect.

"It's nothing," I say, forcing a lightness I don't feel. "Just... foolish rambling, that's all."

"Do you need help with the buildings you have here?" The alien's gaze snaps to the barn itself, skipping across the beams holding up the roof. "Your lodge, perhaps?"

The sudden change in direction has me blinking to catch up. I release a relieved breath, silently thanking God for his mercies. "I had some Raki workmen come out and fix it all up. I think they did a good job. Don't you?"

He hums a sound in his throat. One I can't decide indicates the affirmative or not before he turns slightly, continuing his survey of the building.

"I'm not planning on building anything else. I think I can manage with all the things I have out here for now."

"If you change your mind," he says, leaning on the staff with both hands, "I can assist you with that." His gaze shifts to mine and I go still, every muscle in my body locking into place. Like a startled rabbit, frozen in the sight of a hawk, I don't dare breathe.

It's different this time, his eyes. Different from all the other times he's looked at me. Right now, his gaze is a tangible thing, a silken thread wrapping around me, pulling me taut. It's the kind of look that strips away pretense, that sees right through you, and for a fleeting, terrifying moment, I forget that he's an alien and I'm not supposed to find those slitted eyes the least bit appealing.

The air crackles, the silence stretching between us thick and heavy. It's the kind of silence that hums with unspoken things, with awareness that stretches beyond the boundaries of polite conversation. And I realize I've made a grave mistake. I let my guard down, forgot I'm alone in the boonies with a stranger. And right now, those piercing yellow eyes are fixed on me with an intensity that makes me very aware that we are alone.

He's blocking my escape, too. His massive frame between me and the rest of the barn.

"You've got a wounded foot. You're not helping anyone. What you need to do is help *yourself* and get some rest." I smile, but my attempt at humor doesn't reach my soul. Instead of genuine mirth, the smile feels stiff on my lips.

"I'd endure the pain if it meant I could help you in return."

I'm about to open my mouth and tell him I've got everything I want when he continues.

"Is there anything you need…Donna?"

Oh…good Lord.

The way he says my name sends another shiver down my spine. It's intimate, almost possessive, and it makes me aware of how close we are. Instead of lightening the mood, my joke only served to increase the warmth of the air, making it feel heavy and electric.

Is there anything I *need*? Gosh, that's a complete other basket of troubles than what I *want*, isn't it? What I need…what I need is safety. Stability. Someone who sees beyond the facade, who understands the scars carried beneath my smile. I need trust, built slowly and carefully, not rushed in a moment of passion. And this…whatever's happening here, is exactly what I *don't* need.

I'm not going crazy. I might want to ignore it, but he's flirting with me, isn't he? That makes awareness go through me and I straighten myself, standing taller. I've had enough of that to last me a lifetime and the lessons to go with it, too.

"Ok, listen." My voice is firm and I silently cheer myself on. Better to nip this in the bud right where it is. He's probably sized me up. Noticed I'm all alone on this 'ole big farm. Thinks I'm easy pickings, especially since the only other humans on this side of the planet have formed relationships with his kind.

Well, sorry for him, but I'm not that easy.

I meet his gaze. "Mr. Tovan."

"Just Tovan, Donna." There it is again. He's got a voice like whiskey and honey and it takes everything within me to push past that flutter in my chest. Reaching down for the rake, I place one hand akimbo.

"I'm going to scrape that floor for you so you have some-place to hobble without tripping and then you're going to rest that leg, got it?"

I swear the slits in his eyes narrow. My heart's in my throat beating so hard I can feel it as he slowly jerks his chin to his chest. He shifts slightly, and I take the moment to slip past him, my throat tightening as my body brushes against his.

I've never worked so fast doing any bit of farm work since I was plopped out here by Xarion. In a minute, I've scraped the hay into a big pile and I'm heading out the door.

"Just holler if you need anything," I shout over my shoulder, even though I'm praying to God, Jesus, Mary, and Joseph that he disappears back to wherever he came from before I lose more of the tight control I've had over myself all these years.

Pushing out the door, I take a moment to pause and pull in a big swell of fresh air. The sky's almost completely dark now and a drop of rain hits me in the face.

A shower of blessings. At least, that's what my old pastor would say. A sign that the Lord is looking out for us.

I start walking towards the house, each step an attempt to put distance between myself and the confusing emotions swirling inside me. Because if this is really one of the Lord's blessings, Ma wasn't lying when she used to say he works in mysterious ways.

With every step, I'm aware of the alien's presence in the barn behind me. Of the possibility that he might call out, might need something.

Part of me, a smart part, wishes he won't.

But another part of me—the traitorous, lonely part—hopes he will.

7

TOVAN

A whole sol passes, and then another. The rhythmic patter of the torrent has become my constant companion, a relentless melody that fills the air and drowns out the silence. I lie on the grass-feed, staring up at the beams crisscrossing the roof.

Back in the town, in my nestkan, I rarely listen to the showers like this.

It's nice. I could live out in these plains if it's peaceful like this all the time. But despite my appreciation of the peace, the sol has dragged on endlessly. I've dozed, woken up, sat here in the silence for many hors. When there's a sound, I sit up straight, my focus on the large doors right before me. I lie watching them, each click that passes, hoping to see a certain soft female standing there. But the outbuilding remains empty, save for the occasional rustle of small creatures seeking shelter from the torrent.

I want to see her.

And she does come. The first time she visits, her presence surprises me. I did not expect her to seek my presence even though that was the only thing I'd been hoping for. But when I see what she carries in her arms, I understand. I understand, and a warmth spreads through me that's never graced my lifeblood before. This female braves the downpour, arriving with trays of sustenance, her hair and clothes damp from the short journey between her lodge and the outbuilding. Each time, my heart leaps with hope, anticipating a chance to remain in her presence for even these brief moments.

But Donna's visits are fleeting. She sets down the tray with a quick, "Here you go," sometimes adding a perfunctory, "How's the leg?" before retreating into the torrent. I barely have time to thank her, let alone engage in any meaningful conversation. And on her third visit, it becomes clear that it might be something I have done.

Was I too zealous? I'd cornered her in the back of the outbuilding without intending to. Drawn by the melody in her voice, drawn by *her*. Frakk. How did the Korruk brothers do it? How did they woo these females? All my instincts are telling me to do is smother her with my presence. I want to follow her around as she talks about nothing and everything. Want to hear her sing. I want to study her, know everything about her, and being in this outbuilding with my thoughts alone has only made that need grow deeper.

My gaze skips across the beams above me. Does this mean this female is—could be mine? I've never felt the urge to get to know another female as much as I want to get to know her. The thought of leaving this homestead in the next few hors is actually creating a tangible pain, and not in my foot—that part of me is healing nicely. The pain is deep within.

Again, I close my eyes, searching for about the tenth time this hor. Searching for a rhythm within me. There is none. But there must be *some* sign. With Kari females, the reaction is immediate. Once you are in your mate's presence, your core-rhythm sings and you just know.

But Donna is not Kari.

I am flying in uncharted skies here. No amount of military training can help me now. But I know myself. This is unlike me and that can only mean this female is special.

I just need to know *how* special.

If she is mine, if the gods have blessed me so, I will not stop until she knows it, too.

As the torrent begins to fade, the urgency within me grows. The rhythmic patter that has been my constant companion for two sols is lessening, and with it, my time here draws to a close. I know I should be relieved, eager to return to my work and continue the surveys with Arnak. Work has always been a solace in this unending nothingness. But as I lie here on the grass-feed, listening to the diminishing drops on the outbuilding's roof, I can't leave without knowing.

I need to know if this female belongs to me.

I push myself up, brushing away lingering bits of the grass-feed before I make my way to the large doors, pushing them open. The world outside is drenched, glistening with the aftermath of the torrents.

My gaze drifts to Donna's lodge immediately, and I feel a pull in that direction. I take a deep breath, steeling myself for what I'm about to do. I've rehearsed this speech countless times during the long, lonely hors of the past sol. Now, it's time to deliver it.

As I make my way towards the lodge, I run through the words once more. "Donna," I practice under my breath, "I wanted to thank you for your kindness. My presence has been unexpected and perhaps unwelcome, but I..." I trail off. This is no good. The words sound hollow, inadequate.

I reach the lodge and pause at the door, my hand raised to knock. My core-beat is a wild fluttering thing in my chest and I take another deep breath to steady it before lifting a claw to the door.

I knock.

All that greets me is silence.

I knock again, louder this time. "Donna?" Still no response.

A strange mix of disappointment and relief washes over me. I want to see her again, but perhaps this will give me more time to perfect my speech.

I'm about to turn back to the outbuilding when I hear a distant sound. It's faint, barely audible over the drip of water from the lodge's roof, but it catches my attention. It sounds like…Donna?

Curiosity piqued, I follow the sound. It leads me away from the lodge, past the outbuilding, and towards the field. As I draw closer, I can make out words amidst the grunts and exclamations.

"Come on girl, you have to help me here!"

My core-beat flutters. It's Donna, her voice strained. I quicken my pace, my rehearsed speech forgotten as I head in her direction.

I reach the edge of the field and the sight before me stops me in my tracks. The field has turned into muddy slush and in the middle of it all is Donna. She's knee-deep in the wet earth, her clothes splattered. And she's not alone.

Next to her, equally mired in the mud, is an enormous creature. So caked with mud it's almost unrecognizable is an ooga, one of the large, docile animals that grazes out in these plains. This one, however, is far from docile. It's thrashing about, clearly panicked, its thick legs churning up even more mud.

It's gotten itself stuck.

"Listen, Gertrude, you gotta listen to me, girl. I'm trying to help you." Donna braces against the large animal, trying to help it out of the pit it's put itself in. "Come on, now. You've got this! You're a strong, powerful woman. You are fiercer than you feel. Now, come on, find that inner goddess and pull yourself out of this hole." She grunts, still bracing against the large animal. "You've got this, girl. Come on."

I stare at her for a few moments, her words making humor rumble in my gut. She's frustrated, that is clear, and still her voice is so encouraging even to this stubborn beast.

"You really are a gem, aren't you."

Donna whirls around, eyes wide in her mud-streaked face, and I realize I spoke those words out loud. "Tovan? How long were you—I didn't hear you come up."

I grimace slightly. I wasn't being quiet intentionally. Just a result of years fighting a war that's still haunting me to this day. I'm beside her now, the mud sucking at my boots with each step. "You look like you need help."

The resigned look she's had on her face the past two sols is nowhere to be seen. Maybe because I appeared so suddenly. Those wide eyes are staring at me with a sort of awe that makes me want to stand taller. But she recovers quickly, blinking it away. Her gaze falls to my foot and I wonder if I should have pretended to hobble. I didn't even bring the staff she'd so graciously given me.

But I shouldn't.

I don't want to deceive her anymore.

"You shouldn't be out here," she says. "Your foot's in the mud. Remember, your boot's got a hole in it. Wouldn't want you getting an infection now."

See. There's something special about this female. Or maybe I'm just an old sap, easily attracted to simple generosity.

"I've healed quite well." I give her the ghost of a grin. "I would show you, so you believe me, but it looks like you've got your claws full."

Donna lets out a short, breathless laugh. "Back to the 'capable' act, I see." She shakes her head, body jostling slightly as the ooga she's bracing against bays. "This girl's got herself stuck, and now she's too scared to move. I've tried everything."

And I can see she has. Because, unlike me, it's clear Donna *is* capable. There are large thick branches near the hole, branches she's no doubt carried here to give the beast some leverage. On one side, there's some freshly cut grass-feed, probably to use as an incentive for these food-motivated creatures. Neither has worked.

The ooga bays again, not moving even as Donna gives it another push. "I don't know what to do anymore."

"I do."

When she glances at me, turns those deep brown eyes my way, I see the hope in her eyes and suddenly I want her to look at me like that all the time. As if I can solve all her problems.

"Here, take my claw." I reach toward her and I'm rewarded with her immediately reaching for me. Zero hesitation. I resist the urge to groan with unconcealed pleasure. Pulling her from the hole is easy, and now, by my side, I turn my gaze to the creature even though my complete attention is on the female standing next to me.

Her scent is even sweeter this sol. As if the torrents have washed away every interference. Standing by my side, her chest heaves, the dark tunic she's wearing today doing nothing to conceal those large mounds on her chest. It takes everything in me not to look at them directly. I'm sure they are her teats...and now I'm wondering what they'd feel like against my tongue. Do humans even do such things with their mates?

Apparently, it doesn't matter. My shaft hardens anyway. The thought alone is enough.

"We need to calm him down," I say, the hoarseness in my voice borne from pure depravity. Thank the gods Donna cannot read minds.

"Her."

I don't know what she's referring to. Those thoughts in my head have erased everything else.

Donna grins. "This is my big girl. Her name is Gertrude."

"Ah." My gaze slides to her lips and the grin still there. Her teeth may be blunt but they are perfectly aligned, only adding to her beauty. "Gertrude, then. A fine name."

Donna grunts, placing both fists against her waist and having her elbows jut out in that way she seems to like to stand. "Of course, it is. I named her."

Her grin widens, and I find myself mirroring it, a foolish, instinctive reaction to her infectious good humor. It's all I can do as my mind buzzes with the fact that since the showers, this is the most we've spoken together these past two sols.

Moving around to the other side of the ooga, I grab a bundle of thick rope Donna dropped there. She really *is* capable. Thought of everything. "Here, take this rope."

I hand her one end of the length of rope, trying to keep my gaze low. But I can see how her body moves in just the periphery of my gaze. How her hips sway with a natural grace that sends a jolt of something hot and primal through my veins.

Frakk. This human female…she is a walking distraction, like pure temptation playing out right in front of me. And my senses, honed for battle, for survival, are suddenly attuned to her every movement, her every breath.

This is not a good idea. If she's not mine, I will truly lose all hope in the fates. But even as the thought forms, I find myself leaning closer, drawn to her warmth like a tilgran to a zimi bush.

She holds on tight to the length of rope, following my lead as I move slowly around to the ooga's head.

"Easy now, Gertrude, this big strong Kari is here to help. That's it, nice and calm…" She's soothing the creature, but does she know she's soothing me too? Big strong Kari? Pride makes my scales brighten. So she likes my strength? I can show her more of that. I could put on a show by lifting the bales of grass-feed and helping her tidy up that outbuilding. Would that attract her? And my size… No female has ever outwardly praised my size before. Does she truly like it? Or is she simply saying that for the creature before us?

My gaze shifts to the ooga, meeting its eyes as if it can help me unravel the secrets surrounding this female. If it could talk, it could tell me if Donna often uses such words or if she truly finds me…desirable. If she sees me as a potential mate, or just a helpful stranger.

A low growl rumbles in my chest. I want to know.

Amazingly, the ooga seems to respond to her words. Its thrashing lessens, and its breathing begins to even out. I find myself captivated by the human even more.

"Okay," her brown eyes dance to me. "What now?"

"We'll guide her out. Ready?"

She nods, those delicate digits gripping the rope tightly. We begin to move, urging the ooga forward with gentle tugs and encouraging words. For a moment, it seems to be working. The creature makes an effort to heave itself from the mud, and my gaze shifts to the female still urging it with gentle words.

"You are good with this." I praise. "Younglings must adore you. You speak with such care, such…" I search for the right word. "Such… tenderness." I mean it, too. From the first moment she pushed through that zimi bush to assist me, she's been nothing but gentle. Firm, but gentle still. Her presence, it's soothing, has a calmness about it, a steadiness that I find strangely comforting. It's like… like the feeling of returning to the den after a long, arduous flight. A sense of safety and belonging that I haven't experienced in…well, maybe ever. It's not just the way she cleaned my wound, bandaged my foot. It's the way she speaks, the way she moves, the way her very presence seems to soothe the raw edges of my soul. Like a balm.

I know now why it's been so hard to leave these plains. I met her. I met Donna and suddenly there's a peace I haven't known in orbits. The loneliness that every displaced Kari lives with, the one I thought nothing about because it's simply a fact of life, is suddenly a burden. One I'm very aware of.

I want to say more. I open my mouth to, but then, I see it. The light in her eyes, that spark of warmth and laughter, it flickers, dims, as if a shadow has passed over her soul. Her smile falters, and for a fleeting moment, a look of such profound sadness crosses her face that it steals away my breath.

I have made a grave error.

"Donna—" I move toward her but the fates are playing a game with me. Disaster strikes.

The ooga's foot slips in the mud, and it lets out a bellow of fear. In its panic, it lurches to the side—right towards me. I try to dodge, but it happens too fast and the mud is too thick. The ooga's massive body slams into me and my world tilts on its axis. Time slows down as my core-beat stutters. I go down like a rock, hard and heavy.

For a terrifying moment, I'm completely submerged, my brain taking some time to catch up to what just happened. But then soft claws grab my arms, tugging, urging me up. I break the surface, mud streaming from my face and filling my mouth.

"Tovan! Are you okay?" Donna's voice is filled with concern, but there's an undercurrent of something else. Is she…laughing?

I wipe the mud from my eyes to see her face, streaked with mud and creased with worry, but her lips are twitching as if she's fighting back a smile. The absurdity of the situation hits me all at once, and before I know it, a chuckle rumbles in my chest.

Donna snorts, and that does it. I'm laughing. Great, gulping laughs that shake my whole body.

Her resolve crumbles, too, and she joins in, her laughter ringing out across the muddy field. We're both covered head to toe in mud, standing next to a bewildered ooga, and laughing like we've lost our senses.

The last time I laughed like this was…I…I don't remember.

That makes me aware of everything as I watch Donna's whole body move with the strength of her mirth. So warm. So pure. This stranger…she is…she's perfect.

I don't know why I do it. Why I suddenly tug when her arms are still grasping mine. Perhaps it's the infectious laughter, the joy of the moment, or simply a desire to share this ridiculous situation more fully with her. Whatever the reason, I tug her towards me, into the mud.

It takes only a moment for her to realize what's happening and her eyes widen in surprise. "Tovan, what are you—No!" Her words cut off as she loses her balance, tumbling down into the mud beside me. "Oh, no you didn't!"

I grin at her, feeling sudden mischief. "I believe I did." I chuckle as she tries to sit up, only to slip back down into the muck.

"Let me go, you big oaf!" She laughs, attempting to free her wrist from my grasp. But I hold on, enjoying this playful moment too much to let it end.

Because I will have to go soon. Have to leave her presence after tarrying far longer than I should. And I want these memories. Like a male starved of affection, if this is all I'll take away after these few sols, I want to solidify it all to memory.

"And let you miss out on all the fun?" I tease, using my free claw to scoop up a glob of mud. "I think not."

As if sensing the danger, Donna turns, those wide eyes getting even wider in her head. "Don't you dare—"

But it isn't like when she's warned me those other times. When she made it clear she wasn't to be toyed with. There is laughter underneath her words, a gentle dare that makes me realize that she's enjoying this, too.

With a squeal, she attempts to spin away from me, but it's too late. I've already smeared fresh mud across her jaw, leaving a comical streak across her brown skin. She gasps, mouth opening into a wide circle before I see something glint in her eyes. Before I can dodge it, a clawful of mud comes right at me. It splatters across my chest, and I stare down at it, surprised.

"What? Can't take the heat? Get out of the kitchen."

We're not preparing a meal, but I would very much like to prepare one *with her*.

My gaze lifts, locking on hers, and that confident smile on her face freezes. The air crackles as I stare at this female, knowing I should look away but can't. And I can tell she feels it too, whatever this is. Something in her feels it too because her gaze falls down my face, landing on my lips before going to my throat.

When I suddenly move she squeals again. No longer in my grasp, she tries to right herself, even hanging on to the distressed ooga to pull herself up so she can run away from me. Perhaps I need to leave the town more often. Go into the wilds to run. To hunt. Because right now, I see something I want and the fact she's trying to run away from me is only making the lifeblood in my veins heat so much my skin itches underneath my scales.

I hit her with a small glob of mud and she turns those fiery eyes on me. Maybe I should stop now. I've soiled her quite badly and—

Mud sails through the air, splattering my face. I spit it out just as Donna throws back her head and releases laughter straight from the bottom of her gut. I forget about my doubts. Another glob of mud in my claw and it becomes a full-on mud fight as we try to outdo each other.

In the midst of our playful battle, I lose my balance again, toppling over. On instinct, I reach out to steady myself, my claws finding something warm and soft. I know what it is, should have stopped myself from hanging on. Instinct takes over instead. My arms circle the female's waist as I pull her down with me, and suddenly, I find myself on my back in the mud, with Donna sprawled on top of me.

She shrieks, rich potent laughter making her entire body react as she grabs more mud and plasters me with it. I growl, the sound rumbling through me as I reach for her arms to stop her attack. When I finally have them pinned, I'm three times as covered in mud as she is and she grins down at me, laughing in my face, obvious pleasure in her victory making her unaware of something critical.

The fact that she's pressed up against me.

But I…I'm very aware. Too aware. Despite myself, despite my desperate grasp for control, my shaft hardens in my trouse, the soft weight of her against me conjuring images in my mind that have no place here right now.

I look up into her beautiful face, and I'm struck breathless. Her laughter, so rich and uninhibited, fills the air around us, wrapping me in a cocoon of pure joy. Never have I felt such peace at seeing another being's happiness. It's a strange sensation. Enough, thank the gods, to distract from my quickly hardening shaft.

I look up into Donna's eyes, those mesmerizing brown orbs sparkling with happiness, and I know I would give anything to witness her laugh like this each sol.

A strange thought to have for a stranger. A female I didn't know existed till a few sols ago. But the feeling is there anyway. Solid. Sure. As if it had always been there and was only waiting for me to become aware of it.

Despite the mud streaking her skin, or perhaps because of it, Donna looks utterly radiant. Even her hair, uninhibited by any head covering, is loose and wild, mud-streaked coils framing her face like a halo.

As her laughter subsides, her smile remains, wide and genuine. It's a smile that could outshine Hudo's star. Even thinking that is absurd. But it is true.

I've never been this close to her. She's pressed against me, her entire body settled on my frame, and I can see all of her. Every bit.

In this moment, covered in mud and pressed against me, she is the most perfect being I have ever laid eyes on. And as I gaze up at her, drinking in every detail of her mud-splattered perfection, I feel something shift inside me. A realization, as inevitable as the rising of the star: I am falling for this human. Hard and fast and with no hope of stopping.

She's mine. This is my *kahl*.

My kahl, my true mate, the female who my soul has yearned for over eons, she is here. My core-rhythm is silent but I know. Donna is my kahl. The thought should ground me. Anchor me to this point in time.

Instead, as I continue to gaze up at this treasure, all I feel is terror.

Donna's laughter slowly fades, her entire body stiffening on me as she becomes aware of our position. Probably because I've gone so still, like a cold slab, not even breathing.

She makes a sound in her throat as she eases off me and I have no choice but to release my hold on her arms, despite that I don't want to. Rolling onto her knees, she diverts her gaze as she wipes some mud from her arms.

"That was…" She releases a breath from her nose. "Not something I usually do, to be honest." She wipes more mud away but she won't look at me, almost as if she's too ashamed to. Or perhaps she feels what I do and doesn't know how to say it out loud.

My silence is what makes her glance my way once more. "Is everything alright?" Then she freezes. "Oh God, your leg. That was really stupid of us. Not only have I gotten mud into my hair, but we've probably definitely made your foot worse." She grunts, rising from her knees. "I'm not sure what came over me. I…" She trails off, blinking as she stares into the…

Still on my back in the mud, I open my mouth to respond,

but no words come out. How can I explain this to her? How can
I tell her that in the span of a few core-beats, with everything in
me, that I'm sure she's mine. It's ludicrous.

"Well, I should get Gertrude out and go clean up." She still
doesn't face me. That resigned look she'd had after she'd left me
in that outbuilding is returning. She's locking me out again. I
can't have that. I—

"You're my *kahl*."

The moment the words leave my mouth, I want to snatch
them back. Donna goes utterly still. Her back is turned to me,
but I can see that she's suddenly frozen.

"Your…what?" Her voice, usually so rich and warm, is now
barely above a whisper.

I close my eyes, cursing myself for my lack of control. When
I open them again, Donna is staring at me now, a look in her
eyes I can't quite determine.

"My *kahl*." My courage returns. I've already crossed a line. I
can't stop now. "My true mate. The one I'm destined for."

She says nothing, and that feels like a judgment in itself.

I sit up slowly, mud squelching beneath me. Donna steps
back, putting distance between us, and each inch feels like a
physical blow.

"I apologize," I continue. Words right now are all I have. "I
shouldn't have said anything. But…for my kind, there's
someone out there who's perfect for us. Our other half. We call
them our *kahls*. And when we meet them, the paths of our existence shift ."

She's still silent. Still unmoving. I'm not even sure if she's
breathing.

When I rise to my feet, we stand there together in the mud,
my chest heaving slightly with the gravity of all this as we face
each other. Behind Donna, the troublesome ooga bays,
somehow freeing itself from the mud-hole and ambling away to
go find the rest of its herd. Not even that draws Donna's atten-

tion. She's wholly focused on me, that once expressive face hiding everything from me now.

"It's a feeling. An instinct." I run a muddy claw through my hair, at once frustrated and fearful at the same time. This isn't how I expected it to happen. When I saw the Korruk brothers with their mates, they were aligned. Right now, with that unreadable look on Donna's face, it feels like a chasm has opened between us.

But then she makes a sound in her throat. A laugh—or at least, I think it's supposed to be laughter, except there's no mirth. It's harsh. Dry. More like a mockery of laughter than anything else. "You must be kidding me."

I shake my head. Either my translator is acting up, or she thinks I just made a jest. "I am not. I cannot explain it, but you are my *kahl*. I am sure of it. You are my true mate."

"Stop." Her lips pull back in a curl filled with derision. A snarl. Far displaced from the comforting generosity, the kindness that had shone in her eyes before. She huffs a laugh through her nose, another mirthless mockery, before she shakes her head. A look crosses over her features, so similar to that moment when I'd complimented her about being so gentle with the ooga and younglings, that I stand frozen again.

Donna takes a deep breath. When she speaks again, her eyes are hard and there's a new distance in them that makes my core-beat halt in my chest. "Tovan Kamesh." Gods, the sound of my own name has never made me shiver before. "I think it is time for you to go."

She wants me to leave. Of course, she wants me to leave. I've ruined everything with my impulsiveness. The laughter we just shared, the moments of camaraderie over the past few sols, all ruined. Wasted.

She wants me to leave, so why's there a tightness in my throat? Why have the muscles in my legs locked up? Because I can't move. I can't leave here. Not like this.

"Donna, I..."

She takes a stop forward and it's hard to stand my ground—because I want to fall to my knees before her. Beg her to understand something I can't even understand myself. All I have is a *feeling*. A feeling is not enough to go on. I need confirmation from my core-rhythm. Need it to sing. And not for the first time in the past few sols, I *beg* it to.

It remains silent, and yet, I know this with a surety. I tell no lies. Donna of the line Johnson, this human female filled with color and life and vitality, she is mine.

"What do you think this is?" Her voice is a dangerous whisper. Half my size, she glares up at me. "You think you can just appear out here, get in my good graces, then claim me like I'm some prize to be won?"

I get it now. That unreadable look on her face, that complete shutdown of emotion, it isn't a shutdown at all. It's anger. Raw, pure, hot anger. Her dark eyes flash with indignation, and I can't help but be struck by her fierce beauty even as her words cut deep.

I swallow hard. I've made a mess of this "No, that's not what I—"

"Oh, I know exactly what you thought," she interrupts. "You saw a lonely woman out here on her own and figured you'd swoop in, playing hero. Well, let me tell you something, mister. I've been taking care of myself long before you showed up, and I'll be doing just fine long after you're gone."

Her words hit hard. I flinch. Hers is a rejection that stings more than any others before. But she's right. We are strangers. How can I explain that it doesn't matter? That in realizing she is my *kahl*, she's become the most important being in my universe?

I want to reach out to her, to comfort her, but I know that would only make things worse. Instead, I stay where I am, mud seeping into my garments, feeling more lost than I ever have in my entire existence. Not even when the Tasqals used their power to claim my world did I feel this utter emptiness.

"Upsetting you is the last thing I wanted. If I could explain—"

"Explain what?" she snaps, crossing her arms. "How you think you could fake some injury just so you could waltz into my life and lay claim to me like I'm some damsel in distress?" Fake an injury? Her gaze darts to my boots and she points at my foot. "I'm not an idiot. You sure as hell fooled me, though. I don't know what sort of swamp magic you're using to pull this off, but I've seen enough tricksters in my life to know better."

My core-beat. Everything within me. Is dead. "I—" But whatever words I could say dry up.

"I'm fifty-one years old, born and raised in Tennessee. I've weathered more storms than you can imagine, big boy. I'm not some character in your fantasy. I'm a real person with a real life, and I don't need your fairy tale promises. I sure as hell don't need or want your so-called protection."

I can barely speak. Everything she's saying, everything she's said, is fracturing into a thousand shards of thought, each one sharper, more chaotic, than the last. "It's not about protection. From the moment I saw you—" I stop, because these are just more stupid inadequate words. If she had a core-rhythm, it would sing with mine. Then she would understand. Without that, I have no proof.

"Oh, spare me the romantic nonsense," Donna scoffs. "I've heard it all before, sugar. "

She takes another step forward, and despite her smaller stature, I find myself taking a step back. Her vitriol, I deserve every ounce of it.

"Now, I want you to listen real close." Her voice is a low, dangerous thing. "You're going to turn around and walk right off my property. And if I ever see you skulking around here again, I won't hesitate to call the authorities. You got that?"

I open my mouth to protest, to try one last time to make her understand, but she cuts me off with a sharp gesture, flashing her claw in dismissal.

"I don't want to hear it. Just go. Now."

With that, she turns on her heel and storms away, leaving me standing there. I watch her retreating form, the distance between us growing with each step she takes. The connection I felt, the certainty that she is mine, clashes with the reality that she...doesn't want me.

Within me, a chasm is ripped open, threatening to split me in two. And as she disappears from view, I'm left alone with the crushing weight of one thing.

My failure.

8

TOVAN

*A*s I reach the border of Donna's farm and the transit route, I pause, looking back toward the lodge. I can't see her anymore, but I can feel her. A tugging in my chest, an awareness of her presence. Is this what it means to find your *kahl*? To be forever aware of them, even when they want nothing to do with you?

I shake my head, trying to clear my thoughts. I need to think. Need to figure out what to do next. Because one thing is clear—I can't leave. Not now. Not when I've found my *kahl*.

But how can I stay? Donna made it clear she wants nothing to do with me. The thought of imposing my presence on her, of making her uncomfortable in her own home, is unbearable. But the thought of leaving, of never seeing her again, is even worse.

Turning, I push across the transit route to the other side, the pasture where we first met. I find myself wandering aimlessly through the grass-feed, my feet moving of their own accord while my mind whirls.

All I can think about is Donna. The way her eyes lit up when she laughed. The warmth of her body pressed against mine. The look of cold hardness in her eyes when I told her she was my *kahl*.

I've dreamed of finding my kahl for so long. Imagined the moment countless times. In my dreams, it was always perfect. We'd lock eyes across a crowded space and just know. Our core-rhythms would sync, and we'd fall into each other's arms, two halves of a whole finally united.

I never imagined it would be like this. Never thought my *kahl* would be a human, with no core-rhythm to sync with mine. Never considered that she might not feel the same instant connection, the same bone-deep certainty.

As I walk, lost in my thoughts, I find myself at the zimi bush where I first met Donna. Where she'd pushed through the thicket just to help me, a stranger in need.

That's who she is. Kind. Compassionate. Willing to help others without thought of reward. It's part of what makes her perfect for me. Part of why she's my *kahl*.

But she's also strong-willed. Independent. Not the type to accept being claimed by a stranger, no matter what forces might be at play.

I sigh, sinking down to sit in the still wet earth. The mud on my clothes has mostly dried, flaking off in chunks as I move. I barely notice.

I can't leave. I just...I can't. As I sit there, staring out at the fields without really seeing them, a thought occurs to me. Maybe I don't have to choose. Maybe there's a middle ground.

I could stay in the area, but not on her farm itself. Find a place to make a temporary lodge, somewhere close enough that I can still feel her presence, but far enough away that I wouldn't be imposing on her.

And maybe, over time, I could find ways to interact with her. Not as her *kahl* —she's made it clear she's not ready for that— but as a...a what? A companion?

As I sit there, lost in thought, I look up just in time to spot scales like my own glinting in the light as a large male approaches. I didn't expect to see anyone, didn't want to, not when I'm feeling like this. But I should have known better. Of course, Arnak is out here. He's still completing the surveys. He probably never went back to town.

"Tovan? Is that you?" As he gets closer, his steps quicken. "By the stars, what happened to you?"

I attempt a grin, but it feels more like a grimace. "It's…a long story."

Arnak crouches down beside me, his brow furrowed. "You look like you've been stuck in a pasture and trampled by oogas." His gaze skips over me, his focus intent, even though I'm one of the few beings that knows only one of his eyes works as it should. "Are you injured?"

"Not physically." I rise and he does the same with me. Even without meeting his gaze, I can feel him studying me.

"There's something different about you. If the human threw you out, why didn't you return to your grav bike? I would have enjoyed the company…" His gaze slides over me. "Even if you're a bit surly right n—"

"I think I found my kahl." I start walking, pushing through the grass-feed and leaving him there, stunned.

Arnak catches up with me a moment later, his wild mane blowing in the wind and obscuring his face as he jogs through the grass-feed backwards. "Your *kahl*? The *human*? But that's… that's incredible! Why do you look like the stars have faded across the cosmos?"

I laugh and realize it's the same mirthless mockery of a laugh that Donna did. "Because she wants nothing to do with me."

Arnak almost stumbles and he stops jogging backward and turns around to keep my pace. "Explain. How can that be?"

Slowly, haltingly, I begin to recount the events of the past few sols. Meeting Donna, feeling the instant connection, the disastrous conversation where I revealed she was my *kahl*. As I speak, Arnak listens, his expression cycling through surprise, confusion, and sympathy.

As I climb over the rise beneath which I'd parked my grav bike, Arnak glances at me. "Your core-rhythm…"

"Is silent."

He almost stops walking. "But you're sure?"

I look his way, thankful he's not questioning my stance on this. I nod, chin to chest, my throat tight. "Yes. She's…incredible, Arnak. Strong, kind, beautiful. But she's also human. She doesn't understand what it means to have a *kahl*. I believe my core-rhythm is silent because she has none."

Arnak is silent as we walk up to the grav bikes. I can see an area of flattened grass-feed where he must have made a camp over the past few sols. Even my scanner is here and it's obvious Arnak had retrieved it in my absence.

"What will you do?" he asks.

I release a heavy breath. "I cannot leave. But she doesn't want me to stay. So I will keep my distance…but I cannot leave her alone out here."

Arnak jerks his chin slowly. "Not like that, though. You need to clean up. Need supplies." He looks up at the clearing skies. "It won't shower for a good few sols so you should be fine, but you'll still need a fresh weather cover to camp with. Yours has a hole in it. I know, because I got drenched the first dark cycle."

I stare at him. "You used my weather cover and not your own?" But that isn't what I really want to say. What I really want to say is "gratitude". Even without questioning, he's fully supporting my decision to stay out here until I can figure it all out. This is what you call a true ally.

Arnak grins at me. "Why use mine when yours was available?"

I growl and he grins wider before heading to his grav bike. He hops on the thing, waiting for me to do the same to mine.

"Come on, brother. We have to make it to town before the other Kari fill the queues."

My brow tightens. "What queues?"

His grin widens. "As I thought. I've tried pinging you countless times over the past two sols and there was no answer. You had your comm off, didn't you?"

I blink. Yes, he's right. I forgot about it. "What does it matter?"

"There's been news, brother. News I think will help you."

I STARE at the notification on my comm, hardly believing it. Standing here in the queue, Arnak practically bounces on his feet beside me.

"Isn't this great? We can all know. No more wondering."

ATTENTION ALL KARI and Human citizens.

A voluntary program has been established to analyze the potential for mate bonds between your species. This program requires a simple lifeblood sample and will provide valuable insights into compatibility. Participation is encouraged.

A TEST. A simple test that will tell me with the surety what I already know, that Donna is mine. Not only will it be proof, she will have the surety, too. It's almost hard to believe. Almost too good to be true.

"The two Korruk brothers have mated these females. Found their *kahls* in them," I hear another Kari saying. "I hear there is one other female of this species living here. I hope she will be mine."

They're talking about Donna, no doubt.

"We all hope," his companion says. "Do you know where she stays?"

"Out in the plains, but that area is vast. It will take me some time to find her."

I stiffen, a white hot rage swelling within me so much that I don't realize I'm glaring at the males until Arnak grips my arm.

"Brother," he says, gaze shifting to the two males then back to me. "We are next."

It is with much effort that I move my legs toward the medics waiting before us in this crowded hall. More Kari than I have ever seen before in one place since we came to this world. And all because we're desperate to find our *kahls*.

But I've already found mine.

Arnak is before me. It's a simple extraction. A device on the muscle in the arm and a sample is taken.

"Next," the medic calls and Arnak moves out of the line, his gaze shifting to me for a brief moment.

As I step up to the medic's table, it is only then that I notice the Saffion sitting there. A species with tall ears and fur-covered bodies, this one is all white.

"So far, we have a much larger turnout than we expected," I hear him mutter. "And only one human."

"Has she come in to do her sample yet?" the medic asks as she gestures me forward.

"Not yet," the Saffion sighs. "I think it is best I head out and retrieve it myself. Donna is...strong-willed and might be opposed to this."

Donna...

"But the notification was sent to all humans and Kari on this world, was it not?" The medic gestures me forward again and only then do I realize I'd stopped walking. "It's part of the reason so many have turned up today, for a chance to meet these females."

The Saffion grunts. "There is only one. And as I said, she is...

stubborn. I have another human coming in a few sols, but she has already communicated that she is also not interested. These females might need some reassurance before putting themselves forward."

I grunt and the medic dips her head in apology, thinking it's the device she's just placed on my arm that I'm reacting to. What I'm really reacting to is the fact that this Saffion is right. But not in the way he thinks.

Donna is strong-willed. Strong-willed indeed. She is vibrant. A force to be reckoned with. A female that sets my lifeblood on fire. But maybe what the Saffion says is what is true. That she might need *reassurance*.

I appeared in her life and suddenly declared that she is mine. She knows nothing about me. I must make her trust me first. Make her realize I will be there for her, always.

That's what I will do. That's the plan. My core beat settles a little with this new course of action. Something solid that will help me retrieve the mate I feel like I'm losing.

The medic finishes taking my sample and nods to me again. Finally, the Saffion looks up from the files he's deliberating over. His gaze skips back down to find my name. "Tovan Kamesh, you will receive word via secure comm if we find your match."

I give him a jerk of my chin. This male knows my Donna. Possibly is her companion, too. I hesitate, wanting to say something to him, but there are no words. Everything that happened on that farm is still too fresh.

If I tell him she is my kahl, he will think I'm lying. I have no solid proof. So I jerk my chin to my chest once more and step away, but not before I hear the males behind me in line speak once more.

"Hey, Saffion, you know the female that's available?"

Available? I pause. No, not just a pause. I freeze mid-step, my body completely tensing at the male's words. Slowly, I turn back, my eyes narrowing as I watch the interaction.

The Saffion looks up, his expression neutral. "You're referring to Ms. Johnson? What about her?"

The strange male leans in, a grin spreading across his face. "I heard she's quite the catch. Living all alone out there...bet she could use some company."

The Saffion's red eyes narrow. "If you do not match with the human, I advise that you do *not* seek her out."

The male chuckles. "She doesn't have to be my *kahl* for me to get to know her. I am breaking no law. There are other things I'm interested in, too."

The Saffion stiffens, his ears standing tall on his head. It's a strange sight. His species is usually docile and fearful, but it seems when it comes to these females, when it comes to Donna, he won't hesitate to defend. That immediately puts him in my good graces.

"And what *things* do you refer to..." His gaze slides to the files before him as he searches for the male's name.

"You know what I mean," the male says. At his utterance, there's an approving grunt from his companion.

My fists clench at my sides, a surge of anger rising in my chest. The casual disrespect in his tone, the implication behind his words—it's more than I can bear.

Before I can think better of it, I'm moving.

"Tovan?" Arnak calls, but in three quick strides, I'm back at the table. The strange male barely has time to look up before my fist connects with his jaw.

He stumbles backward, shock and pain mingling on his face as he bares his fangs. "What in the fates?!" he sputters, one hand cradling his jaw.

I stand there, breathing heavily, my claw not even throbbing from the impact. The Saffion is on his feet now, focus darting between me and the other male.

"Tovan Kamesh!" he says, but there's no bark in his tone. Almost as if he's pleased I punched the male.

I know I should feel remorse, should apologize for my actions. But all I can feel is a burning need to protect Donna, even if she doesn't want my protection.

I glare at the male before me. "Don't you dare go near her, or in the name of the gods, I will scale you alive."

"Frakk," Arnak murmurs at my back. "Vicious." But there's a laugh in his tone.

The strange male glares at me, still rubbing his jaw. "What's it to you, Kamesh? The female has no *kahl*. Until then, she is unclaimed."

I take a step forward, halted only by Arnak's claw on my arm.

"Stay away from her." My gaze shifts to the other Kari watching the spectacle, my glare meeting all of theirs. "She is mine."

A hush goes across the room as everyone looks my way.

"Tovan Kamesh," the Saffion says, "what do you mean?" He glances back down at his files then at me.

He wants proof. A core-rhythm that's singing. A positive result from these tests they're doing. I have neither.

My chest heaves as I take in the room.

There are too many Kari, and every single one of them wants my Donna, hopes she is theirs. She is in danger.

I level my gaze with the Saffion one last time before I turn and leave. I thought my resolve to camp out in those plains was sure. Now it is even more critical that I do.

I have to get out there and protect the female who has made my existence pivot. Donna has created a new path for my life. One I won't let any of these hungry males walk over. She is my *kahl* and when my core-rhythm awakens, even if she still rejects me then, I will stay by her side, protecting her until I have no more breath to.

9

DONNA

Stupid, stupid, Donna.

Seems like that bad luck that haunted me back in the States has followed me to this frickin' hoohaa planet off in the middle of nowhere.

Dammit! I thrust the knife so hard it goes right through my bluebread and lodges in the counter. Trying to dislodge it only makes me more pissed off.

'*You're my kahl.*' Must have taken me for a damn fool. How confident was he to say that out loud and think I'd fall for it? How naive do I look?

One whole day has passed and I'm still so angry about it all that it's the single thing I can think about.

I'm so annoyed, I leave the bluebread with the knife still stuck in it and storm into the bathroom, my mood going even lower when I catch sight of myself in the mirror.

A whole day has passed, and I'm still fuming. Fuming because I let this vagrant get under my skin. Yes, he was a handsome vagrant. Strong too. He made me laugh and yes, my heart was beating all sorts of strange in those few days in his presence, but—

"Goodness, Donna. You sure know how to pick them." I frown at myself. Just as I'd told myself before, generosity doesn't always bring you blessings. I shouldn't have been so kind.

Releasing a breath, I run my hand through the two-strand twists I'd done after the hours it took to wash, condition, and detangle my hair. Who on Earth told me it was a good idea to frolic in the mud like some child? I don't know why I did it. Why I allowed him to pull me into the muck with him. Just another bad decision I can add to the long list of experiences with the males in my life.

Whatever had come over me, it's gone now though, thank God.

I didn't think he would listen. To be honest, when I told him to leave my property, my heart was hammering in my chest. My prevailing thought was to get inside and grab hold of a knife, just in case. I was hanging on to that stern facade, praying to every saint I could remember that he wouldn't turn violent at the rejection.

I've seen that kind of anger before. The kind that simmers in a man's eyes when he thinks he's entitled to your time, your attention, your...everything. I wasn't about to become a statistic, some cautionary tale whispered among the women of the Initiative.

But he'd left. Didn't fight. Didn't curse. That utter look of pain I thought I'd seen in his eyes might actually have been real. I've seen no sign of Tovan Kamesh in the day that's passed and that's just fine. My farm is quiet again. My life is quiet. And I am happy.

I force a smile in the mirror before turning away and heading to the front of the cottage. My comm beeps as I pass it and I ignore it. Probably the hundredth notification about some matching program New Horizons has developed. Something about a blood sample to match with a Kari mate.

Xarion has been trying to get my attention from the day

before. Even left a long video message explaining the process. But he said it was voluntary, so I ain't volunteering.

Yea, no thank you.

Inhaling a breath of fresh air as I step out on my porch, I take in the clear pink sky above me. Another day, some more work to be done. If the interaction with Tovan Kamesh taught me anything, it's that I need to get this farm up and running. Need it to be bringing in credits to support my life here. Because, unlike Catherine and Eleanor, I have no mate to help carry this weight. And I sure as hell don't want one.

I step off the porch, grabbing the bucket I'd left there earlier, and head across the field. The ground is still partly wet, causing my boots to sink a bit with each step, but I trudge through it without a bother. I'm really settling into this farm thing, aren't I. The fresh air, the sound of the animals, the soothing peace.

It's a huge effort to push away my anger, my sadness. To face the day. To *pretend*. But I need to distract myself.

It starts as a hum before the song bubbles in my throat. *(Sittin' On) The Dock of the Bay* by Otis Redding. It's a good song, one that immediately eases some of the strain, and I bob my head as I go.

My voice rises and I let the notes carry across the wind. Out here, no one can tell me it's a waste of time and that I need to focus on a job that pays.

I'm singing, feeling the rhythm as I walk through the field when something catches the corner of my eye. My head turns on instinct, even before I realize what I'm looking at.

The song slowly dies in my throat as I frown.

There, across the field is a structure. One that wasn't there the day before.

I squint, trying to make sense of what I'm seeing. "Mmhm, something's not right here."

At first glance, it looks like a natural formation—a cluster of trees and bushes. But that's impossible. Trees don't just sprout up overnight, not even on this alien world.

I take a few steps closer, my heart doing strange, almost cautious, thumps. There's something deliberate about the arrangement, something that speaks of intention. The closer I get, the more I can see and I'm pretty sure the branches are woven together, the leaves arranged in a pattern that provides perfect cover while still allowing glimpses of the interior.

And then I see it—a flash of movement, barely perceptible, but unmistakably there. A shadow shifting within the structure, and the briefest glint of what might be a golden eye catching the morning light.

My breath catches in my throat as a figure emerges from the makeshift shelter. Even at this distance, I'd recognize that large form anywhere. Tovan mother-effing Kamesh.

I go still, not sure I'm actually seeing what I'm seeing. Did he...did he really make a camp near my farm? I stare at him, a swirl of anger, disbelief, and shock making me gape. After I explicitly told him to leave, this alien dares to set up camp on the edge of my property? My mouth slams shut as my nostrils flare with a pressured exhalation, my hands clenching into fists at my sides.

I open my mouth, ready to shout, to demand he leave immediately. But something stops me. Maybe it's self-preservation. After all, I'm alone out here. Better not antagonize him, not when I don't know what he's capable of.

So I clamp my mouth shut, grip my bucket tighter, and pretend I haven't seen him. I turn on my heel and continue on my way, my steps a little quicker, my shoulders a little tenser. But I can feel his eyes on me, watching my every move.

Trying to milk Gertrude while being watched by an alien makes it like trying to get water from a rock. God knows I'm diligent, but I'm no Moses. My hands are sweating, my fingers fumble with the milking pail, and Gertrude seems to sense my unease. She shifts her weight, her massive body bumping against my shoulder.

Oogas have no teats. Her underside is practically smooth, only six sequential dimples near her rear where the milk is supposed to come out . It gets all over my arms and soaks into the dirt, my mood not helping at all.

Glancing over my shoulder, my frown only gets more severe when I catch the alien watching me. As soon as I look his way, he stands straighter. I glare at him, and Tovan has the audacity to *wave*. My frown dives even deeper.

Does he really think I'm going to wave back? I scowl, making it even more obvious I'm ignoring him as I abandon my milking efforts and stand instead. I need to focus on something else. Milking the oogas had been my big plan on supporting myself. Milk and bluebread. I was thinking I could sell them in the town for a modest living. So far, that idea's falling through like sand in a sieve, but I'll figure it out. I always do. So, ignoring the purple alien that stands out like a sore thumb across the way, I carry on with my tasks.

Throughout the day, I try to go about my usual routine. I tend to the crops I've planted in a little square near the cottage, feed the animals, and even repair a section of fencing that's come loose. But every task is colored by the knowledge of Tovan Kamesh's presence. I find myself constantly looking over my shoulder, expecting to see him standing right behind me.

But he never approaches. Never calls out. Just…watches.

It's unnerving. I find myself jumping at small noises, my nerves frayed and on edge. And the worst thing, it's not fear I feel. I'm not afraid of the big alien. I'm just…aware he's there. I don't know if that's worse.

As the sun begins to set, painting the sky in brilliant shades of orange and purple, I retreat to my cottage. I lock the door behind me, something I've never felt such pressured need to do before. Peering out the window, I half-expect to see Tovan's face pressed against the glass. But there's nothing. Just the distant shape of his makeshift shelter on the field next door, barely visible in the fading light.

I sink into a chair at my kitchen table, my mind whirling. What is he doing? He's not approaching. Not trying to convince me of what he blurted the other day. Not trying to get on my land. He's just…there. Is this some kind of Kari courting ritual I don't understand? Or is it something even worse?

Finishing my dinner, I run a hand over my face. "He's not my problem. He'll get bored and leave eventually."

But even as I say the words, I don't believe them. There was something in Tovan's eyes when he called me his *kahl*, a certainty that went beyond mere infatuation or desire. I ignored it, but maybe he believed what he was saying, even if I didn't.

Well, that sucks for both of us.

As I clean up, I catch myself glancing out the window again and again, searching for any sign of movement in the darkness. When I finally make it to bed, sleep eludes me. I toss and turn, unable to rest. What if he tries to break in? What if this is all part of some elaborate plan?

I told him I'd call the guards if he returned, but what will I say? That an alien told me he's interested in me, I told him to leave, and now he's camping next door and it's annoying? It sounds more comical than dangerous. I could call Xarion, but he's the one that's been telling me to put myself out there, not lock my door and tell the aliens to shoo.

When dawn finally breaks, I've barely slept a wink. I drag myself out of bed, feeling like I've gone ten rounds with a wrestler. As I stumble to the kitchen to make some tea, I steel myself for another day of this strange, silent standoff.

But when I look out the window, my heart nearly stops. Tovan's shelter is gone. The point where it stood is empty, as if it had never been there at all.

For a moment, relief washes over me. He's gone. He's finally listened and left me alone. But then something else takes hold. I stare at the spot where his camp was for far too long. Part of me wants to celebrate. This is what I wanted, was it not? The return of my solitude? But another part, a part I'm not quite ready to acknowledge, feels...disappointed.

He gave up.

I frown at my faint reflection in the window. I don't want him here. I don't even like him. There's nothing to be disappointed about. So what? He declared I was his mate and then decided to not pursue me. His loss.

But that twinge of disappointment is still there. Because... because maybe a small part of me wanted the pleasure of that feeling. Of someone chasing me. Of being desired. Even if I wasn't planning on going anywhere with it.

I release a slow breath. I really am a mess.

I spend the morning in a daze. Trying to make batches upon failed batches of bluebread before I finally give up and decide to get on with the other farm work. Without the zimi berries, the mixture just isn't right and I have no idea where to get more from. I'll just have to wait till that bush sprouts some more and that might take a while. The whole idea is exhausting and I'm tired by the time I exit my cottage. There's a slight chill in the morning air today and I wrap my arms around myself as I step off my porch.

That's when I nearly stumble and fall on my face.

"What the—" There, just off to the side of my door, is the thing I almost fell over. A sealed bucket. My brow dives. I didn't leave that there. Going closer, I pry open the thing, my breath stopping in my throat when I see what's inside.

Pure, fresh orange-tinted ooga milk.

My head snaps up as I look behind me. No one's there, but I sure as hell know I didn't sleepwalk and do this in the dead of night. It had to be *him*.

Closing the lid, I step off my porch more cautiously now, my heart a strange thundering thing in my chest as I cast my gaze to the field across the way.

That's when I see it. The shelter.

He's not gone. He's simply moved it. Closer to my property line this time.

The white-hot anger I expect is missing. Now I'm just confused.

I jerk slightly as he suddenly appears. His hair is tousled and he looks like he had as good of a rest as I did last night—basically nada. He lifts an arm to wave again and I ignore him, turning away.

Whatever game he's playing, I'm not throwing the dice.

Going about my daily chores while my mind races is hard. But I manage. Every time I pass that bucket filled with fresh milk, I'm not even sure how to feel. He was clearly watching me struggle yesterday. But what kind of move is this? He hasn't demanded my attention. Hasn't approached me directly. Hasn't tried to speak to me. Just…helping from the shadows?

I can't make sense of it. Men don't do things for nothing. There's always an angle, always something they want in return.

It's not until late afternoon that I notice something's off. The fence I'd repaired yesterday, the one that had been giving me trouble for weeks, is suddenly sturdy and strong. The loose boards have been replaced, the posts driven deep into the ground.

I stare at it, my mouth hanging open. There's no way I did this. I know my own work, and this…this is expert craftsmanship.

As I inspect the fence, I notice other changes. The barn door that was always stuck is now swinging smoothly on its hinges. The barn itself shows signs of being cleaned up too.

I stand there at the door, staring at the work for a long moment. I should be angry. I should be scared. I told him to leave, and he's still here, lurking on the edges of my property like some kind of...what? Guardian angel? Stalker?

But instead of anger or fear, what I feel is...even more curiosity.

I'm a fool, aren't I?

Hissing at myself, I slam the barn doors shut and head in for the night. Purposefully, I keep my head straight, refusing to look in the direction of Tovan's camp.

This time, before I head in, I light the torch I'd found in the supplies New Horizons gave me and set it on the wall.

He'll be gone tomorrow. He can't keep this up forever.

10

TOVAN

It's the third sol since I made camp just outside Donna's homestead. Rising, I blink at the first rays of light signaling dawn.

Sitting up, I stretch out muscles stiff from sleeping on the hard ground. As I do, I become aware of a persistent ache in my chest. It's not physical, not entirely. It's more like a longing. A pull towards the lodge across the pasture, towards Donna.

Is this what it means to be separated from your *kahl*? This constant awareness, this unrelenting need to be near them? If so, staying away from Donna is going to be even harder than I thought. When my core-rhythm sings, it will be near impossible.

I must be prepared for when that happens. I've already notified Arnak. If I don't check in with him each sol, he is to come out here to find me. Just in case. The last thing I want to do is go mad with need and hurt the one creature that's been slowly folding my existence around them.

And Donna has no clue about this. I'm not sure just how much she knows or how much the other Kari have told her about the rut. She is already so wary of me, she will for sure reject the bond once my core-rhythm sings.

It's almost too much to face.

Pushing to my feet, I crawl from the structure, my focus going immediately to the lodge. All is quiet. Donna is still resting. All through the dark cycle, the faint glow of her light pierced through the darkness and I wondered what she might have been doing. This sol, I promised myself I'd find those zimi berries she seems to like so much. I know I saw an untouched bush nearby.

As I set off to find zimi berries in the surrounding area, I feel a glimmer of hope for the first time since my disastrous confession. She hasn't said a word to me. But she hasn't turned me away either. It won't be easy, but I've never been one to shy away from a challenge. And Donna...she's worth any hardship.

The constant glaring in my direction has softened, replaced by curious glances when she looks toward my camp. Her shoulders aren't as tense when she's working in the fields, and once, I could have sworn I saw the ghost of a smile tugging at her lips as she discovered the freshly cut grass-feed I left for her animals.

It's not much, but it's progress. Slow and steady, like the coming of dawn after a long dark cycle.

I pause to pluck a handful of ripe zimi berries from a nearby bush, their sweet scent reminding me of Donna's natural fragrance. Everything about this planet seems to echo her presence, from the rich soil beneath my feet to the vibrant sky above.

I have to hurry and I do so now. Gathering the berries and returning to the homestead. Climbing over the perimeter fence, I leave my offering by her door and hope for the best.

It's a delicate balance, this. One I'm still learning to navigate. But with each passing sol, I feel more attuned to Donna's rhythms, to the ebb and flow of her moods and needs.

Last sol, I noticed her struggling with a particularly stubborn patch of weeds near the outbuilding. It took every ounce of self-control not to rush in and help. Instead, I waited until she retired for the dark cycle, then spent half my sleeping time carefully clearing the area and preparing it for new plantings.

It's the least I can do until she decides to let me in. Till we can at least talk about this. She's my *kahl*, after all. My true mate. And even if she doesn't know it yet, even if she never accepts it, she will always be mine.

I glance at her door before I force myself away and back to my camp. Is she still asleep? Or has she awakened, perhaps scrubbing herself in a warm bath before she faces the dawn.

The image of Donna washing sends an unexpected wave of heat through my body, and I shake my head to clear it. I head back to my camp before I do something stupid like linger too long and she finds me here outside her lodge. The last thing I want to do is erase my progress.

Hors pass and nothing. Sitting in my shelter, even my scales itch with the need to move about. To do *something*. But I must wait. Donna will come out soon.

More hors pass, and there's no sign of her.

As the star begins to rise more fully, I begin to worry. Is she alright? Did something happen to her? The urge to go to the lodge, to seek her out and make sure she's okay, is almost overwhelming.

But just as I'm about to give in to that urge, I see her. She's exiting her lodge and is now walking across the field, carrying what looks like a pail of scraps. She looks...tired. Her gaze is downcast. Those fiery eyes that would at least acknowledge my presence don't even glance my way now and her shoulders are slumped as if carrying a heavy burden.

My core-beat grows sluggish at the sight. Did I do this to her? Is her exhaustion a result of my presence here?

She dumps the scraps for the oogas then turns around.

Only then does she glance my way. "Morning, Tovan. Thanks for the berries."

My core-beat stops.

Did she…did she just speak to me?

It's the first direct interaction we've had since my confession and I think I might have imagined it. It's so unexpected that I don't respond, not realizing I'm standing there like a fool, just staring at her after she *spoke to me*!

But as I watch her retreating form, something nags at the back of my mind. There was something…off about her this sol.

I take a step forward, then stop myself. I want nothing more than to follow her, to make sure she's alright, but I know I can't push too hard. She's only just acknowledged my presence again and humans, I'm realizing, are gentle things. One wrong move and it's really over for me.

So I stay where I am, watching as she reaches her lodge and disappears inside. The door closes behind her with a soft thud, and silence descends once more over the homestead.

Silence that suddenly feels oppressive.

I try to busy myself—tending to my small camp, preparing a meal for myself—but my attention keeps drifting back to Donna's lodge. Something isn't right. I can feel it in my bones, in the very core of my being.

When another hor passes and there's still no sign of her, no sound of movement from inside, no glimpse of her through the windows, my scales begin to prickle. It's unlike her to stay indoors for so long, especially on a sol as fine as this. The grass-feed needs tending, the animals need care. Donna is nothing if not diligent about her responsibilities.

Just as I'm convincing myself that I'm overreacting, that she's probably just catching up on some much-needed rest, I hear it. A crash from inside the lodge, followed by a pained groan.

My core-beat seizes. Donna.

I don't hesitate. I drop everything and I'm sprinting across the field, my core-beat turning wild in my chest. All thoughts of respecting boundaries fly out of my head as I bound onto her porch.

"Donna?" I pound on the door. "Are you alright?" There's no response, just another muffled groan. I try the handle—it's unlocked. A blessing, because I would have punched my way through the thing otherwise. Taking a deep breath, I push the door open and step inside.

The sight that greets me sends a chill through my body. Donna is on the floor, half-slumped against a toppled seat. Her face is pained, her breathing labored. A sheen of sweat covers her forehead, and her eyes are unfocused.

Oh Gods, no.

I'm at her side in an instant, kneeling beside her, pulling her into my arms. "Donna?" I've seen a lot of things. Things that would strike fear into any normal citizen, and none of those things made me shake the way I'm shaking now as I run a claw down my *kahl's* jaw. "Can you hear me, lira'an? What happened?"

Donna blinks slowly, her gaze finally focusing on my face. "Tovan?" Her voice is weak, confused. "You shouldn't be here."

"I know." I'm not going to argue about that. She's right. I shouldn't be here. She told me explicitly to leave several sols ago. "I heard a sound. You're not well." I swallow hard, my claw moving over her jaw again. She's clammy to the touch. "We need to get you to your sleeping cushion. Where is it?"

I lift my head, briefly scanning the room. It's a small lodge. Homely. If my core-beat wasn't stop-starting in my chest, I would have spent more time appreciating the way she's decorated the interior. There's a sweet scent in the room though, one that's not my mate in my arms, and I look up to see a table laden with what looks like several different...I don't know what they are, but they look like food.

She tries to push herself up, but her arms tremble with the effort. She's weak. "You're not taking me to my bedroom."

I could grunt a laugh, but it won't come. Even in this situation, she's indignant. She doesn't want me here. It should hurt, will probably hurt later when I return to my camp and have time to think about it, but right now, looking down at my mate in pain and not knowing why, has erased everything else from my mind.

Without further hesitation, I scoop her up into my arms. The fullness of her body against mine pushes the heat of her body even through my scales. For a moment, she tenses in my grip, and I fear she'll push me away. But almost as if her body's needed this for a while, a sigh causes her to relax, her head resting against my chest.

I head to the room I assume holds her sleeping cushion. It's not. It's the washroom. That only leaves one other door in this small lodge, and I head there instead. It's a small sleeping cushion. If I shared it with her, it would force her to press against me each dark cycle with nowhere else to go. I push the thought away as I lay her down, but as I start to pull away, Donna grabs my wrist. Electricity sparks at the spot, spreading through my entire being.

"Why are you here?" she whispers. "I told you to leave."

"I know." My voice is soft, much softer than it ever has been. "And I will, as soon as I know you're alright. But right now, you need help. Please, let me help you."

She looks at me for a long moment, those eyes, despite the weakness in them, studying me. "You smell like dirt."

I blink at her. The unexpected utterance has me speechless. Again, on another occasion, I would laugh. I can't now.

"You don't have to stay," she continues. "It's just low blood sugar. I forgot to eat. Been too busy trying to figure out how to make the damn bluebread perfect." She takes a moment to rub her eyes as her mouth opens in a yawn. "It's nothing serious."

"You didn't eat?" While I've been snacking on meal squares, my mate was going hungry?

She shakes her head, trying to rise. "No."

A growl rumbles in my throat before I can stop it. "Stay here. I'll make you something to eat."

Turning, I head out the door, my mind a whirlwind of thoughts. But before I can leave, Donna's voice reaches me. "Tovan, you're not supposed to be here."

I stop, looking at her over my shoulder. "I know."

There's a flash of something in her eyes but it isn't anger. It's something else. Before she can force me away again, I head out of the room to the meal preparation area.

My *kahl* needs food, and I will provide it. The fact that I've only ever prepared meals for myself, and rarely, is a minor detail I choose to ignore.

Surveying the room, I take in the various utensils and appliances. I have similar ones in my nestkan but have never had to use them. Meal squares are easy to buy and fulfill basic nutrition. It's what most Kari like me live on. I could go out to my camp, grab a few, but Donna needs a proper meal. So, I push aside my uncertainty and focus on the task at hand.

First, I need something to prepare the meal in. My eyes land on a large cooking pot, and I grab it. Water seems like a good start, so I fill the pot and place it on the heating element. Now for ingredients.

I rummage through the storage units, pulling out anything that looks remotely edible. Dried root vegetables of various shapes and colors find their way into my arms, along with some dried herbs and a package of what I think might be grain.

Returning to the pot, I dump everything in. The water splashes over the sides, and I hastily wipe it away. Now what? Heat, of course. I fiddle with the controls until I hear a satisfying hum and see a faint glow beneath the pot.

As the concoction begins to bubble, I realize I should probably be stirring it. I grab a long-handled utensil and begin to mix, sending more water sloshing over the sides. Okay, slower, softer. The smell that rises from the pot is…interesting. Not necessarily bad, but certainly unique.

After what feels like an eternity, I decide the food must be ready. I ladle a generous portion into a bowl and grab a small curved utensil that will be perfect to scoop mouthfuls into my mate's small mouth. Heading back to Donna's room, I try not to spill the steaming mixture.

Sight of her sends my core-beat into disarray and my skin heats underneath my scales. She's propped herself up on the sleeping cushion and she is…luscious.

I'm a horrible, disgusting male, because my mate is ill and I should be dead inside. Instead, my shaft is hardening in my trouse.

"Tovan?"

My throat goes dry. "I made you something to eat."

Donna pushes herself up some more and those mounds on her chest bounce. Look away, Tovan.

"What…exactly is it?"

I pause, realizing I have no idea how to describe my creation. "It's…a nutritious blend of various ingredients."

She takes the bowl, her brows raised in what I hope is intrigue rather than disgust. Carefully, she uses the small utensil to bring some of the food to her lips. I hold my breath as she tastes it.

For a moment, there's silence. Then she looks at me.

I don't expect her soft smile. I truly expect her derision. But no, she's smiling at me, and oh, does it set my lifeblood on fire. I have pleased her?

"This is…certainly something."

I feel my scales flush even as I try not to stare at her too hard. "I can try again. If you can't consume it, I'll try again or head to town and purchase…" It's the way she's looking at me that makes me pause. She's gone unreadable again and it brings back memories of that sol in the mud. But even if she becomes angry at me, I can't back down, not this time. "You need to eat, Donna. We can't have you starving."

She grunts before gesturing to her body with one of her delicate arms. "Do I look like I'm starving to you?"

There's a sudden tension in the air, her words carrying a sharp edge that catches me off guard. My eyes involuntarily trace the curves of her body, and even though I'm aware of how inappropriate it is, I can't look away. Even though I know how frakking inappropriate it is, I can't stop the hardness still growing in my trouse.

My pupils have narrowed to slits, a visible indicator sign of intent. Of a hunter zeroing in on its prey. And right now, Donna Johnson is the most alluring prey I've ever encountered.

"No." My voice is too low. Much rougher than I intend. "You don't look like you're starving at all."

She grunts again. "Where I come from, some would take offense to that, you know."

Our eyes lock, and I feel a surge of heat coursing through my body. The air between us seems to crackle with an intensity that wasn't there before.

"I mean no offense. You look…" How? How does she look? Beautiful? Perfect? Both true, but neither adequate. My eyes trace the generous curves of her body, drinking in every luscious detail. The soft swell of her hips, the fullness of those mounds on her chest, the enticing roundness of her belly— every part of her calls to something raw and deep within me.

Can I tell her that she is captivating? That her fullness speaks of abundance, of life? That it makes me want to worship every inch of her?

My claws itch to reach out and touch her, to explore the plush landscape of what is Donna. I imagine how she would feel beneath my claws—soft, warm, yielding. The thought sends a jolt of heat straight to my shaft. Spend leaks from my tip.

She is irresistible. Her body is a feast and I am starving for a taste.

I see the moment her breath holds. The moment a flicker of something passes through her eyes. It is what pulls me back from wherever I went, places me back in the present as Donna shifts slightly. The movement sends her sweet scent straight into my nostrils and I almost groan as another bead of spend forms at my tip.

Thank the gods my trouse does not reveal this.

"Tovan." She looks up at me, her voice barely above a whisper. "What are you doing?" For a moment, I freeze. Does she know? Can she scent my arousal? But as she studies me, it's clear she's referring to more than just this moment. She's referring to everything. From the zimi bush to this point.

And I have no solid answer. Only that I'm waiting for a core-rhythm that's taking too long to sing.

"I'm not sure," I admit, not bothering to disguise the huskiness in my tone. "But I know that when I look at you, every point in my existence begins to align."

The tension between us is palpable, a living thing that seems to pulse in the small space separating our bodies. I can almost hear the rapid thrum of her core-beat, or maybe it's mine. Everything else fades away—the room, the food, our past disagreements. All that exists is this moment, this heated, charged connection between us.

But Donna stiffens. "Tovan..."

"I know. I'm not supposed to be here."

Donna stares at me. "Then why are you?"

My throat tightens and I ease back, putting some space between us because I don't trust myself not to reach out and touch her. "I couldn't leave."

She takes the time to put some of the food into her mouth

before her gaze slides to me again. "Are you some kind of creep or something?"

"Creep?" I tilt my head, unsure what she means. "I didn't mean to creep by the border of your farm. I...was out of options. I want to give you space but...I couldn't be far away."

She hums tone in her throat. "Because I'm your *kahl*."

My gaze shoots up and I feel like a fool for being so easy to read.

"I can't be your *kahl*, okay. It's evident you think so, because you've been sleeping in the field next door like a psychopath. But it's about time we talk about this. I thought you were joking, trying to get under my skirt. Clearly, that's not the case here."

My throat tightens some more, making my words sound like gravel. "Why would I joke about such a thing?"

Donna shrugs, her gaze meeting mine before she looks down at the food and takes another mouthful. "You're a man."

Silence descends between us as I replay those words in my mind. A man? Does she mean a male? She didn't believe me because I'm a male? It all makes sense now. Everything she said that day.

"Someone hurt you. Some *male*."

Frakk, what is it with me when it comes to this female? It is like I no longer have control.

Donna grunts, huffing a dry laugh through her nose. "You could say so. I wouldn't call them real men. Boys maybe. There's a big difference."

The growl that rumbles in my throat vibrates the air between us. Enough that Donna looks up, her eyes wide with shock.

"Who?"

She stares at me for a long moment, and that something flickers in her eyes again. "Why do you care? It doesn't matter. It was in the past. Why do you even care about me?"

I take a deep breath, trying to calm the rage that's building inside me at the thought of someone hurting this soft, beautiful female before me. My claws flex involuntarily, and I have to force myself to relax.

"Why do I care?" I repeat, my voice low and intense despite my efforts to soften it. "Because you're my *kahl*. Whether or not you accept it, that's what you are to me. And it's not something I can change or control."

I take a step closer, my eyes never leaving hers. "I care because every time I look at you, I feel like I'm seeing the stars for the first time. I care because your smile makes my core-beat go faster than any battle ever has. I care because the thought of you in pain makes me want to tear apart whoever caused it."

Donna's eyes widen even more, and I see a mix of emotions flashing across her face—surprise, confusion, and something else I can't quite name.

"You don't even know me," she whispers, but there's a tremor in her voice that wasn't there before.

"Then let me." I take a step closer. "Let me know you, Donna Johnson. Let me show you that I'm not here to hurt you. I'm here because…I…I can't imagine being anywhere else."

I'm close enough now that I can feel the heat radiating from her body.

"So that thing in the bush? The wound in your foot…all of this was just so you could get to this point?"

For a moment, her question confuses me, but then it all becomes clear.

"No. That injury was very real. You were singing and your voice…it's strong, Donna, beautiful. Richer than any melody I've ever heard. It disrupted my scanner and I hid the moment I saw you. I didn't mean to. It was foolish. And that's when…" I sigh. "That's when I got caught in the trap."

I expect her to tell me it's all a lie. It sounds like a tale I made up. But she doesn't. She's silent as she watches me. Assesses me.

"But you're healed now," she finally says, and I realize with a jolt that she'd still been worried about me, even though she's been pretending not to be. Another dose of warmth goes through me.

"I'm healed now."

"How is that possible?" Her throat moves but it's the only movement she does. She's utterly still, watching me, a predator assessing its prey. And just like that, the power dynamic shifts, the hunter becoming the hunted. A thrill goes through me.

"We Kari are blessed with a few things. Healing quickly is one of them."

She's looking at me as if she wants me to continue. She still isn't moving and she hasn't even blinked.

"It's why the Tasqals hunted us down. Experimented on us." I'm not sure how much she knows or how much I should even say. "We heal quickly, and their race was dying of a scourge. And our…" I trail off. Just how much should I tell her? What if saying all this will turn her away from me even more?

I have nothing to offer this female. No planet to return to. No kin to create a family unit. All I can offer her is myself.

But she is either more perceptive than I thought or she is one of the few that can read Kari emotions, because Donna sets the utensil down in the bowl as she watches me.

Her voice is soft when she speaks. "They hurt you too? Experimented on you?"

I look away. She's struck a wound there without even knowing it. "No." My admission is almost too quiet. "They didn't experiment on me."

"What experiments?"

I take in a deep breath, remembering scenes of males we'd rescued, the horrors they'd told. "Caged. Tied up. Forced to… forced to release spend. They, the Tasqals, had trouble bearing young. They believed that because we Kari are virile, they could synthesize whatever makes us so. It didn't work. Many suffered." Including the Korruk brothers that she knows so well. I'm sure they bear the scars.

"But you…"

Here it comes. I take in another breath, steeling myself. "I was a fighter pilot. I fought from the skies, not on the ground." There's a sudden rush of shame that goes through me, a sudden rush of unworthiness. My claws clench at my sides. "Many of my people bear the scars of what the Tasqals did to them. They endured unimaginable horrors, fought battles I can barely comprehend. And I…" My voice trails off, and I force myself to look back at Donna. Her eyes are soft, concerned, and it makes my core ache.

"I have no scars to show. No visible marks of what our people went through. I was up there, in the stars, while others suffered below. I tried to help, to fight back, to protect our people. But I know it wasn't enough."

I don't know why the words pour out of me now, things I've never admitted to anyone, not even Arnak.

Donna blinks slowly, those eyes seeing deep into my soul. "It sounds to me like you did the best you could with what you had," she says. Her voice is a gentle balm against the harshness of my self-recrimination. "And sometimes, honey, that's all any of us can do."

There it is again. That goodness that dwells within this female. The one that only confirms to me that I've found my home.

For a few moments, I watch as she moves, a heavy sigh making her shoulders rise and fall as she consumes a few more mouthfuls of the food I made.

"I know you're afraid." Gods, I can't shut up. "I'm not asking for everything. I'm not asking for anything at all. I'm just asking for a chance. A chance to prove myself to you, to show you that this isn't some grand scheme. You truly are my *kahl*."

Donna pauses, looking down into the bowl before her.

"I'm fifty-one years old, Tovan Kamesh. I don't have time for games."

"I do not do this in jest."

She looks up at me then. "And what if I can't give you what you want, hmm?"

I reach out slowly, giving her time to pull away if she wants to. When she doesn't, I gently cup her face in my claw, electricity shooting up my scales at the contact. "All I want is you, Donna. Just as you are. You say I know nothing about you, and you're right. But I want to know. Your fears, your doubts, your past. I want all of it. Because it's all part of what makes you my *kahl*."

She shifts out of my grasp and it feels like the dawn loses its light. "Your core-rhythm has to awaken for you to have a *kahl*. I've seen it happen, Tovan, and you don't look like you're in heat to me."

The utterance is like a barb. As if she's deconstructing everything I've said and calling out a lie. Of course, she's seen it happen. She knows the Korruk brothers. Knows their mates. They're all allies.

Except, I haven't lied. This is true.

"I know it hasn't. That is my failure."

Even now I search within me, hoping it will just spontaneously react. It doesn't.

"You know, I could do that test New Horizons messaged about. And if you're wrong…" She says it like it's a challenge. As if mentioning the test will get me to back down.

"Then you will know I speak the truth."

She stares at me for a long moment before taking another mouthful of the food.

"You can use my bathroom. You've got mud and twigs stuck in your hair and that camp you have out there might be some fancy alien thing I don't understand but I know you sure as hell don't have a shower out there. You're welcome to use my bath if you want."

I blink, momentarily caught off guard by her sudden shift in tone and the unexpected offer. The bath. Her bath. Is she talking about the washroom? The implications of her words sink in, and I feel a mix of excitement and nervousness coursing through me.

"I...thank you."

Donna shrugs, but I catch a glimmer of something in her eyes. "It's just a bath, Tovan. Don't read too much into it."

But we both know it's more than that. It's a tentative step towards...something. I'm not sure what, but I'm grateful for it all the same.

"I appreciate it," I almost whisper, in disbelief of my luck and at the same time suddenly swelling with hope. "And the meal? Is it helping?"

She nods, taking another mouthful. "It's actually not bad. Tastes like alien soul food."

I have no idea what she means, but food for the soul has to be a good thing. "High praise indeed."

There's a moment of awkward silence, and I realize I'm still standing there, staring at her. "I'll...I'll go wash then."

As I turn to go, Donna's voice stops me. "Tovan?"

I look back at her. "Yes, lira'an?"

She meets my eyes, her expression unreadable once more. "When you're done...maybe we can talk. Really talk. About all of this."

I feel another surge of hope in my chest. "I'd like that," I say softly. "I'd like that a lot."

Her expression softens. "Don't make me regret this, Tovan."

"I swear on my life, I won't." And I mean it.

11

DONNA

I sit in that room for far too long. Probably afraid of what just happened between me and Tovan. Probably too scared to face the music.

That he's gotten under my skin—and I'm not a girl that scares easily.

I finish the vegetable soup he made, surprising myself by drinking down the entire thing. Tovan served me in one of those bowls I use to mix batter for my bluebread and I drank it all, anyway. Having finished it now, I feel a thousand times better than I felt this morning, but gosh, I shouldn't have let it get so bad that I ended up collapsing.

What if Tovan hadn't been close by?

Sliding off the bed, I tuck the bowl to my chest as I venture towards my bedroom door and pause. I heard him out there. Soft sounds, like the creak of a floorboard here or the gentle closing of a door there. He's out there and the thought of facing him again…after everything he said…everything he revealed…

I swallow hard.

A part of me doesn't want to open the door because he'll see that he's weakened some of those walls I've erected around myself. That despite his unconventional methods, he's wearing me down.

Stupid, handsome, sweet talker. Why couldn't he look like one of my exes? The hate would be immediate. Then I wouldn't be standing here with a mixing bowl clenched against my bosom, afraid to step into a room in my own home.

"Come on. What's gotten into you?" I whisper to myself. A deep breath, my chin held high, and I push the door open, ready to face him. Ready to set down the ground rules of this…whatever this is. "Ok, Tovan, listen—"

But I'm talking to an empty room. My mouth slams shut and opens again, as I gasp like a fish out of water. He's not here.

"Tovan?" I head over to the bathroom and the door is shut. Pressing my ear against it, I listen. No sound is within. "Tovan?"

Gently pushing the door open, I prepare myself for potentially barging in on him naked, but he's not in the bathroom, either. The room is empty. My cottage is empty, except for me, of course.

That's…not what I expected.

I stand in the middle of my living room, bowl still clutched to my chest, feeling oddly bereft. The silence of the cottage seems to mock me, highlighting an absence I wasn't prepared for. Where is he?

A part of me—a larger part than I care to admit—expected him to be here waiting. Maybe pacing anxiously, ready to launch into another impassioned speech about how we're meant to be together, yada yada yada. That's what I'd steeled myself for when I finally worked up the courage to leave my bedroom.

But this? This absence? It makes me feel like I have no clue what I'm doing here. And probably I don't.

I set the bowl down on the kitchen counter, my mind

whirling. That's when I notice the pot simmering gently on the fire. Curious, I lift the lid and a rich, savory aroma wafts up, making my mouth water. Some kind of stew, by the looks of it.

He rifled through my cupboards and found more food. Guess he's better at reading the ingredients New Horizons left me than I am. I've been eating mostly tinned stuff, relying on the pictures on the labels and taste-testing my way through.

I stare at the stew before taking a ladle and giving it a stir. It's a bit too thick and I add a little water, my lips pursing as my eyes narrow on the food.

Fine. I'm impressed. Not just by the fact that he's cooking—again—but by the consideration. He's not here hovering over me, but he's made sure I'll have something to eat later.

That's…that's more thought than I can say for some of the men I dated on Earth. And I know I shouldn't compare, that my bar is probably far too low, but I can't help it.

"Damn it," I mumble, replacing the lid on the pot. "I can't let him in so easily."

This isn't how it's supposed to go, right? I've seen what happens when Kari find their "fated mates." I've witnessed it firsthand with Catherine and Varek.

Now that was something to behold. Varek had been…well, wild doesn't even begin to cover it. It was like watching a man transform into a beast before my eyes, all frothing need and desperate longing. He'd been mad with the desire to claim Catherine, to mark her as his own. And Catherine, for all her initial resistance, had been just as caught up in it. The love between them had been palpable, electric.

But this thing with Tovan? It's nothing like that.

And…

I swallow hard, setting the ladle down as I step out of the kitchen. Wrapping my arms around myself, I try not to get into my own head. But I have to face the music as well—every heartbreak, every disappointment, every moment I felt unwanted or unworthy.

I've spent so long convincing myself that maybe I'm just not meant for that kind of love, that soul-deep connection I've seen others find. But now…

Now there's Tovan frickin' Kamesh. Tovan with the strong arms and deep voice who claims I'm his *kahl*, his fated mate. Tovan, who looks at me with an intensity that both thrills and terrifies me.

Wouldn't it be just like the universe to finally give me what I've always longed for, wrapped in a package I'm too scared to open?

I let out a shaky breath, closing my eyes. "Nothing good comes easy." It's a mantra I've repeated countless times over the years. No one just frolics through the bushes and stumbles on their Prince Charming like some Disney princess.

But then…has it really been easy? I was abducted, ripped away from everything I knew and loved. I've faced challenges and dangers I never could have imagined back on Earth. Maybe…maybe all of that was leading me here. To this moment. To him.

That I deserve someone who wants me with such a strong bond it would chase my breath away…is it really possible?

My breaths are a bit unsteady as I clutch my chest. Because I would be lying to myself if I said I didn't want it. Everything he's offering with this mate bond. I want it all. For someone to love me, to want me, with such an intensity it consumes me, body and soul.

Like Catherine and Varek; the raw, primal connection between them.

A breath shudders from me and I open my eyes, wiping away tears that brimmed. I've spent so many years giving up on that dream. Am I a fool to even consider it again now?

Giving myself a shake and taking a few huge breaths, I

gather my bearings once more. I stand there for a moment, unsure what to do with myself. The cottage feels different somehow, as if Tovan's brief presence has altered it in some subtle way I can't quite pin down. It's still my space, but now it holds echoes of him—in the lingering scent of the soap he used, even in the stew bubbling on the stove.

Driven by a restlessness I can't shake, I make my way to the front porch. The afternoon sun is warm on my skin as I step outside, but there's a slight wind today. Stronger than usual. For a moment, I just breathe in the familiar scents of hay and earth.

That's when I spot him.

Tovan is out in the field, wielding what looks like a scythe with surprising skill. His movements are fluid, almost graceful, as he cuts through the tall grass. I find myself unable to look away, mesmerized by the play of muscles, the way his scales shift and roll with each swing.

It's...beautiful. *He's* beautiful. Because even though I've convinced myself he's a pest, I can't deny that. The sun glints off his scales, creating patterns of light that dance across his body. I've never seen anything quite like it. He's tall, handsome, strong...thick.

My heart quickens as I remember the way he picked me off that floor as if I weighed nothing. The good Lord knows that the dizziness didn't dampen the feeling of those strong arms or the way his hard body felt against mine.

He makes quick work of the grass and my eyebrows rise a little when I notice even Gertrude seems to be trailing him, her thick frame ambling in the path he's making. At one point, he stops and talks to her and she bays, nudging him with her nose before she nibbles on some of the grass he's cut. Seems I'm not the only one getting too used to his presence here.

I'm so caught up in watching him that I don't realize he's finished until he's walking toward me. Crap. I turn to the hanging baskets, pretending to prune some of the leaves.

"Lira'an, you should be resting."

I try not to react to the warmth that spreads through me at the sound of that deep voice. He's called me that name before. I'm still lost as to what it means.

"I've had plenty of rest, thanks to you." I glance at him, still pretending that I'm busy pruning the flowers. "Your soup really helped."

"Did it?" He sounds surprised and I try not to look at the way he leans on the scythe thing as if it's completely natural for him to be out here, shirtless, working under the sun. "I am pleased."

I snort. "You talk like you're surprised."

He doesn't answer immediately, giving me no choice but to glance his way again. When I look at him, I swear his scales are a little darker.

"It was my first attempt at preparing sustenance for another being."

I snort again, not believing him. "Well, I'm lucky it turned out so well, I guess." But then I sober, my eyes truly meeting his. "Thank you. For earlier. You didn't have to rush to my aid."

He watches me for a few beats, and I can't tell what he's thinking behind those eyes of his. "You didn't have to come help me in that zimi bush either."

His words kill whatever I was thinking to say next. My lips shift into a begrudging smile as I turn away from him once more, actually picking some dead leaves off the plants now. "I guess we can call it even then."

It's so silent I think he's gone off to the barn to put the scythe away. For some reason, I start to sing, something that only happens when my heart is light and I'm happy. It's not Otis Redding this time. It's *Summertime* from Porgy and Bess. My strong contralto rises as I turn to the other plants and pick some dead leaves off it too.

The first stanza rolls from my throat like melted chocolate.

Rich and oh so good. My whole body feels the melody as I pull it from my soul.

I'm about to start the next stanza when I finish working on the plants and turn to find Tovan still standing there. I stop short, the song in my throat and my heart beating hard. I don't often sing for others to hear. That awful ex wasn't the only one to make me push back my dreams of a career in the arts, and I suppose my confidence has waned over the years.

"Tovan, I thought you walked off."

His gaze falls to my lips. "Your voice..." is all he says, and I wish he would continue. What about my voice? He's mentioned it before, too. Said it's what drew him to me. That I disrupted his scanner or something.

"Ah yes." I huff a small laugh through my nose before stepping off the porch and heading toward the well. "If I'd known you were still standing there, I wouldn't have belted out my heart like that."

I only assume he's following me. For such a big male, he's so silent. Careful not to stand on the maintenance hatch for the well, I turn on the spigot like Xarion taught me to and fill a bucket waiting there. From the corner of my eye, I spot Tovan watching me.

Just the outline of his form there, his masculinity in my space, and I'm completely aware of him.

"Why?"

I don't immediately understand what he's asking.

"Your voice is rich."

His praise makes a slight tremble go through me, or it might be the sudden gust of wind that whips around us, tugging at my clothes. I blink against the unexpected force, my grip tightening on the bucket handle.

"Thank you," I manage, my voice nearly lost in the wind. "I don't...sing much these days." Not with an audience, at least.

I try to take a step towards the vegetable patch I've been

working on, determined to water the sprouts despite the weather's interference. The wind picks up again, stronger this time, and I struggle to keep my footing. The water in the bucket sloshes dangerously close to the rim.

Before I can take another step, I feel Tovan's presence behind me, his large frame suddenly enveloping mine. His arms reach around me, his claws covering my hands on the bucket handle. For a moment, I'm frozen, hyper-aware of every point of contact between us.

"Let me." His breath is warm against my ear. "You should be resting."

A shiver runs through me and not because of the wind. I let go of the bucket, allowing Tovan to take its weight. As I do, my back brushes against his chest, and I have to stifle a gasp at the feeling of his scales, even through the barrier of my dress. I can feel the heat of him, the solid strength of his body, and something deep within me—heck, forget poetry—my clit throbs *hard*.

I step away quickly, my heart racing. To distract myself from the lingering sensation of his touch, I speak far too quickly. "I used to sing all the time, actually. When I was younger, I even dreamed of making a career out of it."

Tovan looks at me with interest as he easily carries the heavy bucket towards the vegetable patch. "What changed?"

The question catches me off guard. I follow him, wrapping my arms around myself as another strong gust of wind buffets us. "Life," I say after a moment. I don't want to tell him I put my dream behind me for something much more stable. That the fact I had no one believing in me made me not believe in myself. "Dreams don't always pan out the way you expect them to."

For a few beats, we walk in silence. "Perhaps," he finally says. "But that doesn't mean they can't still come true in unexpected ways."

I pause and he walks a few steps ahead of me as I stare at him. Somehow, it feels like we're talking about more than my singing here. But before I can respond, an even stronger gust of wind nearly knocks me off my feet. Tovan is there in an instant, one arm steadying me while the other keeps a firm grip on the bucket.

"We should get you inside," he says, glancing up at the sky around us. "There's a gale coming. I can smell it in the air."

I look up at Tovan, startled by both his closeness and his words. "You can *smell* it?" A gale? Aren't these plains supposed to be peaceful? But I realize at once that the grasses are tall and lush. Despite the warm sun most days, this isn't a desert, and that means 'peaceful' doesn't mean there is no weather. The strong rains the other day should have warned me enough.

He jerks his chin, those eyes swallowing me whole as they move over my face. "The air pressure is dropping. It will be a significant storm."

I groan. Not another storm. I haven't even gotten to half of what I need done since the rains.

As if to prove Tovan's point, another powerful gust sweeps across the field. I shiver, suddenly cold despite the lingering warmth of the day.

Tovan sets the bucket down and turns to me. The look he's giving me is so soft, it holds me speechless. He reaches out, his claw gentle as he tugs my headscarf down on my forehead. The touch is brief, but it sends a jolt of electricity right through me again.

"Go inside, Donna." That voice of his is a low rumble that I feel as much as hear. "I'll secure things out here."

For a moment, I'm lost in his gaze, in the intensity and warmth I see there. Then I give myself a mental shake and nod. "Okay," I manage. "Be careful."

He gives me a small smile, a small twist of his lips that shows me the tip of one fang, and my gaze zones in on it. He'll want to bite me with that. Sink his teeth into my skin. Why doesn't that scare me?

"I have more to live for now than just the blessing of another sol," he says, gaze still eating me up. "I will be careful, lira'an."

Lira'an.

I watch as he strides towards the vegetable patch, his movements sure and purposeful despite the strengthening wind. Then, with a last look at the sky, still calm and bright despite the rising wind, I hurry inside.

CALL me a fool for standing by the door, pacing.

The wind had picked up so much outside that I can hear it whistling now. It's so strong, I wonder if my new roof will hold.

It's a sound that takes me straight back to those sweltering Tennessee summers, the air thick with humidity and the scent of honeysuckle. The way the sky would darken without warning, the wind whipping up into a frenzy, the ominous wail of the tornado sirens piercing the stillness.

I swallow hard, daring to peer through the window. The oogas have all hunkered down, lying low on the ground. From here, they look like small boulders with their heads tucked close against their bodies like that. Even they know to take cover.

My gaze shifts and I search for the telltale glint of pink and purple scales, but I don't see Tovan. Frowning, I'm a bit annoyed at myself for even searching for him. He's a grown man and at least there's some boundary between us while we work this out, but...where is he? If the oogas have the sense to hunker down, so should he.

The wind picks up, and my worry grows. I don't know what to expect with this windstorm. Should have asked Xarion whether there was some sort of basement for me to take cover in if a twister appears. I didn't even think of that.

I pace again, pausing once or twice to look through the window. Still no sign of the alien. Damn. I haven't felt this kind of unease since the day I watched a twister rip through my neighbor's farm, leaving nothing but splintered wood and shattered dreams in its wake.

Making sure the windows and the door are shut firm, I force myself to head farther into the house. The meal Tovan put on has finished cooking, and I focus on serving two bowls. He cooked it, he might want to share the meal with me. That will mean him being in my space again, though. My hand pauses with the ladle as I force down a lump in my throat, searching for any part of me that hates that idea. I swallow hard when I realize I don't. Don't get me wrong, I'm still a bit wary, but I don't think he's here to harm me. I'm not scared of him in that way, not since that first day. That fear is long gone and the fear in its place stems from a whole other source.

Meal served, I shudder when a particularly powerful gust screams past the cottage. I swear the building shakes as if I'm being transported to the land of Oz. I'm almost too afraid to look out the window again, but curiosity, and a growing worry for the alien who's out there braving the elements, gets the better of me.

Peeking through the curtains, I gasp. The once-peaceful landscape is now a whirlwind of activity. Leaves, a kaleidoscope of reds and yellows, swirl through the air like confetti, branches thrash wildly, and the orange grass bends low, bowing to the wind's fury. I scan the field, searching for any sign of Tovan, my heart clenching with each gust that howls past the cottage.

But he's nowhere to be seen.

"He must have hunkered down in the barn," I grunt. I should hunker down, too. Right now, this seems like the perfect weather to go lie down with the sheets right up to my chin and a good book to keep me...

I'm just turning away from the window when I spot a flash of purple. Tovan. He's running for cover, but not in the direction that makes sense. Not toward my barn. He's heading toward his camp. Is he so insane that—

The thought cuts off because he *is* insane. I've seen it first-hand, camping by my property line, even though I explicitly told him to leave.

For a moment, I think maybe he's just grabbing something he forgot, some vital piece of equipment or supplies. But as the seconds tick by and he doesn't emerge, a cold realization settles in my stomach.

He's not coming back.

This man, this *male*, he's still trying to respect my boundaries, isn't he? Even when it's clearly not safe for him to do so. Oh hell. I bite my lip staring in the direction of his camp before a large sigh lifts my shoulders.

"Damn it." Because I already know what I'm about to do.

Stupid generosity. Stupid kindness. Ma should have raised me to be a cold-hearted bitch like Aunt Mary. How she managed to snag so many fellas with that icy stare and a tongue sharper than a butcher's knife, I'll never know. Course, Aunt Mary could also charm the scales off a snake, so maybe that's why she never needed kindness.

I grab a large, sturdy piece of cloth from a seat nearby. It's the same cloth I've used for curtains at my window, but this is a makeshift shawl I'd been using to keep warm on cooler evenings. Wrapping it tightly around myself, I take a deep breath and push open the door.

The wind hits me like it's a person, nearly knocking me back inside. For a moment, I tell myself Tovan Kamesh is a fool for thinking he can wait this out in a house made of sticks while the wind is screaming "Let me in. Let me in." But then again, he doesn't know the story of the Big Bad Wolf. I grit my teeth and push forward, my legs straining against the gale. Each step is a battle, the wind tearing at my clothes and even my hair, threatening to sweep me off my feet.

As I struggle across the field, I curse myself. What am I doing? He's insane, but I'm a fool, too. The journey seems to take an eternity. The wind whips stray pieces of grass and debris across my face, stinging my skin, and each step feels like I'm battling with God himself. I keep my head down, focused on each step, willing myself not to be blown away.

Finally, I reach the edge of Tovan's camp. The structure is shuddering violently in the wind, looking like it might take flight at any moment.

"Tovan!" I shout, my voice nearly lost in the howling wind. "Tovan, are you in there?" I ask the obvious. Even though I know this alien who is slowly taking over more of my thoughts than I'd like to admit is definitely stuck inside the little thing.

But for a heart-stopping moment, there's no response. Then, a piece of the structure shifts and Tovan emerges, those yellow eyes wide with shock.

"Donna?" he calls back, disbelief evident in his voice. "Is something wrong? You shouldn't be out here!"

We're screaming against the wind.

"You can't stay out here!" I yell, gesturing wildly at the chaos around us. "It's not safe!"

He stares at me, seemingly frozen in place. And there is… conflict in his eyes.

"Come on!" I reach out, grabbing his arm across the fence. "We need to get to shelter!"

For a moment, he resists, but then another powerful gust rocks us both. When I tug again, hardly able to even open my eyes wide enough now to see, I feel him relent. He climbs over my fence as if he's a gymnast and his warmth is suddenly by my side.

We turn back towards the cottage, leaning into the wind and I pray we make it back without being lifted up like a kite. Tovan leans closer, his large frame practically like a shield trying to protect me.

"You shouldn't have come, lira'an. It's not safe."

Lira'an.

"You see this, right?!" I gesture with one hand, the other gripping the shawl for dear life. "Do you really think you could stay in that little camp?! Why didn't you go to the barn?!"

He leans closer, protecting me some more, but he doesn't answer. He doesn't need to. We both know why he didn't take shelter in the barn.

Pressing on, I have to grip him to keep steady. My fingers dig into his side, into his scales, and I try not to think of how soft they feel against my palm. We're almost at the edge of the field when a particularly vicious gust catches us off guard.

The world switches orientation. I feel my feet leave the ground, a scream torn from my throat as I'm lifted into the air. But before panic can fully set in, I'm grounded. Thick, strong arms surround me as Tovan pulls me close, shielding me with his body as we both tumble to the ground.

We roll once, twice, before coming to a stop in the tall grass. Breath knocked out of me, I'm only aware that the effect of the wind isn't as heightened as before. That I can actually open my eyes although I can feel it all around me—just not *on* me. And that's when I realize it's because something else is on me—or someone. *Him.*

I'm pinned beneath Tovan's solid form, his body a warm weight above me. The grass around us bends and sways, creating a small cocoon that offers a moment's respite from the wind's assault.

I'm stunned, my body lighting up in ways that shouldn't occur as I stare up at him. In this moment, with his focus on the wind around us, he doesn't realize I'm staring. That I'm drinking him in.

The strong line of his jaw, the furrowed concentration in his brow, the way his eyes narrow against the wind—I commit every detail to memory. A stray lock of hair falls across his forehead, and I fight the urge to brush it away.

My breath catches as I realize how close we truly are. I can feel the steady rise and fall of his chest, the warmth underneath his scales seeping through the thin fabric of my clothes. The scent of him envelops me—a mixture of earth, sweat, and sweetness.

I tilt my chin up a little, inhaling again. So sweet. He smells good. I've never…never wanted to dip my nose into the crook of a man's neck and just inhale his essence before. Not like this.

For a heartbeat, the howling wind fades away, and all I can hear is the thundering of my own pulse. Every point where our bodies connect threads electricity underneath my skin, each touch sending sparks through my system.

Suddenly, Tovan's gaze snaps to mine. His eyes widen slightly, as if he too is only now grasping the intimacy of our position. For a moment, we're frozen, caught in a wordless exchange that seems to stretch into eternity.

We should move. We're in the middle of a storm.

But…

I watch as something shifts in his expression, and our position becomes even clearer. He's settled between my thighs. In a position I haven't had a man in…how long? Forever? A position I've wanted to be in so many times, lying alone in my bed with a battery-operated friend that, while effective, just always left something missing. Something like this. His weight. His heat. *Touch*.

Tovan doesn't make me feel too big or clumsy.

I feel like a *woman*…and that…that is slowly breaking me.

When his leg presses hard into my thigh, I blink, before I realize it's not his leg at all. My eyes widen at the same time that my core reacts, clenching, a whimper that I wish gets lost to the wind leaving my throat. But the wind raging around us is not my ally. Tovan hears the whimper and I see him react.

It's his eyes. They get…hungry.

I don't know why I do it. I'm in a field, the wind raging around us, and maybe I've gone a little mad from the hypoglycemia. Because I tilt my chin up.

I tilt my chin up and I hesitate for a moment.

Then I press my lips against his.

DONNA

The moment my lips touch his, the world around us fades away. The howling wind, the swaying grass, the looming danger—all of it recedes into the background, overshadowed by the electric current that surges between us.

At first, Tovan is still, his body rigid with surprise. I can feel his confusion, his hesitation. But then, as if a switch has been flipped, he responds with a fervor that takes my breath away. His lips move against mine, clumsy at first, then with growing confidence as he mirrors my movements.

The kiss is unlike anything I've ever experienced. It's been a while, I'll say that. A while since anyone has touched me like this. Kissed me like this. But there's a rawness to this, a primal intensity that makes my toes curl and my heart race. His lips are softer than I expected, the contact between us more enjoyable than I thought it would be. The sweetness I smelled earlier is there too, a hint of something exotic and intoxicating on his tongue.

I lose myself in the sensation, my hands moving of their own accord to tangle in his hair, pulling him closer. Tovan responds in kind, one hand cupping the back of my head while the other presses hard into the grass at my side.

This is insane, I think, even as I arch into his touch. *What am I thinking? What am I doing?* But the rational part of my brain is quickly being drowned out by the flood of sensations over-whelming me. I'm caught in a whirlwind of desire and doubt, unable and unwilling to break free.

The kiss deepens, grows more urgent. I can feel the heat building between us, threatening to consume us both. Tovan's body shifts against mine, every point of contact slowly shat-tering my will—the press of his chest against mine, the weight of him between my thighs, the unmistakable evidence of his arousal.

But just as I'm about to lose myself completely, Tovan pulls back. His eyes are wild, pupils almost invisible, chest heaving as he struggles to catch his breath. For a moment, I fear I've crossed a line—my own line, and probably his too. Afraid that he'll pull away and I'll be left to face the consequences of my lapse in good judgment. But then he speaks, his voice a low, rumbling growl that sends a delicious shiver down my spine.

"Not here," he says, the words more felt than heard over the roaring wind.

Before I can process what's happening, Tovan is moving. He rises to his feet, bringing me with him. I gasp as he lifts me effortlessly, cradling me against his chest as if I weigh nothing at all. It's a stark reminder of his strength, and rather than fright-ening me, it sends a thrill of excitement instead.

Instinctively, I wrap my arms around his neck and tuck my head against his shoulder. From this vantage point, I can feel the rapid beat of his heart, smell the intoxicating scent of his skin. I'm still breathless from our kiss, my mind reeling from the intensity of it all as I tighten my legs around his waist. He grips me with those arms, his palms splaying over the expanse of my behind. Even that makes a skitter of electricity shoot straight to my core.

I tell myself I'm not this easy. That these simple touches shouldn't affect me so. That I need to resist this, whatever it is. But another part of me is suddenly defenseless.

Tovan turns, facing into the wind and I press more into him, shielding myself against his hardness. I can feel the tension in his muscles as he braces himself against the gale. For a moment, I worry that even his strength won't be enough against this wind. But then he's moving, each step deliberate and sure, carrying us both back towards the safety of my cottage.

The journey seems both endless and far too short. Part of me wants to stay like this forever, safe in Tovan's arms, sheltered from the storm. Another part is eager to reach the cottage, to safety. And yet, another part is terrified of both.

There are a thousand reasons why this is a bad idea.

A thousand reasons and a million lessons in the past as to why I should end this here. End it now.

As Tovan carries me across the porch, as he kicks the door open and we step inside away from the storm, I expect him to set me down. That I'll get a moment to breathe and think clearly.

I'm wrong.

Tovan presses me against the door as soon as it closes, caging his body between my thighs as my back presses into the wood. Outside, the wind rages. A loud howl that screams through the windows. But not even that can pull my attention away from this moment. For a beat, we stand like that, both breathing heavily, the air between us charged with enough electricity to create a thunderstorm. Tovan's eyes search mine, seeking permission. Reassurance.

And I am weak.

Desperate for more of a touch I didn't know I'd been yearning for so badly.

I answer by pulling him in for another kiss, my hands, which should be pushing him away, find their way to his shoulders, pulling him closer.

This time, there's no hesitation. Tovan meets me halfway, his lips crashing against mine with a hunger that almost startles. His claws roam my body as if he knows this is just a moment's lapse in my judgment, one chance before I push him away again. He's hungry, starved even, and I can feel the intensity of his desire in every touch—in a way I've never felt from anyone, any other man, before.

Tovan is…consuming.

When his claws slide up my sides, thumbs brushing the underside of my breasts, I jerk with the jolt of pleasure it sends through me. I arch into his touch, a silent plea for more, one I'm too scared to put into words.

With a growl, those claws move to cup my breasts, fingers kneading the soft flesh as if it were a ground he's desperate to claim. Through my dress, I can feel the pressure of his touch and it's not enough. I want more. I want the barrier gone, even though that would mean opening up myself some more.

Tovan grunts against me, shudders more like, as he slowly breaks our kiss. Both of our chests heaving, he meets my gaze before his eyes drop to my chest where his claws are still pressed against me there. His throat moves, probably a silent plea in itself, one that's screaming at the fever pitch of my own need growing within me.

Because my doubts are quickly fading away. In their place is a simple, powerful thought:

Fuck it.

Life is short. Unpredictable. How many chances do we get for moments like this? How many chances have I gotten? How many more will I get out here on a world that's not my own?

Without another thought, without letting fear take hold, I reach up, my fingers gripping the neckline of my tunic. It's one of those stretchy ones the Initiative provided, thankfully designed to accommodate a variety of human body types. I tug it down over my shoulders, the soft fabric whispering against my skin as it shifts down my arms, revealing my neck, my shoulders, and the rise of my breasts. For a heartbeat, I freeze, exposed, the cool air a shock against my heated flesh. Shame, hot and fast, threatens to overwhelm me.

I'm not twenty-two anymore. My body has changed. I—

It's Tovan's low rumbling growl that erases every thought in my head. His focus holds me captive.

His claws, still resting against my breasts, tighten. It's such a possessive gesture that sends a shiver of both fear and anticipation down my spine.

Gently, he shifts his claws to hook into the neckline of my dress, tugging it the rest of the way down my chest, exposing me fully to his gaze.

"Frakk," he mutters.

His eyes, already dark with desire, turn molten as he takes in the sight of me. I swallow past the slight lump in my throat, my body too hot, too needy. I should say something. I should stop this. I should—

But Tovan suddenly leans down, capturing one taut peak in his mouth, his tongue swirling around the sensitive bud. I gasp, my body jostling in his grip where he still has me pressed up against the door.

I don't know what I expected. But I know I never expected it to feel this good.

"Oh," I moan, my hands moving to his hair, gripping the strands tightly as waves of pleasure wash over me. He growls against my skin, the vibration sending another shock of electricity straight to my core.

There's a rumble in his throat, one that momentarily deafens the screech of the wind just outside my door as he moves to lavish the same attention on my other breast.

"Tovan," I breathe. That's all I can say. The sensation, the pleasure, I feel myself moisten and drip. With the heat of those lips he's sent me past my last boundary.

Tovan sucks, tongue swirling, while his claws slide down to grip my hips. They sink into my flesh again, his touch possessive, hungry. He's not gentle, but I know he's trying to be. I can feel the restraint in his touch, the delicate balance between his strength and his desire not to hurt me. I can feel the hard length of him pressed against me, too, only the thin fabric of his pants and my dress separating us. I grind against him, seeking friction, seeking more and he groans, a deep, guttural sound as he lifts me again, pulling me off the door.

We stumble further into the cottage, neither of us willing to break the contact between us. I'm dimly aware of the fact that his lips are leaving my nipple, traveling across my skin as he heads up to my collarbone, my neck, my throat.

When they meet mine again, I lose sense of time and space.

Dimly, I can still hear the wind outside. Still hear the storm raging. But it's drowned out by the heavy beats of my heart. Of the rumbling sounds coming from the male against me as he pulls down what's left of my tunic just as we reach my bedside. Those hungry claws rove over me again, stopping at my panties as he does an almost comical pause in his movements. He's never encountered panties before, that's clear, but his pause is momentary. In the next second, he strips them too.

Tovan sets me down but doesn't release me. His claws are notched into the flesh at my hips, kneading as his gaze swallows me whole.

"Lira'an," he rasps, voice low, so gravelly it's hard to hear the actual words. "You're perfect. So soft. So frakking beautiful."

Oh, to be praised. Where I would usually brush off such words and get on with my day, Tovan's make me tremble. Maybe it's the way he's staring down at me, those golden eyes swirling with hunger. No one has ever looked at me like that. Not even those who claimed they loved me before.

His throat moves, his claws still kneading the flesh at my hips as his gaze slides over my form. He takes everything in, every part of me, every imperfection, every bit I'd normally try to hide, and the look in his eyes doesn't change.

His gaze roams my body with an intensity that makes me feel simultaneously exposed and cherished. But when his eyes meet mine again, there's a vulnerability there that catches me off guard. I don't know how I see it, staring into eyes so yellow even the dark hole of his pupil seems non-existent. Maybe it's the way he's paused, contemplating, kneading my hips as he drinks me in.

Maybe it's that hesitation that makes me realize something.

Despite my openness, my bare skin before him, Tovan isn't rushing to take advantage. His touch is reverent, almost worshipful, but restrained. There's a question in his eyes, a silent request for permission that speaks volumes about who he is as a male.

This is the male that declared I'm his *kahl*. The male I thought wanted me—not because he thought he met someone who he could truly see a future with, but someone who he thought was vulnerable enough to fall into his trap.

I'm struck by the realization that this isn't just about physical desire for him. The way he looks at me, it's as if he's trying to memorize every detail, every curve and line of my body. As if he truly wants *me*.

"Donna," he finally says. "I am at the precipice of control. I do not want to hurt you. Your trust is more important than this."

This is it. The moment of truth. One last chance for me to turn back. But as I look up at Tovan, feeling the weight of claws clutching me as if I belong to him, the depth of emotion in his eyes, I know there's only one answer I can give.

"Yes," I whisper. "I'm sure."

Tovan releases such a deep groan that I swear the air vibrates.

His gaze drops to the center of my thighs, and for the first time since we collapsed outside in the wind, his pupils shift, suddenly growing larger. The soft patch of curls between my legs does nothing to hide what's there. And now he can see it. My most sensitive place.

Tovan parts my legs, his touch reverent, almost hesitant, as if I'm a delicate flower he's afraid to bruise, but despite his gentleness, I'm suddenly hit with the fact this is probably the first human female anatomy he's ever seen.

"You are…" He trails off, his voice an even huskier whisper. "You are… extraordinary."

The heat that flares in my cheeks is almost visible against the richness of my skin. Because I thought he was looking at me like a man obsessed before? Now he's looking at me like I'm the most beautiful, the most fascinating creature he's ever laid eyes on. In that moment, as his fingers trace a slow, lingering path along my inner thigh, sending shivers of delight dancing across my skin, I know I've made the right decision.

Tovan utters another harsh growl. When he suddenly dips, bracing low over me, it puts him face-to-face with my folds. Before I can even grunt in surprise, his head lowers and my thoughts disengage from my mind.

Tovan drags the flat, broad surface of his tongue over my entirety, another growl going through him as he barely takes a breath before diving for more again. My toes curl, my head throwing back, my fingers digging into my sheets as I take in a deep breath. Tovan grips my hip with one claw, the other forcing my legs open and he groans into my pussy before taking another taste.

He's eating me like a starved man.

His long tongue delves between my folds, lapping while making a map of every single inch of me.

"Exquisite," he rumbles, as his nose presses hard into my clit, that tongue of his seeking out my folds until it slips inside me. "The sweetest gift..."

I jerk at the sudden invasion, seeing stars.

The desperate sounds that spill from my lips only urge him further, coaxing my thighs to fall impossibly wider as he thrusts his tongue deep. The room is suddenly filled with the wet, slurping sounds of his mouth on my flesh, punctuated by my moans and gasps. I've never felt so exposed, so vulnerable—and yet, for the first time, I don't feel the need to launch a defense. I don't feel the need to find some strength within me to protect myself.

Tovan groans, curling his tongue as he pulls it from within me only to run it through my folds once more. When it hits my clit, I jerk again, pleasure disguised as a sob leaving my lips as he pauses. He does it again and again, eyes flicking up to watch my face contort and my body jerk. And then I see the pleased glint in his eyes. He laps at my clit now, flicking it gently with the tip of his tongue before sucking softly. The sensation is pure bliss, sending electrifying jolts straight to my core. I arch my back, my hands gripping the sheets so tightly that they might tear. I can't help but moan his name. I call it out as if I've screamed it before in moments just like this.

Tovan's response is instantaneous. He growls, the vibration of it echoing against my core. He presses a little harder, shifting a claw to my clit as his tongue penetrates me more deeply now, the movements slow and deliberate. It's as if he's drawing out every last drop of pleasure, every ounce of sensation.

I'm close, so close to the edge.

"I'm going to—" Oh God, I'm really going to. It's been so long, it almost feels too powerful. As if this orgasm is going to ruin me forever.

With one final thrust of his tongue, Tovan sends me over. My convulsions grip his tongue, my body shuddering as I cry out his name again. The orgasm is powerful, waves of pleasure crashing over me like a tidal wave. I've never experienced anything like this. Yes, I've had sex before. Yes, I've orgasmed. But never, never like this.

"You taste like the sweetest nectar," Tovan rumbles, but I can't see him. Either my eyes are closed or I've gone blind. All I can hear is the wind raging outside. All I can feel is the warmth still rushing through my core, weakening every fiber in my body as my whole frame jerks with the aftershocks. "I will never tire of this feast."

I'm still trembling, when I'm finally able to open my eyes again. Tovan is still bent over me, his lips glistening with evidence of what just happened. He slides his tongue out to take another lick of me and I groan, sensitive.

When his gaze finally meets mine, another shudder goes through me.

That focus of his doesn't waver as he licks his lips clean, his golden eyes sweeping over me in another slow, reverent appraisal. His chest swells with every heavy breath—he looks like he's holding himself back, like he could lose control at any second. But still, he makes no move to climb over me, to claim what I'm now almost desperate to offer.

My breaths come shallow, each exhalation filling the space between us, but when a long pause stretches between us, I blink in confusion. What is he waiting for? I thought he would—

It hits me like a wave. He's waiting for me.

He's not assuming. He's not taking. He's waiting. For permission. For affirmation. For *me*. And there's something sweet in it—a sweetness that only makes the hard ache between my thighs pulse all the stronger.

"Tovan," I whisper, voice still breathless from my release. I push myself up slightly, my weight supported on my elbows as I meet his intense gaze. He shifts ever so slightly, withdrawing just a fraction, as though to allow me space, like he's giving me room to change my mind.

But I'm not changing my mind.

For the first time since I met him, I think I'm thinking clearly.

"Come here," I say, and it comes out like a plea. My fingers beckon for him, and for a split second, his entire body freezes. Then something ripples through him—some deep, primal emotion, raw and uncontainable. His claw, which had been resting on my thigh, tightens slightly before he pulls away just enough to stand. He's staring at me with something between reverence and disbelief as if he can't quite make sense of my words.

"You...*want* me?" he asks, his voice low, filled with uncertainty. Surprise.

My heart thuds against my ribs. He's braced himself for rejection all this time? Shit. Perhaps he even expects it.

I don't know whether it's the battles of my past. I don't know if that's why his actions are making me melt inside. But for the first time in a long while, I don't fight it anymore.

"Yes," I whisper. "I want you."

Tovan's pupils narrow, his breathing becoming more jagged as my words sink in. With a grunt that sounds almost pained, he starts to undress, his large hands working quickly at the clasp of his trousers. My entire body hums with anticipation, and I can only watch. God, I've already seen how strong he is, how powerful his body is, but as he reveals more and more of himself, I'm struck by the sheer masculine beauty of him. Every line, every muscle—it's like he's been carved from stone, honed by battle and time.

And then my eyes are drawn down, down, to where his length juts out, hard and proud.

Painfully aroused, Tovan's inhuman cock juts proudly from

between his thighs, so much larger and stranger than anything a human male could boast. Ridged and curved, the dark purple shaft pulses with every beat of his heart.

His skin is smooth there, like mine. No scales except for a splatter at the base. Small frilly protrusions decorate the upper part of his shaft alternating between raised bumps that form a line straight to his tip.

He's already slick with arousal, the evidence of his desire for me clear and evident. I swallow hard, my body throbbing with a need so intense it's overwhelming. I push myself up further, my gaze never leaving him as he climbs onto the bed, his movements slow and deliberate, as if he's afraid he might startle me.

But I'm not startled. I'm entranced. I'm eager. I reach out, my fingers grazing his cheek, his jaw, tracing the line of his neck down to his shoulder. His scales are warm, almost feverish, and I can feel the tremor that runs through him at my touch.

Tovan leans into my hand. "Lira'an," he rasps, "Are you sure?"

In response, I lie back, pulling him with me. His body covers mine, his weight a delicious pressure that sends shivers of pleasure coursing through me. I can feel him, hard and hot, against my thigh, but he makes no move to rush, to claim. Instead, he presses his lips to mine. Still unsure of what to do, he rests them against mine before he kisses me, slow and deep.

I wrap my legs around his waist, my heels digging into the small of his back, urging him on. I can feel his length, slick and hot, pressing against my entrance, but still, he waits. His hand cups my face, his thumb brushing gently against my cheekbone.

"Tovan," I whisper against his lips, "Please."

With a groan, he shifts his hips, the head of his length pressing against my entrance. He's slow, so slow, as if he's savoring every second, every inch. I gasp as he pushes into me. Just an inch and yet it feels like he's already filling me, stretching me, the sensation overwhelming and exhilarating all at once.

He pauses, his body trembling with restraint, as he gazes down at me. "Is this…am I hurting you?"

"Not enough."

He pauses, a strange look coming over his face as he reaches up and taps his ear. I think it's because he hasn't heard me, so I shake my head instead, my hands sliding up his arms to grip his shoulders. "You feel," I whisper, "…incredible."

A shudder runs through him at my words, and he starts to move, his thrusts short and slow. He's watching me, studying my reactions, adjusting his movements to draw out every gasp, every moan. It's as if he's learning me, memorizing me, with every stroke. "You're so perfect. I don't want to hurt you."

Oh, but he's making me ache. Making me ache for something I'd convinced myself I couldn't have.

I arch into him, my body meeting his, urging him deeper and Tovan stiffens, a strange look going across his face before he bares his fangs and growls deep in his throat.

"Lira'an," he warns. Funny. I've never felt such power before. Not like this.

"I won't break."

A moan slips from my lips as I tighten my legs and force him deeper.

Tovan jerks, still trying to stiffen against my movements before I feel him shudder. Battle lost, he presses into me with another deep growl.

"Yes," I pant, as his pace quickens, his breath coming in ragged gasps that match my own. The room fills with the sound of our bodies coming together, the wet slide of his length inside me, the harsh symphony of our breathing.

As his claw slides down to grip my hip, Tovan utters a rumbling moan. His claws press into my flesh, not hard enough to hurt, but enough to leave marks and when his lips find mine again, his kiss is hungry, desperate. His tongue moves in time with his thrusts, and I'm drowning in sensation, overwhelmed by the sheer intensity of it all.

My body tightens around him, clenching as I feel another orgasm building, and Tovan groans, his body shaking with the effort to hold back. "Lira'an," he rasps, "I...I cannot...much longer..."

That's when I feel the swelling at the base of his cock. He's all the way inside me apart from that bulge, that swollen hardness that he's grinding against me. I shift my hips, lost in sensation, and meet his thrust, forcing the bulge just past that barrier of my swollen flesh.

Oh...fuck.

My eyelids flutter as my body quivers. The stretch. It's almost too much.

"Lira'an." Tovan's voice is strained as he shifts, pulling back. But I don't want him to. This is the most I've felt in years and I don't want to let go. Not just yet.

As my orgasm crashes through me, I clench hard, stopping him from pulling back and Tovan groans, a deep, guttural sound that resonates through his entire body. His claws tighten on my hips as he pushes that swollen bulge deeper inside me.

My eyes widen as the stretch becomes even more profound. It's as if every nerve ending in my body is concentrated on that single point. A mix of intense pleasure and a stretch that borders on pain. A pain that only heightens my ecstasy.

I can feel every inch of him, every ridge, every vein, as that bulge swells further, locking us together. My whole body shudders, my heart pounding like a drum in my chest, as my lungs burn, each breath harsh and ragged. Tovan groans too, his breath hot on my forehead as his body trembles with the effort to hold back, but there's no holding back now.

The room spins as some sensation rips through me. Not an orgasm, no. Something sweeter. Something more filling. More intense. I cry out, my nails digging into Tovan's back, holding on to him as if he's the only thing anchoring me to this world. The sensation of that bulge, fully engorged and locked inside me, is unlike anything I've ever felt. It's all-consuming, a connection so deep and primal that it defies words.

And then his body convulses, his release pulsing into me, filling me with a warmth that spreads through my entire being. He growls my name, his voice hoarse with passion and desperation. We're locked together, riding out the storm of our shared pleasure, matching the intensity of the storm outside. Out there it's cold. Frigid. But in here our bodies are slick with sweat, our breaths mingling in the air between us. Heated. Intense.

We cling to each other, our bodies shuddering, our hearts pounding in sync. The world around us fades away, leaving only this moment, this feeling.

Leaving only him.

13

TOVAN

Stars.

I am at peace.

Of all the ways I expected this sol to end, I could have only dreamed of this.

I lie, spent, nestled against the soft frame of my female.

My female. Mine. Donna of the line Johnson is *mine*.

Pressing my face against the softness of her mane, I tug her even closer to me as I roll onto my back. She settles on top of me so well, her body limp from my ministrations, her entire frame fitting against mine like a puzzle piece I'd lost and had always been searching for.

Her head rests on my chest and I tug the bed covering over her, enjoying how her softness and her weight shift with my movements. Enjoying that she's stuck with me like this until this knot loosens.

I hadn't intended to knot her, but my mate is irresistible. Knotting is often only done during the rut. My shaft should not even have responded in such a way because I am not in heat. Not yet, at least.

But this can only be good news. My body is responding to

this female in ways it has never responded to any other female before. Surely, that is a good sign.

"Mm." Donna releases a sound from her throat as she turns her head on my chest. There are tiny beads of perspiration on her thin skin and I lift a claw and brush away the spectacle. "Tovan?"

"Yes, lira'an?" A breath shudders through her frame and I almost groan again. Her nakedness against my scales is not something I could have prepared for. "You are so soft everywhere," I whisper, trailing a claw down her spine.

She makes another hum in her throat at the same time that her slit clenches. I jerk, the sensation both pleasurable, threatening to make me harder than I already am, and painful. She's so small inside. So tight. When I explored her with my tongue, I was sure it wouldn't work. I am still amazed we fit.

Donna lifts her head, those dark eyes meeting mine in surprise. "You didn't come? I thought you did."

"I did." And she can probably feel I'm getting harder thinking about doing it again.

"But you're still hard."

I grunt. "Of course, I am. You are here."

She stares at me for a moment before her gaze softens and her lashes flutter ever so slightly. "You're a sweet talker."

Did she say sweet talker, or something else? Lifting a claw, I tap my implant, forcing it to reset again. The frakking device is failing more often than it should, and while I'd not updated it because I'd had no need to, now there is a sense of urgency. Because I have Donna.

I want to understand every word she says.

She looks away briefly, her composure slipping just enough to reveal a hint of vulnerability. And then she jerks. "Oh, let me get off you!"

She shifts her hips upward, only to be stopped by my claw

pressing firmly on her behind and, of course, my knot. She freezes, eyes widening, at the same time that I grunt.

"Don't move, lira'an."

Her throat moves. "I—" She shifts her hips again. "I...can't." Deep inside her warmth, I feel her core-beat pick up. "Tovan, I...I *can't* move."

She shifts her hips again and I hiss at the twinge of pain.

"Lira'an," I warn.

Donna stiffens, eyes still wide. But instead of moving her body, she clenches her tight slit around me. I hiss again.

"We're stuck. Your cock it's..." She trails off, looking down between us but she can't see farther than my chest. "You can't pull it out?"

The slight panic in her voice kills something inside me. She *didn't* want my knot? *Doesn't* want it?

But...she's my mate. My *kahl*. My lira'an. Our joining, the knot, it's...it's supposed to be the ultimate expression of our bond, the physical manifestation of our destinies entwined.

"Oh my gosh," she whispers, still staring between us. I feel her clench around me again, testing, and I try to remain still. "You can't take it out, can you?"

"No," I manage, my voice rough despite that I'm trying not to make it so. "Not...yet."

My grip tightens on her hip, not to restrain her, but to ground myself, to anchor myself to the reality of her warmth, her scent, the rapid thumps of her core-beat against my chest. I can feel her tremble, a fine tremor that runs through her like a current, and a wave of protectiveness washes over me even though I'm the reason she's suddenly afraid.

What have I done?

"It is...temporary," I say, forcing my voice to remain calm, steady, even as my own instincts scream in protest. "The knot... it will release. Soon."

Even as I say the words, I will my cock to deflate, to release

Donna before this turns sour and this rocky foundation I've managed to build sinks beneath my feet.

Donna doesn't answer, but the way her muscles are locked tells me everything. I have to do something, to ease her fear, to soothe the panic that's rising within her like a tide.

"Look at me, lira'an." My voice softens, a low rumble that I hope conveys reassurance, even as my own core-beat thrums a chaotic mix of desire and uncertainty. "I didn't—"

"You didn't want to knot me." Donna's gaze meets mine and the fear I thought I'd see is overshadowed by something else— guilt, perhaps even shame. "I forced it in, didn't I. It felt so good that I…Oh shit, you didn't… You didn't want that to happen, did you." Her throat moves and she looks away, a furrow marring her brow.

She thinks…she thinks she's *forced* this upon me?

If she only knew…

"No," I say quickly. When she winces, I curse inwardly, realizing how my answer sounded. "I mean, yes." Frakk, this is too important to fumble. "Donna, I wanted to knot you. More than you know."

She glances up at me, but her gaze has gone unreadable. Just like those times when she's pushed me away before. Gods, I must make her understand.

"I wanted you from the moment I first saw you. But my knot, it's…" I pause, studying her face, hoping for some revelation, a look into her thoughts. "It's large and you are small, my *kahl*. I didn't want to rush, didn't want to risk frightening you or pushing you away."

She's studying me now. Her gaze moving across mine.

I have no choice but to continue. "The knotting…it's a part of being a Kari. I should have warned you, explained it beforehand. That's my fault, and I apologize." Now it's my turn to look away, because if she rejects me now, while I've knotted her, I have no doubt I will die. "If anything, I worry that I've pushed you too far, too fast. This bond…it's intense, more so than I expected. I would feast on you every chance I get, if you let me."

My voice drops lower, a rumble that I can feel resonating in my chest. "I want you, Donna. All of you." Frakk. Am I making this better or worse? "I read all I could in the archives. I know your species doesn't form bonds like this. But it is different for me. I want you." I *need* her. But will she run if I tell her that? It's a lot to put on a female whose species doesn't form mate bonds like this. "I want to learn every part of you, to share myself with you in ways I've never wanted with any other female."

I pause, suddenly aware of how much I've revealed. Yes, surely, I will die if she rejects me now. But as I shift my gaze back to Donna, my core beat skips.

She's looking at me strangely, thoughts behind her eyes that I can't read. "So…we're stuck like this?"

"Joined? Yes."

"For how long?"

I hold back a groan of pleasure as she wiggles her hips, testing the knot once more. "I…do not know."

She goes silent, studying me once more. But there's a slight smile on her lips. The only thing that makes me settle down a bit.

"Must really be something," she finally says and I'm tempted to tap my implant again or rip it out altogether. But then Donna laughs. She drops her chin to my chest as a chuckle makes her entire frame vibrate. "What do you do if you only want a quickie, but you end up knotting the woman?"

Quickie? "I want nothing quick about this. I want to savor you for hors. Always."

Donna snorts. "C'mon, sweet talker. I'm talking about when you had sex in the past and were forced to cuddle because of your knot."

My brow tightens as I stare down at her, unable to soften my glare. "I would never do such a thing."

But despite my rough voice, despite the snarl on my lips, my Donna isn't fazed. Her pointed gaze meets mine, undeterred.

"I don't understand," she says.

"You are the first female that has ever taken my knot." I grip her behind, groaning at the sensation of her flesh under my claw. "Do you not understand how special you are to me? How rare?"

She goes silent, the humor that had been building on her lips slowly dying. Finally, she rests her head against my chest. For long moments, I hold her like that and she says nothing. Her warmth, her softness, they both envelop me even as my thoughts grow chaotic, wondering what my female is thinking.

"Tovan?"

"Yes, lira'an?"

"What were you scanning for out there? The day we met."

I shift slightly, still enjoying the way her body moves on top of mine. Her question is strange. Not the question I expected her to ask.

"Ore. Ore of the rare kind is out in these lands. We were surveying that pasture on that sol, Arnak and I."

"Arnak?" She lifts her head now. "You weren't out there alone?"

It feels like I've just opened up another well shaft to fall into. "No. I was not."

Donna studies me and I fear she may take this as some form of deception. And she'd be right to, because it was.

"Arnak is my survey partner. We often work together on field assignments."

Her brow furrows slightly, but she doesn't seem upset. Instead, there's a glimmer of curiosity in her eyes. "So...he saw me that day too?"

I nod, feeling a strange mixture of pride and possessiveness. "He did."

She chuckles. "But you shoo ed him off because you wanted me all to yourself."

"Correct."

Donna's mouth falls open before she snorts again.

Resting her head against my chest, silence surrounds us once more.

"How much is this ore worth? The one you're looking for?"

I shrug. "A clawful is worth enough credits for a lifetime."

Her head snaps up from my chest, eyes wide. "Could you... could you survey my farm? Check if any ore is there?"

It is my turn to study her now. "If there is, we would have to destroy your farm to retrieve it. It is buried deep. There would be nothing left of this place."

Something dims in her gaze. "Oh." She rests her head again and there is more silence.

"Why, lira'an? Are you low on credits?" If that is her worry, she need not. I have enough to take care of her and twenty other Kari generations without trouble. As my mate, she will be well-provided for.

I feel when her throat moves. When a sigh makes her body shift against mine, reminding me of just how close we are together. "It's just...I need to find a way to make money out here. It's not urgent, but...I have to put things in place now. Bluebread isn't working for me and I'm not a great farmer. I guess I'm just worried. It's only me and—"

I growl, stopping the words in her throat. Donna looks up, meeting my gaze.

"It's not just you," I grunt. "Not anymore."

Something changes in her gaze. A hesitant hope. A flicker of trust that makes my core-beat thrum with a joy I haven't felt in orbits. My shaft pulses in her heat as those dark eyes of hers take me in, seeing me, truly seeing me, for the first time.

"You really see me in your future..." she whispers, her voice a breath against my scales.

I growl again, a sound of possession, of promise, as a wave of pleasure, so intense it borders on pain, washes over me. My knot loosens, releasing its hold, and a guttural moan escapes my lips, mirroring the soft cry that escapes hers as our bodies convulse in unison. A wave of my essence spills between us. Warm. Marking her as mine.

"Not *in* my future, lira'an," I murmur, my voice hoarse as I pull her closer. "You *are* my future."

14

DONNA

Where do I go from here?

I wake up feeling so completely sated, I don't feel like myself at all.

The blanket is tangled around my limbs, still warm from Tovan's embrace, and the scent of him, that sweetness, lingers in every fiber.

I dip my face in it, inhaling deeply, even before I can stop myself. When a deep groan rumbles in my throat, I freeze.

Oh Lord, *what is happening to me?*

The question comes clawing at the edge of my consciousness. I've crossed a line, a galaxy-sized line, and there's no going back. I've given myself to an alien, a creature from a world I barely understand, a creature who claims I'm his…lira'an. His *kahl*. His mate.

His *future*.

The thought sends a tingle right through me, starting at the base of my spine and spreading right through to my fingertips. I take a deep breath, forcing myself to calm down, but what only happens is that I pull in more of the scent of him and our lovemaking.

I groan again, another shiver going through me.

"Tovan?" I hazard, but thankfully, there's no answer. I don't think I can face him just yet. What will I say? He revealed so much yesterday. *I felt so much.* Rolling over, I lift my comm from where it rests near the bed. As the screen lights up, it looks like Xarion has been trying to ping me and there's still that notification blinking in the corner, too, the one about that blood sample New Horizons wants me to give so I can hopefully find my Kari match.

Before, I'd decided not to do it simply because I didn't want to invite trouble into my life. But now, the thought of that test confirming everything Tovan's been saying has something strange settling deep in my gut.

Because I'm starting to believe him. I'm starting to believe every word he says.

Damn.

"Computer," I speak to the comm, "what does lira'an mean?"

For a moment, the device does nothing. I'm still figuring out how to use the thing, and it makes my head spin. I open my mouth to try again, but it suddenly replies, its synthesized voice echoing in the quiet bedroom.

"Lira'an is a word from the Kari old tongue."

"Okay, but what does it mean?" I brace myself for what the device will say. What am I hoping for? Part of me hopes it won't know, that it will say the word is untranslatable or unknown. But another part, a part that's growing stronger with each passing moment, yearns for confirmation of everything Tovan has told me.

"In the language that you speak, lira'an from the Kari old tongue means 'melody of the sun'."

I stare at the comm, something hard forming at the base of my throat that I just can't swallow down. "Melody of the sun?" I breathe.

Because of my singing? The phrase is so beautiful it holds me speechless. I don't know what I expected. It wasn't that.

Everything this alien says and does, he's slowly pushing past all my defenses.

Placing the comm down, I brace on my elbows, scanning the bedroom. I don't hear him in the front room, so maybe he's gone outside for a bit.

Or maybe he's left, Donna. That could be the case, too.

I stop that thought right there, despite how true it might be. Maybe he's not gone. Maybe this isn't like other times. Maybe...

Maybe I can give all this a chance.

Sighing, I start to rise, only for my thighs to rub against each other and for me to become aware of a more immediate problem: the sticky evidence of me and Tovan's joining. There's a lot of spend still clinging to my skin, more than I think I've ever encountered before, and that only reminds me of the lovemaking, the way he handled me with care *and* possession, and...the knot.

My God, the knot.

I clench just thinking about it. In all my years...

Good God, Donna. Get up.

I slip out of bed, stretching as I gather the blanket around me and push the bedroom door open. It's silent. I don't know why I tiptoe like a fool sneaking by as I hurry to the bathroom. Door locked behind me, I take a breath.

I'm nervous. He's really gotten under my skin. My heart's beating hard and my ears are perked. Forcing myself to calm as I fill the tub with water and sink in. All through my bath, my thoughts revolve around one thing. Him.

Where do I go from here?

I don't have an answer. Not yet.

I finish my bath and dress quickly, pulling on a fresh dress that falls gently over my curves as my mind still reels from the events of the day before.

By the time I'm dressed, there's still no sign of Tovan in the house. But on the table, I find a bowl covered with a clean cloth. Lifting it, I discover a steaming bowl of that thick stew. I bite my lip.

He even cooks. I am in so much trouble.

I'm halfway through the stew, savoring each bite, when a sharp rap on the door makes me jump. I set the bowl down, my heart suddenly pounding against my ribs. Tovan. But why is he knocking?

Without hesitation, I unlock the door and swing it open, a welcoming smile already forming on my lips. Play it cool, Donna. Don't look too enthused, just a little interested. A little curious. Not overly ecstatic. Whatever you do, don't make him realize you're still weak in the knees.

But whatever words I had die in my throat, my smile becoming stiff as I take in the sight of the alien standing on my porch.

It's not Tovan.

This is someone else. Someone who makes my skin crawl. Someone I can immediately tell is surrounded by a whole lot of juju.

"Uh...hello?" I glance behind the mountain of the Kari male before me, but he appears to be alone. His scales are a deeper shade of purple than Tovan's, and his features, though sculpted like Tovan's, come off as sharper, angular, giving him a severe look. What's worse, his expression is as unreadable as stone.

"Good sol," he rumbles, his voice lacking the warmth I've come to associate with Tovan.

"Yesss," I drag out the word, shifting a little so I can see up the road behind him. There's a transport by my gate. Something that looks like a metal balloon. But I see no one else. "Are you Arnak?"

That's what Tovan said his friend was called, right? I put some hope in that. That this stranger is just here looking for

Tovan and that he hasn't arrived at my door for some other reason. Because the vibes I'm getting aren't good, and they're all I have to go on.

"I am not." His face shifts and I figure he's smiling? God. It doesn't look like that when Tovan smiles and I'm immediately grateful. The alien before me looks like he's baring his teeth over a bit of steak. "May I come in, Donna of the line Johnson?"

He knows my name. Alarms ring loud in my head.

"I...who are you?" It's as if all my senses sharpen and my hand tightens on the doorframe. I have no weapons. Nothing to defend myself. My closest weapon is all the way in the kitchen!

"My designation is irrelevant." He takes a step closer, and I instinctively shrink back, my other hand squeezing the door-knob. I want to slam it shut; to bolt it. Everything about this male screams *threat*.

"We've been waiting for you to register." His voice is so flat, emotionless, that his words fade into the background of his looming presence.

"We?" I lift my chin.

"Many males. We wait for the result of your test. You are the only female we have to hope for." His head tilts slightly and a cold dread tingles along my spine. "It is...disappointing...that you have chosen to delay this process."

"The blood test," I whisper, more to myself than to him.

He does that thing again that suggests he's smiling. All that happens is I see more of his fangs. "Aye. Just a sample of your lifeblood is all we need."

I try not to swallow hard. To not reveal the sudden increase in my heart rate. "That program is voluntary, and frankly, I'm a bit put off by the fact you are here at my door requesting that I comply. Are you a representative of the program?"

But I know he isn't. It isn't run by Kari. It's run by New Horizons.

"Not a representative." He leans closer, slanting his frame to brace against the door jam and blocking my view of everything behind him. "A hopeful. For all I know, you could be my *kahl* and we are ignorant of that fact because we have no sample of your lifeblood."

So he's here to what? *Make* me comply?

The thought almost makes me want to vomit. This is leagues away from the apprehension I felt around Tovan. This…this is something dark. A violation of my very being.

"I'm not interested." My voice is stronger now, defiance replacing fear. "I want no part in it." I move to close the door, but it doesn't shut. And that's because at the last moment, the stranger blocks it with one boot.

My heart lurches and I force the lump down my throat. I'm alone out here. For all I was hoping that Tovan might have been different, that what we shared meant something and he wasn't just spewing lies like every other hopeful in my life, I might have been wrong. Because he's not here now. He's gone.

I have to be smart about this. I have to be there for myself, just like I've always been. This…this weight of independence. Of always having to fight battles on my own. I'm tired. I'm so damn tired.

So tired of dealing with things like this. That and the fact this alien has dared to approach me in the sanctity of my own home pushes past my fear and reaches my anger instead. My brows dive. "Now listen here." I press a fist into my hip as I glare at him. It's the same look I used to give stubborn old patients who would have rather died than take their medicine. "I don't know who you think you are, but you better pick on up and *leave*."

"That is not your choice, human." The stranger growls, muscles bunching as he leans even closer. He sniffs, inhales deeply, and something withers inside me. Not like Tovan. Not like Tovan at all. This is all wrong. "We have been patient, female, but your…resistance…ends now."

He lunges then, his arm shooting out, grabbing my shoulder like a vice. Pain explodes in my flesh and I scream. Instinct takes over and I lash out, my fist connecting with his jaw. It barely sounds like a punch. Pain shoots through my fist, anyway.

The stranger roars, more surprised than hurt, and I use the momentary lapse in his grip to wrench myself free. I stumble back, adrenaline pumping through my veins, fear warring with a fierce determination to fight, to survive.

"Get out!" I scream, my voice raw with fury. "Get out of my house!"

But he's already advancing, his eyes narrowed. I scramble back, my hand searching for a weapon, anything to defend myself. A vase? A chair?

But there's nothing. Nothing but my own trembling hands and the frantic beat of my heart against my ribs.

He advances so fast there's just a single moment when there's a single terrified beat of my heart. When he grabs me again, this time by the waist, he lifts me off the ground like I'm a rag doll. I kick, I scream, I fight with everything I have, but it's no use. He's too strong. Too big.

This is it? This isn't how I expected this day to go. Yesterday was so wonderful, like a new world opened up for me, and then today...

"Put me down!" I claw and scream at him, but those scales that I admired on Tovan Kamesh, their smoothness, their softness, also turn out to be impenetrable. My fingers do nothing. I'm screaming, struggling, vaguely aware that it's having some effect. Stools topple and the stranger bangs into the dining table. I continue screaming, thrashing. I will not make this easy for him.

Just when he grunts, his arms tightening even more around me, a new voice, a familiar voice, a voice that sends a surge of hope through my terror, cuts through the chaos.

"Get your claws...off my mate."

Tovan.

Suddenly, there's a blur of motion. Tovan appears as if from nowhere, his eyes blazing with fury. He slams into the stranger with the force of a freight train, forcing him to let me go. I fall, barely managing to land unsteadily on my feet as I lift my head, trying to get a sense of what's happening.

I look up in time to see Tovan punch the stranger hard enough that he staggers backward, crashing into the door before stumbling off the porch.

Chest heaving, Tovan turns, his gaze finding me.

"Donna," his gaze skips over me, assessing, "are you hurt?"

I'm speechless, the words stuck in my throat as I shake my head.

There's a sound outside, a growl coming from the stranger, and I see the moment Tovan snarls. And then he's gone.

I'm frozen in place, watching in horror as the two Kari males trade vicious blows. Tovan fights with a ferocity I've never seen, landing punch after punch on the stranger's face and body. It's then that I realize I've never seen him like this before. The soft, agreeable male that's been stalking me is nowhere to be seen. Instead, I see a warrior. A fighter who's seeking blood.

But the stranger is just as large as Tovan, and his strikes, when they land, seem to shake Tovan to his core.

"Tovan!" I cry out as the stranger lands a devastating blow to Tovan's ribs. I hear a sickening crack, and Tovan stumbles back, gasping for air. It feels like the sun is going down, cloaked by a heavy rain cloud as I watch the stranger press his advantage, driving Tovan to the ground with a series of strikes that feel like they hit me too. Blood trickles from a cut above Tovan's eye and his breathing is labored. But still, he struggles to his feet, placing himself between me and the Kari stranger.

The sight of it shatters something inside me. Something I've been pushing against for so long.

I like Tovan.

I like Tovan Kamesh.

Seeing him get hurt like this, I can't, I can't stomach it. I have to help him.

I hurry to the kitchen, heading toward the knives when I spot the still-bubbling pot of hot stew. Gulping, I grab a towel and lift the pot instead.

"Leave." I hear Tovan growl as I head back to the front. His voice is a mix of raw pain and determination. *"She is not for you."* He's standing but he's gripping his chest with one arm, even as he glares at the stranger, who looks like he's got a busted leg.

The stranger wipes blood from his split lip, but with his back turned to me he has no idea what I'm doing. "You fool," he spits. "You cannot keep her for yourself. We are all waiting. Every single one of us. Waiting for our *kahls*."

Tovan stands taller. "She already has a kahl." He speaks with such surety, such finality, that for a moment, I can only stare at him. This alien that stumbled into my life and is claiming me with such conviction it rocks the ground at my feet. "She has me and I'm not going anywhere."

For a beat, there is silence and then the stranger laughs. It's a grating hollow thing. A sound that makes me shake with the pot in my hands.

"Liar," the stranger growls. "There is no core-rhythm. Just as you lied at the registration, you lie now." He laughs again. "You should be ashamed." He wipes his lips again. "You think you are better than us with your masses of credits. Better than we who were on the ground during the war. We who had to fight with our fists. We who bear the scars of those experiments. You are no better, Tovan of the line Kamesh. *You do not deserve this female.*"

Tovan's jaw clenches, his scales glinting in the light as he stands taller. "Deserve?" he snarls. His voice is low, so deadly, it doesn't sound like him at all. "You speak of deserving? You who would force a female against her will? You who would violate the sanctity of her home, her life? You are no Kari. You are a disgrace to our kind."

His words are sharp. Cutting. They hang in the air like a challenge, a condemnation. The stranger flinches, his bravado faltering for a moment before his anger flares again. I can see it in the way he stands that he's about to make a move, and I grip the pot tighter, ready to react.

But before he can retort, Tovan steps forward, his gaze never leaving the other male. He's injured, vulnerable, yet the power radiating off of him, the raw intensity of his possessiveness, makes the stranger take a step back.

"This female," Tovan says, "is my *mate*. She is under my protection, and I will remain by her side until my last breath, until she herself casts me away." His gaze is fierce and unwavering. "I will stand beside her. Always."

His words are a promise, a vow, and a warning, all wrapped up in one. And as I watch him, standing there, tall and proud, defying both pain and convention for a woman he barely knows, a warmth spreads through me, a feeling I haven't dared to acknowledge, a hope I thought was long gone.

Maybe, just maybe...Tovan is right. Maybe I do have a protector. Maybe I'm not alone after all.

"What a pest." The stranger snarls, crouching lower, and I know he's about to attack. No more lingering around. Time to move.

"Hey!" I shout. There's not much warning. I don't allow it. It's almost painful wasting the food, but I don't hesitate. As the stranger looks over his shoulder in my direction, all he sees is a hot pot of good stew descending on him. Shock makes him howl as he spins to face me, his spine bending back as he roars in pain.

"You've really got some *nerve!*" I shout. I still have the pot in my hands and I'm about to clobber him with it, but I don't get a chance to.

Tovan tackles him to the ground, landing some hard punches that have blood streaking across the dirt just outside my porch.

The stranger fights back. "Admit it, Tovan Kamesh. You don't deserve this female." He punches upward, landing a solid one in Tovan's jaw.

"You're right. I don't."

The stranger laughs, coughing blood. "Even you know it's true. You, who spent the war safe in the skies. You, who have never known true hardship, true loss. You think you can just claim this female as your own? You—"

Tovan silences him with a punch. But he doesn't stop there. I watch, heart in my throat, as Tovan unleashes a torrent of fury, his fists pounding against the other alien's flesh, each blow punctuated by a guttural growl. It's terrifying, the raw power he unleashes, the primal rage that contorts his usually handsome features. It's like a different creature has taken over, a beast fueled by a protectiveness that borders on madness.

He's going to kill him.

The realization hits me like a cold wave of horror washing over me. I can't let that happen. Not on my doorstep. Not because of me.

"Tovan!" I scream, my voice barely audible over the roar of their struggle. "Stop it! You're going to kill him!"

But my words are lost in the wind, swallowed by the chaos. I have to do something, to stop this madness, but what?

Without thinking, I drop the pot and rush forward, throwing myself against Tovan's back, my arms wrapping around his chest, pressing myself into his spine as I hold on tight.

"Tovan...please." My voice breaks as I hang on, knowing this isn't going to work but not sure what else I can do.

But Tovan stiffens beneath my touch. His arm pauses midway in the air, his fist still clenched tight. Beneath my breast, I can feel his whole body vibrating with a tension that makes me tremble. I feel the shift, the slow, grudging release of his fury. His shoulders slump, his breathing becomes less ragged, and the heat of his anger cools as his arms drop to his sides.

He's still trembling, his breathing ragged, but I hold him tight, my cheek pressed against his spine. "It's fine. We're fine."

"No. I could have failed. It isn't enough." I can feel the vibration of his words all the way through his back and I press into him some more. Because his words don't sound like he's talking about only right now. It feels like he's talking about more than just this incident. Of horrors past. Memories. Ghosts that still haunt.

With the pause in the onslaught, the stranger drags himself away. It's slow, every second like a full minute as I hang on to Tovan, stopping him from moving.

The stranger grunts and anger flares as my gaze slides to him. Every one of his movements is slow and pained as he shifts away, pausing only when he's far out of reach of Tovan's fists. He looks like a crumpled broken thing now, far removed from the confident asshole that knocked on my door.

"Leave." I lift my voice, my anger evident. "And if you know what's best for you, you don't come back here."

As the other alien drags himself to his feet and stumbles away toward his transport, I keep my arms wrapped tight around Tovan, feeling his tension bleed right into me. Feeling his pain.

He watches the other alien leave, his claws still tight fists at his side, and I realize that I'm not just holding him back.

I'm holding him together.

15

TOVAN

It's quiet in here. Outside, the plains are silent. All is well.

Except it isn't.

I lie in a bath my lira'an forced me to take, the warm water barely covering my form as I hear her bustling around the lodge.

We still haven't spoken about what happened, how I lost control. She still hasn't mentioned the fact she saw me in my anger. The fact that I must have scared her to death.

The fact she must be thinking the worst of me now.

Instead, she led me inside, bolted the door, and started the warm bath. She dropped herbs within, forced me down into the steam, and hurried away again.

My throat feels tight as I listen to her moving around within the lodge. The memory of her cry for help still reverberates in my mind like a haunting signal.

What if I hadn't been here?

Frakk.

I lean back, the water sloshing as I adjust my frame. The wounds and bruises beneath my scales don't even concern me as I listen to my female move. Knowing she must be frightened is tearing at me. Not knowing what she will do after this is even worse.

I'm tense, all my muscles tight, when the door to the washroom opens and my lira'an steps in. Her gaze finds me immediately, her brows twisting.

"How are you feeling?"

She's brought heavy pieces of fabric, 'toh-wells' as she calls them, and there are round tins of ointment in her arms. A warmth immediately floods through me. She's caring for me, even though she must be rattled by that other Kari's sudden appearance.

But the warmth that suddenly rises within me quickly recedes. Because this is my Donna. She will care for me even if she will cast me away later. That is simply her nature. She is too good to let me bleed and suffer. Even if I deserve it.

That other Kari was right.

There are many others, many that have flocked to our small town, that deserve a *kahl* more than I do. He was right. I—

"Tovan." Donna crouches, setting the things down as her soft claws skim over my chest, her soft digits rubbing away the blood that's stuck beneath my scales. "You're bleeding, but I can't see the wound."

Her fingers tremble and my core-organ aches.

I could end all this. This waiting. This ache. If I could just force my core-rhythm to sing, then it would all become clear. The others would leave her alone. They wouldn't dare come to her farm on the off chance that she could still be claimed.

I could protect her with just my name, my lifeblood. All would know she is mine.

But my core-rhythm won't activate. It...frakk.

I growl a little, my frustration evident. Evident enough for Donna's fingers to stop moving against my scales. Her brown eyes shift to mine, searching.

"You're hurt. I'm worried."

I shift my body, and the water sloshes over the rim of the tiny bath, soaking her garments. She doesn't even blink. Her other claw touches the water too, her touch as light as the wind as she brushes her digits across my jaw.

"You have to tell me this will heal. Like your foot did. You know, your magical alien mojo." She grunts a soft laugh, but it's different from the other times she's laughed before. Almost hesitant. She's…unsure. Scared even.

"I will heal." I press a claw over the one she has resting on my chest. "It is minor, the injury."

She nods, her digits shifting underneath mine. "Good."

She doesn't pull her claw away, and the one that's gently brushing my jaw remains there too. Of all the times for my shaft to grow hard, now is the worst of them. It does so, anyway.

"I am sorry, lira'an. I was tending to your outbuilding. I wanted to clear it out for your oogas." I pause, fighting the growing thing between my thighs as all my attention wants to go to how her soft claws feel against my scales. "I should have heard him sooner."

"It's not your fault. He's a prick."

That translates to him being a big, hard cock, and I'm tempted to reset my translator again.

"I'm happy you were here…" She doesn't meet my gaze but the words alone settle something inside me. She doesn't hate the fact that this male arrived because of my own body's failing? She is too forgiving. Even of a male like me. "And you're not undeserving."

My whole being stills and she notices.

"Tovan…"

I can't face her. Shame burns in my throat, a bitter taste. "You don't know—"

"About the war? No. You're right. I don't know. But I come from a planet that's seen its share of conflict, too."

This makes me look up, meeting her eyes. Donna takes a deep breath before continuing. "My brother...he was in the Air Force. I saw firsthand how hard it was on him, the toll it took. The nightmares, the guilt, the struggle to adjust to civilian life afterward." Her gaze meets mine. "I didn't see your war, but I know you must go through the same thing. War leaves scars, Tovan, and not all of them are visible."

My throat tightens. Words fail me. For a moment, I wonder if my translator is on the fritz again, translating the exact words I want to hear. Of all the people to understand the ache in my soul, I would have never thought a female as soft and lovely as this ever would.

But this is why I'm sure she's my *kahl*. She understands more than I realized.

Her claw shifts against the weight of mine, rubbing the scales on my chest. Her touch is so warm, so reassuring, some of the tension leaves my shoulders. "We've both been through things that have left their mark. But that doesn't make either of us undeserving of happiness, of connection, of...whatever this is between us."

My core-beat stops. Did I hear right? Or is my translator chip—

When Donna suddenly leans forward and her lips brush against mine, the rumble that goes through me makes the surface of the water vibrate. Water sloshes as I lean over the bath and reach for her, groaning again as our tongues meet and her softness presses against me.

Oh gods. I will never get enough of this.

Before my mind can catch up, my body is already out of the water, lifting my female against me.

"Tovan." She's breathless, but her lips press against mine again. Water drips everywhere as I press her into a counter at her back, and when her legs open, inviting me in, I can't help but growl into her throat.

It makes her whimper. Makes her go limp. And my whole being lights up with need.

My cock bobs, already seeping pre-spend and I try to press it into the counter to keep it away from the center of her thighs. But my female protests.

Donna whimpers again, tugging me closer as her hips roll and shift.

Breathless, I pull my lips from hers. "We can't," I pant.

"Why not?"

"I knotted you last time and you are so small, my kahl."

"I can take it."

Frakk. My cock aches against the hard wood.

"Not here. Not like this."

Donna pauses, gaze meeting mine before she runs her tiny pink tongue across her lips.

Leaning in, she presses her nose into my neck, pulling in a deep lungful of air. "You smell so good." She shifts her hips and reaches down between us. When her digits come in contact with my heated flesh, I jerk, a ripple of sensation going through me.

"Don't knot me right now. Just...just make love to me. You can do that, right?"

Frakk. I will do anything she wants. "Yes, my *kahl*."

I can't resist anymore. Shifting my lips, I allow my cock to bob upward, pressing between her thighs.

"Wait." She reaches between us and shifts away a piece of fabric that's covering her beautiful slit. "Now."

Gods, I wanted to take it slow, but the moment her softness begins to close around me, I lose control. And Donna pulls me in. With a moan and a jerk of her hips, she pulls me in deeper.

Her warmth envelops me and the pleasure is so intense I can only see stars. A groan reverberates through my chest as I begin to move, slow at first, but she urges me on with her heels against my spine, her claws clutching at my scales.

"Yes," she whispers, her breath hot against my ear. "Oh shit yes. Don't stop. Don't you dare stop. I need this. I need...I need..."

Me?

I can hear the fact she wants to say it. But she's not quite there yet. No matter. I am a patient male. I will wait. And in the meantime, I will make her slit weep.

My hips snap forward, driving into her with a force that makes her cry out in quick succession. Her body takes all of me, every inch, fitting perfectly around my length. And I bury myself inside her.

Her moans fill the room, mingling with my growls and the sound of our bodies meeting. I can feel her core-beat racing, her breath coming in quick gasps.

"Don't stop. Just..." She's frowning, eyes squeezed shut tight, and if not for the way she's gripping me, surrendering to me, I would think she's in pain. But this isn't pain. This is something else. She's close, I can sense it. "Don't stop. Don't stop."

And so I don't. I keep doing the exact thing. I keep the rhythm, the pressure. I keep my tight hold on this delicious morsel of a female, *my* female, and I drive my cock into her just the way she's begging for it.

"Tovan!" Her nails dig into my scales as she climaxes, her body convulsing around me. The sight of her lost in pleasure, the feel of her pulsing around me, sends me spiraling.

With a final, deep thrust, I let go, pouring myself into her. My body shudders with the force of my release. It's so much that it comes streaming down onto the counter, the scent filling the air of mating and spend.

Donna's legs are still wrapped around me, her body limp and satisfied. I press my face into her neck, inhaling like she did before I nibble her face, her lips. She smiles against my mouth, her eyes still closed.

"See," she murmurs. "We fit just fine."

I can't help but chuckle, my chest vibrating with the sound. "Yes, my *kahl*. We fit perfectly."

In this moment, everything else fades away. Still buried inside her, I tug her closer. I know, with a certainty that shakes me to my core, that I will never be free of this female. And I don't want to be.

I am hers.

Completely.

Utterly.

Hers.

16

DONNA

The days that pass feel like I'm living in a dream.

I wake and Tovan is there, showering me with kisses, his arms encircling me each morning as he tells me how beautiful I am. How lucky he is.

And each night, after a long day working on the farm, we tuck in together, his arms around me again, his hardness deep inside me, and my whole body singing as if I'm floating on a cloud.

It's probably why I wake each morning with my heart thundering in my chest, thinking it's all been a dream and I've now woken up. Probably why, each dawn brings an anxiety that lingers even now with the sun fully risen.

Standing at my front window, I stare outside, a cold drink clutched in my hands and that same anxiety in my heart.

What am I afraid of? What's making me so scared?

I swallow hard, pushing away the emotion as I take a sip of the drink and turn away from the window. My dining table is filled with batches of bluebread. Tovan's been an excellent taste tester, but I'm starting to wonder if he's just being nice because he thinks everything I do is amazing.

The bluebread just doesn't taste…right. Or maybe I'm just hoping for it to taste like a place that I'll never see again. Not only that but it's becoming increasingly clear that unless I use this farm for its original purpose—crops and livestock—I'm going to be in deep financial trouble.

I need a plan. A way to make this farm work, a way to secure my future. A way to stand on my own two feet.

And then there's Tovan.

He's weaving himself into my life. I've never felt so desired, so cherished, so completely… possessed.

Are we truly mates? Or is this just…what? A fleeting attraction? A desperate attempt at connection in a strange new world? The trouble with having so many men disappoint me is the fact I can't even trust *myself* or my heart.

It's led me astray before.

Shaking my head, I try to clear the swirling thoughts. This isn't getting me anywhere. I need to do something to feel productive. So I head back into the kitchen, humming the familiar strains of "Amazing Grace" as I clean up the kitchen.

I hear the moment Tovan steps in. The front door closes quietly behind him, and as if there's some electric current between us, I sense the moment he stands at the kitchen door.

"Lira'an."

My cheeks heat and I stop humming, now knowing what that word means.

"I will wash myself."

Looking over my shoulder, I give him a slight nod.

Tovan's eyes drop to my lips before he licks his own and my entire body heats. Not once in my life have I reacted to any man like this.

I watch him as he heads to the bathroom and soon I hear water filling the tub. There in the kitchen, my fingers twitch on the kitchen cloth before I say "fuck it" and head after him.

"Donna." His head pops up the moment I step into the bathroom. His pupils narrow slightly, a mix of surprise and desire flickering across his face and I'm immediately taken back to the fact that he's taken me, made me climax, in this very room.

What am I doing? "Need help?" I've never been this bold.

"I would be honored," he says softly.

As he settles back into the water, I reach for the soap, working up a lather in my hands before beginning to scrub his broad chest.

The simple act of washing him is strangely calming. My hands glide over his skin, tracing the contours of his muscles, memorizing every detail, every texture.

And my mind wanders. I think about how quickly I've gotten used to this male's presence, how natural it feels to have him here. He's thrown himself into the work on the farm with a dedication that leaves me in awe. From dawn to dusk, he's out there, tilling the soil, repairing fences, doing all the things I have no idea how to do.

And...I like it. I like him. Not just for the work he does, but for the comfort he brings, the sense of safety and belonging I feel when he's near.

But even as I acknowledge this, the fact remains that...I have no idea if I really am his true mate.

I finish washing him and Tovan steps out of the water, all tall and proud and undeniably male. As he towels off, I watch him, wringing my hands as my thoughts go awry. I allow him to get dressed before I take his hand and lead him to the porch. The big male is so pliant, he does everything without protest, not breaking the silence between us. Maybe because he can feel the tension rising in my blood.

As he sits between my legs, massive arms thrown over my thighs, I sigh.

I need to know. I need to know if this is it.

Tovan relaxes against me, eyes on the sky as I begin braiding his hair. The texture is different. Soft, yet each strand is as strong as rope. I focus on the repetitive moments when his voice suddenly breaks the silence.

"Lira'an. Will you spin a melody for me?"

I pause. "You want me to sing for you?"

Tovan tilts his head back, gaze meeting mine. "I could listen to your voice for eons, my kahl. I know many beings would pay high credits just to hear you."

I scoff. "You're flattering me."

But his face is deadly serious. Popping out his comm, he does something I don't understand on the device before his lips shift, a fang flashing. "Sing me a melody. I will show you this is true."

I roll my eyes before readjusting his head, smoothing down a stray lock of his green hair. *Such a drama king.* But there's a smile on my face, one that I indulge in since he can't see. For a few moments, I don't utter a word. But the music is there, right at the tip of my tongue. And maybe, maybe I like Tovan Kamesh enough to let him hear me sing.

I start with the beat first, a soft tapping of my foot against the porch floor, a slow, sultry rhythm that echoes the beat of my own heart. Then, my voice, low and husky, wraps around the melody. *Careless Love*, a whisper of desire against the backdrop of the twilight sky:

"♪♪ Love, oh love, oh careless love ♪♪"

My voice is a low, husky murmur that hangs in the air between us. I watch him closely even as I continue the single central braid, gauging his reaction. He's still, so still, his breathing slow and even. For a moment, I think he's regretting asking me to sing, but then, his claw, warm and rough against my skin, slides up my leg to grip my thigh in a hold that's both gentle and possessive.

Encouraged, my voice grows stronger, bolder.

"♪♪ You've caused me pain enough ♪♪"

I almost pause. Because this song, each note is a confession, a release. The years of heartbreak, the loneliness, the fear I'd locked away…it all pours out, transformed into something beautiful, something powerful. The seat creaks as I shift on it, a rhythmic counterpoint to the melody, the air thick with the scent of the cool air and Tovan's sweet musk.

"♪♪ But this time, a different tune I hear♪♪"

I pause, my gaze meeting his. His eyes are open now, head tilted back as those golden orbs fix on me. He's not smiling either, but there's something in his gaze, a warmth, a wonder, that makes my heart soar.

I lean closer, my voice dropping to a whisper, my lips brushing against his brow.

"♪♪ A love that conquers all my fear… ♪♪"

The last note hangs in the air, a promise and a plea. I pull back, searching his face, waiting for his reaction.

Tovan doesn't speak, but his grip tightens on my thigh, and his gaze, burning with an intensity that makes my knees weak, holds me captive.

And in that moment, as the stars begin to twinkle in the twilight sky, I know, with a certainty that goes beyond words, that this alien warrior has heard my song.

And he's listening.

"I'm going to do it," I whisper and it feels like the air stalls between us.

Tovan's throat moves but he remains silent.

"The test," I continue. "The blood sample. I'm going to do it tomorrow."

His throat moves again.

He doesn't have to say anything. We both know what this means. After tomorrow, we'll either be together, or we'll break apart.

The weight of it all is almost too much, and I release a soft breath through my nose. Because, looking at this Kari male sitting between my legs, allowing me to braid his hair as if it's a very natural thing he's always done, I know that whatever happens tomorrow, I'll still be happy for this.

Happy I got to experience even a moment of this.

This peace.

Tovan's grip tightens on my thigh, and I see a flicker of something in his eyes, a mix of hope and fear, that mirrors the storm raging within my own heart.

I give him a soft smile and readjust his head as I finish the braid in silence. He puts his comm away and it's like neither of us is breathing. Now there's a big question mark between us and I don't know what the future holds.

I open my mouth and close it. Words that mean too much on my tongue.

I want to tell him I've fallen in love with him. That despite the rocky start, I can't imagine not being with him anymore. But I can't. I can't say all that. Not with that test looming before us. Not with the chance that I might open my heart one last time and lose it all.

Just as I finish the braid, the lights from a transport break the growing dusk.

Tovan sits up straighter, immediately alert, and so am I. If it's another stranger…

But as the transport comes to a stop, Tovan's shoulders relax.

I can already tell it isn't Eleanor or Catherine, but Tovan's lax in alertness soothes some of my caution. "You know them?"

"Aye. It is Arnak."

Oh, his friend.

I sit up a little straighter. This is the closest person to Tovan's family that I'll ever meet and although I'm a grown-ass woman, a skitter of nervousness goes through me, anyway. Only more proof of how much this alien has come to mean to me. But that nervousness quickly turns to confusion as the Kari male hops out of the transport and twin bunny ears follow behind him. "Xarion?"

The sight of Xarion's bunny ears bobbing behind Arnak's imposing figure is so unexpected that, for a moment, I wonder if I'm hallucinating. But no, there they are, clear as day in the fading light.

Tovan rises to his feet, his massive frame blocking my view for a moment. I can feel the tension radiating off him now, a stark contrast to his relaxed state just moments ago. He stands watching them as they walk into the yard.

"Arnak," Tovan's deep voice rumbles. "And the Saffion. What brings you here?"

Arnak's gaze flicks from Tovan to me. He's a bit shorter than Tovan, not as thick, but still imposing as hell. He studies Tovan for a moment, his expression unreadable. "We need to talk, old friend. It is...urgent."

I stand up, moving to stand beside Tovan. His claw immediately finds my back, resting there over my spine.

"What's going on?" I ask, gaze shifting from Arnak to Xarion who now comes to stand by his side.

"Kahlesta..." Arnak does a slow bow that makes my eyes widen slightly. My gaze shifts to Tovan before sliding back to the two males before us. Xarion releases a breath before folding his arms behind his back.

"Donna Johnson," he says, before his red gaze slides to Tovan. "Tovan Kamesh. There is trouble in the town. Rumors. Concerning ones."

My heart sinks. Somehow, I know this has something to do with that stranger who showed up at our door. The one Tovan chased off.

Tovan shifts his arm so it slides around my waist, tucking me into his side. He's still focused on the two males. I don't even think he's realized what he's doing. "What rumors?"

Arnak sighs, running a hand over his face. "That male who came here a few sols ago..."

"You know about that?" My eyes narrow slightly and Arnak

focuses on me once more. I wait for the shiver, the disgust like when that stranger appeared at my door and I had the instinct to run. But there's none. His presence doesn't bother me. Despite the fact I've only just met him, he doesn't give me the same vibes that stranger did.

"Everyone knows," he says. "He's been spreading stories in town."

"Concerning ones," Xarion repeats.

My stomach churns. "What stories?" But I think I already know.

Xarion releases a heavy breath as if the whole world is on his shoulders. "Apparently, Tovan Kamesh is holding you hostage. Keeping you here against your will, while using you for his own pleasure."

I sputter, my eyes widening as I choke on a laugh. "What?" But not one of the males standing around me share my humor. "That's…that's ridiculous! How could anyone believe that?"

"He is Kari and you are human. You do not have the means to fight back," Xarion deadpans.

I shake my head, scoffing again. "Alright, I know where this is going. Listen. I haven't been forced to do anything. I—"

"So you *have* mated with the Kari." Xarion's words make mine die in my throat. I never thought I'd be confessing what happened in my bedroom to anyone—not even myself, to be honest.

I open my mouth and slam it shut. Crossing my arms over my chest, I meet Xarion's gaze. "Yes." Before he can say another word, I continue. "I know I said I wanted nothing to do with these males but—"

"But you tried for the sake of the Initiative." Xarion does a slow nod.

Oh, bless him. He's so clueless. "Yep. Completely for the Initiative."

Arnak's expression is grim. "You have to understand, Tovan.

Humans are still new here. Many Kari have never interacted with one before. And with the fact that you have claimed she is your *kahl* without activation of your core-rhythm…"

My heart stutters. Of course. It all boils down to that. To the very uncertainty I've decided to end tomorrow.

Arnak continues. "There's unrest in town. Some of the more vocal Kari are talking about coming here, to 'liberate' your female."

"The hell they are," I blurt out. The very idea is so absurd that I almost want to laugh, but the gravity of the situation stops me. This is serious. People could get hurt. Tovan could get hurt.

"I'm doing the test tomorrow." I shift my focus to Xarion, giving him a tight smile even as that anxiety returns, churning in my chest. "I'll give the blood sample."

Xarion's nose twitches. "We have to do it now." He turns his gaze to the skies. "The test we developed is reliable. It will find your mate and once the mate bond is underway, his core-rhythm will sing. He will go into a rut and you will need to decide if you wish to risk your life by accepting his bond."

Right. I knew some of this before, of course. But back then, it wasn't me who was the subject of all this. It had been Catherine.

"Because he'll be driven out of his mind with…" I clear my throat, now completely aware of the warmth of Tovan's arm around my waist. "With need."

"Affirmative. And once you accept the bond, we hope there will be kahl sigils that will carve their way into your flesh, proof you are his and that your lifelines are embedded. That should be enough to quell this unrest. If not, the presence of a core-rhythm should." Xarion sighs, his gaze dropping from the skies. "This visit will require a significant update to the Initiative, Donna Johnson. If you are truly this Kari's *kahl*, your lifeline will extend. I'll be documenting your antics for eons."

I snort, unable to help myself. "You aren't getting rid of me… but lifeline extending? What do you mean?"

Xarion shifts his gaze between me and Tovan before his nose twitches. "I should not say. We are still researching this. But, the two other humans, Eleanor and Catherine, have shown signs of cell regeneration."

I freeze. "What now? They're getting younger?"

Xarion shrugs. "Or aging incredibly slowly for your kind."

My eyes widen, and I look up at Tovan, who is now staring at Xarion with an intensity that could melt steel. His face is tight, his tension clear.

"Well, shoot," I say, leaning back against Tovan's chest, forcing a lightness I don't quite feel. "Why didn't you tell me that before, honey? We could've skipped all this drama and gone straight to the altar!"

I swear, these men are a tough crowd. Nobody laughs.

"Just wait here. I'll go get my shawl."

Tovan stops me, his arm still around my waist.

"Lira'an," he says softly.

"Lira'an?" Arnak whispers in shock under his breath.

"Don't, Arnak." Tovan slides a side eye his friend's way before the glacier melts as he looks at me again. "Are you certain? This is not how I wanted this to happen. You shouldn't feel pressured."

"I was already going to go, sugar." I lift my hand, cradling his jaw. "Besides, weren't you the one who was so certain about us from the beginning?"

A flicker of his usual warmth returns to his eyes. "I am still certain."

Arnak makes a sound in his throat. "The medic will still be open. If we leave now, we can have the results before the dawn."

I nod, a strange mix of nerves and determination settling over me. "Let's go, then. The sooner we put these rumors to rest, the better." And the sooner I find out if Tovan's really mine, that this love will be different from all the others, the sooner I can move on.

Turning, I head toward the door, my hand trailing down to grab Tovan's claw as I pull him along behind me.

"Donna?" Xarion questions.

"Just a minute," I say as I shut the door, blocking him and Arnak out.

There, in the small cozy interior of my home, I throw myself into Tovan's arms, all my fear, my hope, my longing, all in this one desperate act.

Our lips crash together, a collision of need, of a love that I'm only beginning to let myself feel. I kiss him like it's the last time, pouring every ounce of my being into that single, searing contact. When we pause to take a breath, Tovan leans his forehead against mine.

"Donna?" It's a ragged whisper. One that breaks me in two.

Before I know it, his arms tighten around me once more, crushing me against his chest. His tongue invades my mouth, tasting, devouring, taking, and I give it all to him, freely, recklessly, lost in the heat of his embrace.

This kiss, this moment, it's a goodbye and a promise all wrapped into one. A goodbye to the life I knew, to the woman I once was. And a promise of a future I can barely comprehend, a future where the melody of my heart beats in time with the rhythm of his soul.

17

DONNA

*I*t's strange arriving in town with this tension over my head. Every one of us in the transport is silent. All except for Xarion, who takes the moment to inform me of all that will happen after I'm matched. *If* I'm matched.

The rut. The danger. The fact I will be wholly consumed by the Karl who calls to my soul.

Everything he's saying is almost terrifying—because I can't imagine going through all of that with some male other than Tovan.

My gaze shifts to Tovan now, sitting beside me in the back of the transport. He's been watching me the whole time, but wherever I look his way, he pretends that he hasn't been. Even gives me a soft smile, flashing just a bit of fang. Meanwhile, his claws clench and unclench consistently.

He's worried. And I am, too.

I wrap the shawl tighter over my shoulders as Arnak pulls up outside a small building. My heart leaps into my throat as the transport comes to a stop. The small medical building looms before us, its windows glowing softly in the growing darkness. But it's not the building that catches my attention—it's the gathering of Kari males outside, their massive forms silhouetted against the twilight sky.

"Lord have mercy." My whisper is almost silent as my hand finds Tovan's arm. There must be at least a dozen of them, their low rumbles of conversation drifting through the night air. As soon as our transport stops, their heads turn in unison.

"They're here for me." I'm frowning, but it's in complete disbelief. Meanwhile, Tovan has gone as stiff as a rock.

Xarion sighs. "I will have to speak to New Horizons about dispatching security for any other humans that arrive. We did not prepare for the fact the Kari would react like this."

"They're not here to hurt you." Arnak glances over at me. "They're just...we're all just...finding a *kahl* it's..."

"Life changing," I whisper. I give him a small smile because I see the desperation in his eyes, too. "You all just want to find love." I turn my gaze back to the crowd just outside, huffing a soft, sad laugh through my throat. "Unfortunately, I will be disappointing quite a lot of these males today. If all goes well, I'm destined for only one."

My gaze shifts to Tovan and his throat moves. He lifts a claw, brushing it over my jaw in the barest of touches. As if he's afraid that if he touches me fully, he won't be able to let go.

I swallow hard now, taking a deep breath. "Let's just...let's just get this over with."

As we step out of the transport, the crowd of Kari falls silent. I can feel their eyes on me, burning with curiosity, suspicion, and something else I can't quite name. Something I refuse to acknowledge. Their need.

Instead, my grip on Tovan's arm tightens as we make our way towards the entrance of the building.

Xarion and Arnak flank us, creating a protective barrier, but as we pass through the crowd, I catch snippets of whispered conversations.

"...the human..."

"...Tovan's kahl?"

"...impossible..."

I keep my head high, but inside, my heart is pounding so hard I worry everyone can hear it.

The interior of the medical building is a stark contrast to the tense atmosphere outside. It's clean, sterile, and blessedly quiet. A medic greets us, the same species as Xarion.

"This way, please," she says, gesturing towards a small examination room.

As I follow her, I suddenly realize that this is it. This tiny room, this simple test—it's about to change my entire life. The weight of that realization nearly stops me in my tracks.

Tovan must sense my hesitation because he gives my hand a gentle squeeze. "I'm here, lira'an," he whispers, his words meant only for me. But I choke anyway.

"What if I'm not your lira'an?" I'm not crying but I might as well be. My throat is closing up and it's getting hard to breathe.

"Nonsense." Tovan grins, hiding whatever emotion is present in his eyes. He dips his head, inhaling my skin before he whispers in my ear. "You'll always be my lira'an."

Oh, my heart. I think I've more than fallen in love with this male. Wouldn't it just be my luck for this to all go to shit. I dread it. Lord knows I half expect it to all come crumbling down.

The actual blood draw is quick and painless. As I watch the vial fill with my crimson life essence, I know this tiny sample will determine my future, my fate, my very destiny.

As the medic labels the vial and prepares it for analysis, Xarion clears his throat. "Donna," he says, his tone so uncharacteristically gentle that I frown at him. "I think it would be best if you *didn't* return to your farm this dark cycle."

I blink, surprised. "What? Why not?"

Xarion's ears twitch slightly. "Given the... current situation, it would be safer for you to remain here. Just until we have the results and can address any...misconceptions."

"I can't just stay here. I didn't bring any clothes. Toiletries. I'm not staying in the hospital with a host of Kari just at the door."

"I've arranged for a private room in a secure lodge," Xarion continues. "It would be…advisable for you to stay there. Alone."

The implication hangs heavy in the air. If the test results come back positive, if Tovan and I are truly meant to be…well, we all know what comes next. The rut. The bonding. The irrevocable joining of our lives. But if it doesn't…

I glance at Tovan, seeing the conflict in his eyes. He wants to protect me, to keep me close, but he also knows that Xarion's suggestion makes sense.

We're all adults here. What Xarion suggested…it's the right thing to do.

I swallow hard, nodding slowly. "Okay."

Tovan's claw tightens on mine, and I turn to face him. The pain in his eyes mirrors the ache in my heart. We both know this could be our last moment together as we are now—two individuals, separate but yearning. After tonight, everything could change.

"Tovan," I breathe, reaching up to cup his face in my hands. "I…"

Words fail me. How can I possibly express everything I'm feeling? The fear, the hope, the love that's bloomed so unexpectedly in my heart?

He leans down, pressing his forehead to mine. "I know, lira'an," he murmurs. "I know."

We stand there for a long moment, breathing each other in, memorizing every detail of this moment. Then, with a gentleness that belies his massive size, Tovan presses a soft kiss to my lips.

"Until dawn." The words come out rough, as if he's holding back tremendous emotion and I nod, not trusting myself to speak. As I turn to follow Xarion out of the medical building, I can't help but look back one last time. Tovan stands there, his golden eyes locked on mine, and with Arnak at his side. I take comfort in that. At least he won't be on his own. When the news comes, at least he'll have someone there with him. And I will be...

Alone?

I swallow hard. It's nothing new. I've weathered a shit-ton of storms alone. I can do this one, too. But there's an ache. That ache Tovan had been starting to fill.

I don't want to do it alone. Not anymore.

The walk to the inn is a blur. Xarion takes a series of corridors and back roads all while chatting about procedures and protocols, but I barely hear him. My mind is consumed with thoughts of Tovan, of the test, of the future that hangs in the balance.

Turns out the inn is like a luxury apartment building. The room is large, comfortable, and gives a view of the street below. I stand there for a few moments, watching the Kari mill about around the medical center. Every one of them waiting for the news that will soon come.

"If Tovan Kamesh is not your mate," Xarion begins.

I shake my head before stepping away from the window. "If he's not my mate, I really don't want one."

Xarion sets down a pack that looks like it has a bundle of fresh tunics, soap tubes and other things. "You have bonded with him that much?" He steps closer, crouching before me as I settle into a soft feathered seat. Those red eyes search mine before his ears fold back on his head. "Oh, Donna Johnson...you have bonded with him. Deeply. Removing such a bond will bring hardship if he turns out to not be your kahl."

I snort. "Hardship. I'm no stranger to that, honey."

Xarion stretches a furred hand toward me before pausing and pulling back. He rises. "This is certainly not what I had in mind when I encouraged you to 'integrate' with the Kari,

Donna. Though, I must admit, your approach is…far more interesting than what would normally go in my reports."

"I've got a few choice words you can put in your report." I scowl at him and his mouth twitches in a rare smile.

"Farewell, Donna Johnson. I will see you on the dawn of the next sol."

I look away, eyes on the open window. He's leaving. I don't think I want to be alone. Not now. And I can't have Tovan.

As soon as Xarion leaves, I sink further into the feathered seat, the events of the day finally catching up with me. I'm exhausted, emotionally and physically drained.

I'm not sure how long I sit there, lost in thought, when a knock at the door startles me back to reality. For a wild moment, I hope it's Tovan, protocol be damned. But when I open the door, I'm greeted by the familiar faces of Catherine and Eleanor instead.

"Surprise!" Eleanor grins, holding up a basket filled with what looks like food containers. "We thought you might need some company."

Catherine, more reserved, offers a gentle smile. "And some food. We remember how…demanding the whole process can be."

My heart leaps even as I try to hide it. "Demanding?"

Stepping back, I let them in.

"Yes," Eleanor says. She's already halfway across the room and setting the basket she brought down on the table with a thud. "The rut. You'll be drained. We brought vitamins and an energy shot that should get you through it. Not to mention the food. You'll be so achy you won't want to get up and cook a thing."

My mouth is slightly open as I close the door and lean on it, my gaze darting between my two friends, their cheerful faces, and that basket overflowing with goodies. For a moment, I'm speechless, caught between the sheer absurdity of the situation and a wave of relief so profound it makes my knees weak.

I hadn't realized how much I needed this—the comfort of friendly faces, of women who understand exactly what I'm going through.

"Oh, honey." Catherine's face falls, and she rushes toward me, throwing her arms around my shoulders. "Why didn't you call? You're not alone out here, you know? We're here for you."

A breath shudders through me as I return her embrace. "I guess I've been a bit overwhelmed."

"Tell me about it," Eleanor murmurs. As she unpacks the basket, revealing an array of carefully prepared meals and snacks, Eleanor turns to me with knowing eyes. "How are you holding up?"

I let out a shaky laugh as Catherine walks with me to the table. "Honestly? I have no idea. It all feels so…surreal."

Catherine nods. "Xarion pinged us. Updated us about everything. And…" She clears her throat. "A Kari named Tovan pinged Varek."

I blink at her. "What? Why?"

"He…well…when we first met him, we were thinking of introducing him to you. You know, just in case. Funny how destiny works." She grins. "It's nothing. He pinged because he thought you might want us here with you."

My lips press into a line as I hold back the surge of emotion.

"He's the one, isn't he." Eleanor drops her voice. "The one you like."

I snort. "It's way past that now. Way past the "like" stage. It's just…we don't know, you know."

Catherine nods. "I remember that feeling. Like you're standing on the edge of a cliff, about to leap into the unknown."

"Precisely," I whisper. "And I don't know if I'm terrified or exhilarated. Maybe both?"

Eleanor reaches out, squeezing my hand. "That's normal.

What you're about to go through…it's intense. Life-changing. But Donna, it's also beautiful beyond words."

"The rut," Catherine says, her eyes distant with memory, "it's overwhelming. But in the best possible way. It's like…like every cell in your body is singing in harmony with his."

Eleanor nods, a soft smile playing on her lips. "And when the bond forms… Donna, there's nothing like it in the universe. It's like finding a piece of yourself you never knew was missing."

As we settle in, sharing some of the food and talking quietly, I feel some of the tension begin to ease from my shoulders. Their words paint a picture of a future I'm only beginning to imagine—a life intertwined with a Kari mate, filled with challenges but also with a love deeper than anything I've ever known.

But everything I've always dreamed of.

18

DONNA

Maybe it's the slight buzzing in my veins that makes me wake. The sense that something phenomenal is about to happen. Or maybe it's the commotion just outside on the street.

For a moment, I'm disoriented, the unfamiliar surroundings throwing me off balance. Then it all comes rushing back—the test, Tovan, the agonizing wait.

Judging from the dim light streaming in, it's barely past dawn. The test results should be in by now. So why hasn't anyone come to tell me?

A low rumble of voices draws me to the next room to find Eleanor and Catherine both standing at the window, looking down into the street below.

"Girls? What's..." They turn in unison, the look on their faces making me hurry over to the window to see for myself. "What's wrong?"

"Oh, darling." Catherine releases a long breath, as she gives my shoulder a comforting squeeze.

The street below is filled with Kari. Even from here, I can

tell they're restless, agitated, and the tension in the air is almost palpable.

Something's wrong.

As if on cue, my comm unit pings. It's a message from Xarion:

"Donna, we need you at the conference center immediately. There's been a...complication."

My stomach drops. Complication? What the hell does that mean?

With trembling hands, I get dressed. Eleanor and Catherine like two comforting columns of support behind me all the way. By the time we get outside, Varek and Zynar, Catherine and Eleanor's mates are there, waiting. Going through the brief greetings feels like it's all happening to a version of myself that's not really there.

We take a back road, walking around the buildings as Varek leads us to the conference center. I can tell both he and his brother have already heard whatever news that's flooded the streets—the same news that obviously involves me—but it's clear they're not wanting to speak on it.

And that can only mean one thing.

I was wrong to hope. To hope that it would be different this time. That I, Donna Johnson, could actually find true love.

As we approach what I assume is the conference center, I spot Xarion waiting at the entrance. His ears are flat against his head, a sure sign of stress.

"Donna," he says as soon as I'm within earshot.

"Just tell me."

His ears flatten even more. "The results of your lifeblood sample. It's...inconclusive."

The world slows down a little. Inconclusive? I press my fists into my hips, arms akimbo. "How can a mating test be inconclusive?"

"Perhaps because this is all still new. There are markers in the other mated humans' lifeblood. We had hoped…" He studies me and I know that this male, my friend, is feeling regretful. "You should come inside before the Kari arrive."

At first, my heart leaps because I think he's talking about Tovan, but then Zynar speaks.

"We will try to get them to calm down until she is ready to see them."

I frown. "What's going on, Xarion?"

He sighs, running a hand over his folded ears. "We've seen nothing like it before. Your hormones are…compatible with Kari physiology, but there's no clear match. It's as if…"

"As if what?" I press.

"As if you could potentially bond with any of them."

The words make the air go still.

"Oh hell, no." I'm already gathering my skirts and turning around, ready to leave. I'm done. Done with this hullabaloo.

"Donna," Xarion's tone stops me. "New Horizons has decided to give them all a chance. To woo you, as it were, in the hopes one of their core-rhythms sings."

I stare at him, incredulous. "You're kidding, right?" When he doesn't answer, I feel my temper rise. "You can tell New Horizons to kiss my big black ah—"

"This is great!" Eleanor practically dances, and I glare at her. It does nothing to stop the grin on her face. "Let them come, Donna, or this will never rest. You can simply turn them away one by one. Otherwise, they won't give up. Kari are persistent."

My lips curl. I don't want all the Kari. I want Tovan.

My gaze shifts from each member of this new family of mine, feeling a mix of frustration and amusement. "What, am I supposed to sit on some fancy throne, have them parade in front of me one by one, and just say 'next, next, next' like some reincarnated version of Queen Elizabeth I?"

Eleanor's eyes light up. "Oh! That's brilliant! We could totally set that up!"

"Eleanor!" I exclaim, but I can't help the huff of laughter that escapes me. The absurdity of the situation is starting to get to me. "I was joking. I'm not actually going to do that. Hell, I ain't no choir director tryin' to pick out the best voices for Sunday service."

Catherine, ever the voice of calm, steps in. "Donna, I know this isn't ideal. But Eleanor has a point. The Kari won't let this go unless they feel they've had a fair chance. They really are persistent."

I blow out a full breath, making my lips balloon as I breathe out. "But I already know who I want." Fuck. Hell. Shit. I'm really admitting this now? Out here? In front of these people who will be in my life for the foreseeable future? "I want Tovan. It's always been Tovan."

There's a grunt. A deep pleased grunt of a laugh and I look up to see Zynar and Varek both smiling enough that their fangs are visible.

"Then prove it," Eleanor whispers almost like a dare.

"The heart knows, Donna," Catherine adds.

I swallow hard.

"Once you turn them away, they will no longer have the right to attempt to woo you," Xarion says. "I have already arranged for your farm to be guarded and any Kari that breaks that covenant will be taken care of."

I close my eyes, releasing a long breath.

Finally, I look at Xarion. "And Tovan?"

Xarion studies me and I know he's only trying his best. "That...I cannot speak on, Donna Johnson. That is up to you... and the fates."

Another sigh and I bite my lip. Fuck it. "Fine. Let's do this."

As we enter the conference center, the cacophony of voices hits me like a wall. At least fifty Kari are packed into the room, all talking at once. But as soon as I step through the door, a hush falls over the crowd.

All eyes turn to me, a sea of golden gazes filled with hope, curiosity, and something more primal that makes my skin tingle.

I scan the crowd, searching for one particular pair of eyes. My heart begins to fall, dropping to the pit of my stomach and lower, the longer it takes for me to spot him.

Tovan. Where is Tovan?

But he's not here.

Xarion guides me to a raised platform at the front of the room. As I climb the steps, my legs feel like jelly. What am I supposed to say to them? How can I possibly navigate this impossible situation? And Tovan...

My gaze shifts to my friends, falling on Catherine and I watch her mouth the exact words she just said to me. "The heart knows."

Only, my heart isn't in this room anymore. He's not here.

The ache comes sudden and fast, even as I clear my throat, the sound echoing in the sudden silence. "I, uh... I'm not really sure what to say."

A low rumble goes through the crowd. I take a deep breath and continue.

"I know you're all here because the test was...inconclusive. And I know something like this has never happened before. To be honest, I'm as confused as you are."

I pause, gathering my thoughts. Hell, this isn't what I'm supposed to be doing. This wasn't the plan. But as I stand here looking at all the males before me. Males who are simply hoping, hoping for a chance at love, I know I can't do it. I can't simply turn them away with a harsh dismissal. Not me who knows how much the heart aches for something it's always wanted but was never destined to have.

"I came to this planet looking for a new start," I begin. "A chance to belong somewhere. And I've found that here, on my farm." My eyes search the crowd again. But he's still not here. I guess...I guess he's not coming. Maybe he already got the news and decided to not bother. Decided to give up.

My heart aches some more. The disappointment threatens to overwhelm me and the demon in the back of my mind whispers that this is what I deserve. That I'm used to this disappointment.

But another part of me, something new, pushes back.

Tovan wouldn't just give up like this, would he? No. Not the Tovan that slept in my barn, pretending to have a life-threatening injury when he could simply get up and leave. Not the Tovan who camped near my property because he just couldn't keep away. Not that Tovan. Not the Tovan who held me. Kissed me. Loved me.

I refuse to believe he's like all the others of my past.

I refuse to believe.

"I know I'm supposed to be impartial. To give everyone a fair chance. But the truth is...my heart has already chosen." I meet the eyes of as many Kari as I can. "My core-rhythm as you would call it."

Murmurs of surprise and discontent rise from the crowd. I raise my voice, speaking over them.

"I'm sorry if that's not what you want to hear. I'm sorry if it goes against your traditions or your expectations. But I can't pretend that I don't feel what I feel."

And maybe I'm a fool to be declaring it so loudly for a male who isn't even here.

My throat tightens and I'm about to bid all the males farewell when the door slides open with such force that it rebounds off the wall, the sound echoing through the suddenly silent room. Every head turns, and I feel my heart leap into my throat as I see Arnak stumble in. His chest heaves, and there's a wild look in his eyes.

I immediately fear the worst.

"Kahlesta!" he shouts. It's a rough, urgent sound, one that rattles something inside me. "We need to get you out of here. Now!"

The crowd of Kari males parts like a sea as Arnak pushes through, his powerful frame easily clearing a path. Murmurs of confusion and concern ripple through the gathering, but I barely hear them. My focus is entirely on Arnak, and the palpable sense of urgency radiating from him.

As he reaches the base of the platform, I can see the tension in every line of his body. Something is very, very wrong.

"Arnak?" Do I even dare to ask?

He takes a deep breath, his eyes darting around the room as if searching for any immediate threat. When he speaks, his words send a shockwave through me.

"It's Tovan. His rut has begun."

The words hang in the air and the world slows down. I can only blink.

"His core-rhythm," Arnak continues. "It's singing for you, kahlesta."

The room erupts into chaos. Kari males start shouting, some in outrage, others in confusion. I can barely make out individual words over the din.

Xarion steps forward, his voice cutting through the noise. For a dude that looks like a soft thing, his voice is commanding. "Silence!" He turns to Arnak. "Explain. Quickly."

Arnak's eyes never leave mine. "I was with Tovan when it happened. Early this dawn, it started. His eyes glazed over, and he started trembling. I've seen ruts before, but this...this is different. More intense." He pauses, taking a breath before he continues. "He told me to lock him in and wait. To give you a choice. If you chose another Kari then…"

I glance over at Catherine, who's standing near the edge of the platform. Our eyes meet, and I can see the recognition in her gaze. A small, knowing smile plays on her lips.

"That big, noble idiot," I mutter, shaking my head. The words come out fond and exasperated in equal measure.

Catherine's smile widens, and she nods in understanding. Of course, she does. Varek had done the same thing, putting her choice above his own needs and desires. It seems Kari males have a penchant for self-sacrificing gestures when it comes to matters of the heart.

I turn back to Arnak, my voice steadier now. "He was going to lock himself away? Give me a choice?" The idea of Tovan suffering alone, fighting against his rut while I stood here oblivious, makes my heart ache.

Arnak nods solemnly. "He was adamant about it. Said you deserved to make your decision without any…influence."

I snort, my gaze shifting to the sea of men before me. Who would have thought. Maybe the universe isn't so much of a bitch but a fairy godmother after all. Dangling candy and actually making me eat without demanding my sacrifice for the pleasure.

"Where is he?" I'm already helping myself down from the dais. "Where's Tovan?"

"Surely, you cannot let the female leave without proper proof of this…*bond*, Saffion," a voice snaps. The one who speaks comes to block my path. "Tovan Kamesh has lied before."

I can tell, even from the corner of my eye, that Xarion has had enough. He stands tall about to answer, but I know the brute that spoke. The same stranger that had come to my home.

I walk right up to him and he has the sense to flinch. "Listen here, you sanctimonious *prick*." I jab a finger at him. "You came to my home, uninvited and unwelcome. You tried to intimidate me, to make me doubt myself. Well, guess what? It didn't work then, and it sure as hell isn't going to work now. So unless you want to find out just how creative I can get with more than just *stew*, I suggest you shut your mouth and step...aside. The only thing I need right now is for you to get the hell out of my way before I show you exactly what this *female* can do."

Murmurs go through the crowd. In the back, I hear Eleanor clapping. Turning back to Arnak, I open my mouth to tell him to take me to my man when there's another crash at the entrance of the building.

Xarion exclaims beside me. "I thought you said you locked him up!"

Arnak's expression tightens. "I did. I didn't say it worked."

My breath catches in my throat as I turn around.

Tovan.

He stands there, silhouetted against the light from the rising sun, his massive frame filling the entire doorway. His chest heaves with each breath, and even from this distance, I can see the wild, almost feral look in his eyes. His gaze sweeps the room, and I can see the moment he spots me. His entire body goes rigid, every muscle tensing.

"Donna," he growls, his voice so low and rough that it sends shivers down my spine.

Then he takes a step into the room, and all hell breaks loose.

The Kari males nearest to him immediately move to intercept, whether out of a sense of protection for me or competition, I'm not sure. But Tovan reacts with explosive violence. He roars, a primal sound that seems to shake the very foundations of the building, and launches himself at the closest male.

The fight is brutal and swift. Tovan moves with a speed and strength I've never seen before. Not even when he was fighting the stranger at my home. He throws one Kari across the room as if he weighs nothing, then grapples with another, both of them crashing to the floor in a tangle of limbs.

"Stop!" I cry out, but my voice is lost in the chaos.

Arnak grabs my arm, trying to pull me towards the back of the platform. "We need to get you out of here," he insists. "In this state, he could hurt you without meaning to."

But I resist, my eyes locked on Tovan as he fights his way through the crowd. Despite the madness in his eyes, despite the raw, animalistic nature of his movements, I'm not afraid. Something deep inside me recognizes him, calls out to him.

"No." I pull my arm from Arnak's grasp. "I'm not running."

I take a step forward and even in the chaos the movement catches Tovan's attention. His head snaps up, our eyes meeting across the room. For a moment, everything else seems to fade away. It's just him and me, locked in a gaze that feels like it could burn the world down around us.

"Tovan," I speak with every ounce of mental strength I can muster. "I'm here. I'm right here, baby."

He freezes, his whole body going still as a statue. The Kari he was grappling with takes advantage of the moment to scramble away, but Tovan doesn't seem to notice. His focus is entirely on me.

Slowly, deliberately, I start to walk toward him. I can hear Arnak and Xarion protesting behind me, can see the other Kari tensing, ready to intervene, but I keep my eyes on Tovan, willing him to see me, to recognize me beyond the haze of his rut.

"It's okay," I say softly, taking another step. "I'm not going anywhere. And I don't want them." I gesture blindly to the room and I swear a male whimpers. "I want you. I'm right here, Tovan."

He's breathing heavily, his chest rising and falling with each ragged breath. His hands clench and unclench at his sides, and I can see the struggle playing out on his face. The rut is pushing him to claim, to take, but the Tovan I know is fighting it, fighting to remain in control.

I take another step, and another, slowly closing the distance between us. The room is so quiet now that I can hear the pounding of my own heart, the soft shuffle of my feet on the floor.

When I'm just a foot away from him, I stop. This close, I can actually smell the musky, wild scent of him. It stirs something in me. Something that makes my heart beat harder and my blood grow warmer.

"Tovan," I say again, softer this time. "It's me. It's Donna."

I see a flicker of recognition, a moment of clarity amidst the storm in his eyes.

"Donna," he growls, his voice rough and strained. "You…you need to run. You need more time. I can't…I can't control it."

But I stand my ground, shaking my head. "I'm not running, Tovan. Not from you. Not anymore."

I take a deep breath, gathering my courage. Then, slowly, I reach out and place my hand on his chest. There, in the center, is a wild vibration that feels like it thrums right through my arm and straight into me.

The touch seems to shock him. He inhales sharply, his entire body trembling. For a moment, I worry that I've made a mistake, that this small contact will be enough to shatter his control completely.

But with a gentleness that belies the storm I know is raging inside him, he leans down and presses his forehead to mine. I can feel the heat of his scales, can hear the soft rumble in his chest that's almost like a purr.

For a long moment, we stand like that, foreheads touching, my hand on his chest and his covering it. I'm dimly aware of the room around us, of the shocked silence from the gathered Kari, but none of it matters. All that matters is this moment, this connection.

But then he sniffs. *Loudly.* Tovan dips his head to my arm and he inhales before a snarl makes his lips pull back. His gaze snaps to Arnak immediately and I realize the moment we made a mistake. The exact moment Arnak had gripped me and tried to pull me away.

Tovan snarls, the scent of his friend on my arm making that wildness flood his gaze immediately.

"Oh, frakk," I hear Arnak whisper.

Tovan growls, the sound reverberating through the room, shaking the very walls.

"Go, Arnak!" I shout, my voice barely a whisper against Tovan's rising growl. I wrap my arms around him, holding him tight, just like I'd done when he'd protected me from that stranger.

For a heartbeat, he's frozen, his body a coiled spring, his muscles trembling with restrained power. Then, with a suddenness that makes me gasp, he scoops me up into his arms, holding me close, my body pressed against the hard planes of his chest.

"Donna!" Xarion cries out, his voice laced with alarm.

"I'll be alright!" I shout back, my voice surprisingly firm because my heart is pounding a frantic rhythm against my ribs. "I'll ping you later!"

But even as the words leave my lips, I know, with a certainty that chills me to my core, that I won't be pinging anyone later. The scent of another male on my skin is a betrayal Tovan can't ignore. Tovan is no longer in control.

He carries me swiftly from the stunned room, his gaze fixed on some unseen point ahead. Out on the road, he heads in a direction I don't know when I spot the building Xarion prepared for me.

"There!" I'm not sure if Tovan even hears me, if he's even capable of rational thought right now, but he follows my direction. People, beings, dodge out of the way as we go and I can't help the blush that rises on my cheeks. This is wild, but maybe I needed this over-the-top kind of love. Maybe it's always been what I needed.

Tovan kicks the door open, a splintering crash that echoes in the stillness, and then he's inside and the door is slamming shut behind us, the lock engaging with a heavy thud. With purpose, he finds the bedroom, setting me down gently, almost reverently, and for a moment, our gazes meet, a flicker of recognition passing between us, a fragile spark of humanity in the midst of the storm.

But then he's gone.

I ease up on my elbows, confused when realization dawns. As the lights dim in the room, I realize he's pulling all the blinds closed. Locking all the windows. Affording us some privacy before...

Before he takes me.

When he appears at the door again. my throat goes dry.

His pants are tented, his cock straining hard to get through and his chest is still heaving, claws still clenching and unclenching.

"Tovan..."

With a speed that makes me gasp, he's upon me, his body covering mine, his weight both terrifying and exhilarating.

As his lips find mine, his kiss a consuming fire, I surrender to the inevitable, to the primal force that's drawing us together, body and soul.

I surrender to this male. To his love.

I surrender to everything.

The rut. It has begun.

19

DONNA

The world explodes.

That's the only way I can describe the moment Tovan's lips meet mine. It's not just a kiss, it's a supernova of sensation, a collision of need so powerful that it shatters the last of my control, my sanity.

His scent fills my senses, an intoxicating sweetness that makes me dig my fingers into his scales, urging him closer. They press against my skin, a delicious friction that makes me arch into him, craving more even as his claws roam my body, mapping my curves, claiming me as his.

He growls against my throat, a low rumbling sound that vibrates through me, stirring something deep within my core. It's a wild, untamed response that's never happened to me before. As if my body is waking up because of this intensity, this need radiating off him.

And his mouth is everywhere, devouring, tasting, branding me with his possession. He sucks on my earlobe, nipping at the sensitive skin, making me cry out, pleading for more. But he doesn't linger. Not for long. His tongue traces a path down my neck, leaving a trail of fire in its wake, and then he finds my breast, his mouth closing over it, sucking, teasing, driving me mad with pleasure, my whole body lights up, electricity like sparks going through my veins.

I writhe beneath him, my hands clutching at his scales, pulling him close, wanting to climb inside his skin, to become one with this creature who's both alien and familiar, dangerous and comforting.

"Lira'an," he growls against my skin, his voice thick with desire, with a possessiveness that both terrifies and excites me. "You are mine. *Mine.*"

With a swiftness that makes me gasp, Tovan flips me onto my stomach, his weight pressing me into the soft mattress, his heat enveloping me. He pulls my tunic up, baring my backside to him, and I shiver, a mix of anticipation and apprehension rippling through me.

With a growl, he snaps my panties, flinging them away with a careless flick of his wrist before his claws whisper down my thighs. He's staring at me and I'm completely open. Completely vulnerable. But never have I felt so safe.

As his growl deepens, he parts my legs with a slow, deliberate motion that has me trembling. The moment he leans down, I get a single second of warning before his tongue traces a molten path up my inner thigh. I gasp, the sensation overwhelming, but it's nothing compared to the shock that rips through me when his mouth finds my core. He devours me, his tongue darting and probing, rolling over and through my folds as he groans in pleasure, grabs my hips and holds me still as he presses his face into my core.

I cling to the sheets, my fingers tangled in the fabric, as waves of pleasure crash over me. Tovan growls again, and I'm not sure whether it's in pleasure or possession. His mouth is relentless, every stroke of his tongue heated and wet.

"Tovan," I whimper. He responds with a feral sound, his claws digging into my flesh enough that I cry out. The pain melds with pleasure, a heady mix that prolongs the fever building within me.

His tongue thrusts deeper, finding a rhythm that matches the pounding of my heart and my body arches out of my control. Every lick, every nip, every growl pulls me deeper and I feel the bond between us strengthening, an unbreakable tether that ties our souls together. It's intense, raw, and beautiful in a way that defies words.

The world narrows down to his mouth on me, his claws on my skin, his growl in my ears. I feel myself unraveling, the pleasure building to an unbearable peak. And then, with one final, deep thrust of his tongue, I shatter.

The orgasm rips through me, a storm of sensation that leaves me crying out, gasping for breath. My body convulses, each wave of pleasure cresting higher than the last. Tovan's grip tightens, his claws anchoring me to him as if he's afraid I will just up and float away.

His growl is one of satisfaction now, as his tongue slows, drawing out the last shudders of pleasure until I'm left panting and boneless beneath him.

But he doesn't stop there. With one fluid motion, he's up, turning me onto my back once more. When my heavy-lidded eyes meet his, I can hardly see his pupils. So narrow, I know he's at the edge of his own control but that he's still somewhere in there, holding back, trying to make this good for me.

As I look at this male who saw me and immediately knew I was his, my eyes tear up. This…this is exactly what I've always wanted. To be seen. To be wanted. To be claimed. This isn't just passion or desire—it's a recognition, a claiming of souls that goes beyond the physical.

This isn't just another relationship. This isn't just another attempt at love that will fizzle out or end in heartbreak. This is different. This is real. This is forever.

I'm looking at my future.

But he's holding back. Fighting the intensity of his need because he doesn't want to hurt me. I see it in the way his jaw clenches, the way his claws tremble against my thighs, the way he keeps whispering my name under his breath like it's a plea, a prayer.

I don't want gentle.

I want *him*.

With a confidence I've never felt quite like this before, I reach up and grab my breasts, teasing the nipples as my lashes dip, a soft moan escaping my lips. I shift my hips, tightening my thighs to urge him closer as I knead my breasts before sliding one hand down my belly toward my center. I'm so wet down there, my fingers come back glistening.

Tovan's response is immediate, a groan escaping his lips as he cages me in with his arms. As I lift my hand, he catches it with his lips, tongue swiping out across my glistening fingers.

"Tovan..." I pant. I shift my hips again, grinding against him, feeling the hard length of his arousal pressing against my core. I need him.

"Donna," he rasps. His voice is barely understandable, merely a rumbling growl. "I...don't want to hurt you—"

"You won't," I whisper, reaching down to release his trousers. The moment his cock bobs out and my fingers close around it, my eyes roll back in my head just imagining how good he will feel. "I want you, Tovan. You can lose control. I want all of you."

I give him a stroke and feel him shudder, his control shattering, his growl a primal echo of my own desire, and I know I've won.

He's mine now.

His claws slide underneath me, cupping my shoulders, lifting me slightly as he positions himself at my entrance. His length presses against me, hot and hard, as his body jerks with his last restraint.

"Lira'an," he rasps. "I will claim you now. Completely. Irreversibly."

"I'm all yours."

With one powerful thrust, he sheaths himself deep inside me. I cry out, not from pain, but from the sheer intensity of it. He fills me completely, stretching me, branding me from the inside.

Pulling back, he sheaths himself deep inside me again. This isn't gentle. Tovan's hips pull back to snap forward again as he buries himself in me over and over, and I become lost to the rhythm.

The room spins, the walls blurring as wave after wave of pleasure crashes over me. And as I shatter, falling apart, coming undone beneath the force of his lovemaking, I know, with a certainty that transcends language, that I am his.

WE BECOME LOST to the wave of insanity. Time passes. Days? I'm not sure. I wake with Tovan's cock buried deep inside me and I'm pretty sure I fall asleep on his knot, too.

In moments where there's clarity, I feel food and drink being offered to me. Tovan places a piece of sweet fruit to my lips, pressing it gently against my mouth. I part my lips, taking the fruit into my mouth, savoring the burst of sweetness. He feeds me slowly, patiently even as his entire body trembles, those eyes never leaving mine as a soft growl of contentment rumbles in his chest. I reach up, my hand brushing against his scales, feeling their warmth, their life, as he allows me a moment of respite.

Water follows, cool and refreshing, poured gently into my mouth. Some of it sloshes with his fevered tremors. But he fights back anyway, granting me a moment of calm within the storm.

But that calm is fleeting. As soon as the basic needs are met, the urge takes over once more. Tovan's eyes darken, the gold turning to molten fire, and I can feel the heat between us building again. His scent envelops me, becoming a drug that I can't resist, can't deny.

He takes me again and again, each time with a ferocity that leaves me breathless, my body a canvas for his passion, my soul imprinted with his mark. His knot becomes a familiar ache, a constant reminder of his possession, of our destinies entwined and when he sinks his fangs into my neck, sheathing himself completely in my slit as streams of spend fill me, I know I am lost.

Tovan touches me, explores me, and worships me with an intensity that brings actual tears to my eyes. And I respond with an abandon I never thought possible.

As the days blur, the world outside fades away, and this little room becomes our universe, a sanctuary filled with the scent of him, the taste of him, the sound of his grunts, his groans, his whispered words of love in a language I'm slowly beginning to understand.

And within that universe, within the safe haven of his arms, I find a peace I've never known before. A belonging that transcends language, culture, even species.

I find the one thing I've always truly been searching for.

I find my home.

TOVAN

My eyes snap open to darkness.

For a moment, I'm disoriented, my mind hazy and my body aching in ways I've never experienced before. Slowly, the fog begins to lift, and awareness seeps in.

I have a *kahl*.

Deep in my chest is a new vibration. A song that sings only for her.

I blink, letting my eyes adjust to the dim light filtering through the curtains. As my senses sharpen, I become acutely aware of the warm body pressed against me. Donna. My mate. She's tucked against my side, her breathing soft and even.

Carefully, I shift to look at her. Even in the low light, I can see the marks of our passion on her skin. A wave of tenderness washes over me, mixed with a hint of guilt. I know the rut is intense, but seeing the evidence of it on her delicate human form makes my core-beat stutter, makes my new core-rhythm falter.

I ease myself off the sleeping cushion, wincing at the protest of my muscles. As I stand, I survey the room, taking in the aftermath of my frenzy. The destruction is...substantial. Furniture overturned, drapes torn, personal items scattered across the floor. It's as if a storm passed through, which, in a way, it did.

Me.

Glancing back at Donna, more guilt fills me. I have no idea how she will react to all this. Yes, she accepted my call. She accepted my bond…but she is human. Humans do not mate like this.

Her soft body accepted my every demand, but that doesn't mean this was not a great sacrifice for her. For the rest of my days, I will make sure that she is taken care of. That she wants for nothing. That her happiness is profound.

It is a pledge I make as I stagger across the floor, taking a moment to brace against one wall.

I am weak. Need sustenance.

Something clenches within me as I cast my gaze back to the sleeping cushion. Vaguely, I remember pushing food and water into my mate's mouth, but my memory is hazy. It could all have been a dream.

Leaving her to rest, I stagger into the front room, searching for food. There's an open energy tab with one missing and I pray to the gods that Donna had been the one to take it before my rut claimed me. Taking the remaining tab, I lean against the wall, waiting for it to work.

Distantly, I hear a comm buzzing. Most likely Donna's. I have no clue where mine is.

I stagger toward the sound, falling to my knees to retrieve the device from underneath a broken table.

My chest heaves with strained breaths as I accept the transmission.

A human female's face is on the screen and I blink at it, recalling her visage. I met her once before. I remember now. I'd been in my nestkan, the sounds of her and her mate bonding echoing through the walls and making me yearn for something I thought I would never have.

Only, I have it now.

"Oh, hello Tovan. It's good to see you. This means...this means it's over?" Her piercing green eyes rival the color of my mane.

"It is finished," I murmur, keeping my voice low as my gaze shifts to my mate. She's still resting and I don't want to disturb her. "We are one."

"Fantastic!" The human screeches and I wince. "Oh, sorry. I remember how sensitive everything was after me and Varek..." She makes a sound in her throat. "I'm Catherine, by the way. Might as well introduce myself now, since you're practically my brother-in-law." She smiles, but it is hard for me to focus on anything except the fact all my muscles feel like string. I collapse on the floor, holding the comm up so I can see the screen. "Is... can I speak to Donna?"

"No."

The human's brow rises in, I suppose, surprise.

"She is still resting. It has been...hard on her."

This Catherine nods. "That's fine. I just wanted to check on you guys. Will it be alright if we stop by in a few days? We want to give you enough time to settle in together, but we also want to see her, if that's okay."

I want to growl. To tell them I don't want to share my mate for the next few sols. That I want to tend to her in peace. But I am not barbaric. Donna needs these females. And...it is not only Arnak and me, anymore. She is right...I have new family now.

"A few sols, yes," I breathe.

"Great," Catherine flashes her blunt teeth. "It's nice meeting you, Tovan."

I tilt my head slightly in respect and the ping ends. The device slides from my claw to rest on the floor again as I settle back against the wall.

But there's a grunt. A slight shifting of the female wrapped in the covers on the sleeping cushion. I'm moving without even thinking, crawling over to her, my gaze searching every inch of her that I can see.

"Tovan?" It's a soft whisper, so unlike my Donna that for a moment, I fear the worst. Only, when my gaze snaps to her face, Donna's eyes are still closed. She's still sleeping, but calling out my name.

Warmth spreads through me as I dip my face into her neck, inhaling the scent of us and the many sols of our mating.

"I am here, my kahl." I stay there for a few moments, enjoying the feel of her before I rise with a sigh.

It is slow going, but I set about putting things right. I move quietly, not wanting to wake Donna. Once the room is somewhat presentable, I return to the sleeping cushion. Donna hasn't stirred. Gently, I lift her into my arms, cradling her against my chest. She mumbles something incoherent but doesn't wake.

Moving slowly, I carry her to the washroom. The bath is large enough for both of us, and I fill it with warm water, adding some soothing oils I find on a nearby shelf. Their scent reminds me of Donna's cottage, of comfort, and for a brief moment, I wonder if she'll want us to return there.

I never discussed this with her. I have enough credits to get somewhere else. A bigger place. One where she doesn't have to worry about a farm or animals. I also didn't tell her that while I was working on her homestead, I surveyed part of the soil, found traces of the ore. That she will have enough to survive on for a long time, if she chooses to give up on the farm.

I know she's been trying to think of a way to support herself. Saw how she worried about the bluebread she was making.

But she has ore. Donna doesn't need me or her farm.

The thought almost makes me stumble. It is hard pushing it away as I lower us both into the water. She doesn't need me. But I pray to the gods, that after this, after this claiming, she still wants me.

My throat is tight with this turmoil as her eyes flutter open briefly.

"Tovan?" Her voice is thick, husky with exhaustion.

"I'm here, lira'an." I press my lips against her forehead. "Rest." My treasure.

She nods, her eyes closing again as she relaxes against me. I begin to wash her with utmost care, my claws as gentle as I can manage as they glide over her skin.

Turning her so her back rests against my chest, I wash her arms, my claws sliding over them and down to her teats as I make my way down to—

I stop, core-rhythm rising in my chest.

"Gods," I whisper, because before me is something I didn't think I'd see.

There, etched into my mate's skin, is a series of carvings, a design that calls to me at the very core. *Kahl* sigils.

It's a Kari bonding mark. The symbol of our connection, etched permanently into her being. They say only the truest of mates bear *kahl* sigils, a blessing from the universe itself that we have found our home. My core-beat swells with a mixture of pride and awe.

Gently, I wash the sigils, using a single digit to trace their entirety. It is...beautiful. Just like my mate. Silently, I vow to always cherish and protect the precious gift the gods have given me.

Her.

Over the next few sols, I devote myself entirely to Donna's care. She drifts in and out of consciousness, her body recovering from the intensity of the rut. I ensure she eats when she's awake, help her wash, and hold her close as she sleeps.

As she begins to regain her strength, I see a new light in her eyes when she looks at me. A depth of emotion that mirrors what I feel for her. Something I never realized I was yearning so much to see.

One sol, as the star rises, painting the room in hues of gold and orange, Donna stirs beside me, her lashes fluttering open, those dark eyes, so full of life, meeting mine.

"Tovan?" she murmurs, her voice hoarse with sleep, but there's a smile playing on her lips, a hint of mischief in her gaze. "Is that you? Or am I still dreaming?"

I can't help the warmth that goes through me. I've never... I've never felt like this before. As if there'd always been a piece of me missing, and now I am complete. "It is me, lira'an," I whisper, my claw tracing the delicate curve of her cheek. "And this..." I lean down, my lips brushing against hers, "is no dream."

She sighs, a contented sound, and snuggles closer, her body fitting perfectly against mine, her warmth a haven I never want to leave.

"How long..." She murmurs into my chest. "How long has it been?"

"Six, maybe seven sols." My gaze traces the delicate contours of her face, memorizing every detail, every freckle, every curve.

"Seven days?" She sits up, a sudden panic in her eyes. "Oh Lord, my farm! My oogas! They must be..."

I chuckle, pulling her back down, my arms encircling her, holding her close. "Worry not, lira'an. Your farm is thriving. Arnak has been taking care of everything."

"Oh god, Arnak?" Her eyes are still wide. "He doesn't even know me. I'll have to pay him handsomely for—"

I growl. "You will do no such thing. He was honored to do it. You are his kahlesta after all. Worry not, I will reward him for his time."

She settles against me slightly. "Did you apologize to him?"

"For what?" I grunt, pressing my lips against her skin, my tongue flicking to sample a taste of her. She trembles, shuddering in my grasp.

"You almost attacked him at the conference center."

I stop moving, my nose still pressed into her soft neck.

There lies the proof of my bite. My claim on her and with her pressed against me like this, her scent, her sweetness, I can feel myself growing hard again. I want to claim her once more.

It's an effort to control it. My mate must rest. Recover.

I groan. "I was not in my senses. But yes, I did apologize."

"Good," she smiles into me. "Nevertheless, I'm glad you came to me instead."

I stiffen, my claw tangling in her thick coils. "You should have run, lira'an. I would have suffered…but if I had hurt you, I might as well have died."

She settles against me some more. For a moment, she says nothing. But then, "Tovan…I didn't run, because I'm tired of running." Then she looks up at me. "But this is real. I don't have to run anymore."

It's like a question. As if she needs me to confirm something, and as I press my lips against hers, I do.

"You are mine, Donna Johnson," I murmur against her lips, my voice rough with emotion, with a possessiveness that is no longer a threat, but a vow. "And I will never let you go."

She smiles against my lips. "Is that why you call me your lira'an? Your melody of the sun?"

I grunt. So she knows what it means. "Your voice…it's like the first dawn after a long, harsh cold. Warm, radiant, full of life. And you, lira'an…" I pull her closer, shifting so I fall between her thighs, my whole body lighting up as if I didn't just spend sols buried inside her. "You are like the star itself, Donna. A fiery heart that burns away the shadows, a light that guides me home."

A soft shiver goes through her as she watches me. There's a slow smile on her lips, and her body is lax, not an ounce of tension.

"I enjoy your warmth, lira'an."

Donna snorts but her soft smile is still there as she lifts a hand to trace patterns down my arm. "Don't you think you've had enough of that warmth to last you for a while now?"

I inhale sharply before I release a playful growl. Pinning her arms above her head, I lean in to her, letting her feel just how much I want her right now. I see the moment she senses it pressing between her thighs. The same moment her breath catches.

"Never," I whisper. "I will never have enough."

TOVAN

When Donna feels well enough to travel, I suggest returning to the farm. Her eyes light up at the mention of her homestead, and I'm reminded of how much the place means to her. We make the journey slowly. Instead of my grav-bike, I purchase a transport with a cab so she can ride in comfort.

The journey is short but there is no rush. It's just me, my *kahl*, and forever ahead of us.

Passing through the town, I see the looks the other Kari send our way.

Envy flickers in some eyes, a resigned acceptance in others. But there's also hope, a renewed sense of possibility that wasn't there before. They see us, Donna and me, two beings from different worlds, bound by a love that defies logic, and they see a reflection of their own deepest desires. I understand their longing, the ache of loneliness that has haunted our kind for so long.

I understand, because I, too, was once lost.

As we approach the farm, I feel a mix of emotions. This place holds so many memories now—our first meeting, the days spent working side by side, the growing attraction between us. And now, we return as mates.

But...how do I fit into this world she's created? Does she truly see me living here, in her lodge?

The transport slows to a stop in front of the cottage, its vibrant walls a beacon against the backdrop of the orange fields, and Donna turns to me.

"Welcome home, Tovan." Her smile is filled with a warmth that melts away my apprehension.

"Come on," she says, her hand clasped in mine as I open her door. "I'll show you where you can put your things."

We're walking down into the yard when movement catches my eye. A large male coming from the side of the cottage. The bale of grass feed he's balanced on his shoulder is slowly placed on the ground as he faces us.

"Good sol, kahlesta." Arnak's uncertainty is reflected in his grin. "Tovan." He dips his head.

"Arnak." Donna walks over to him and I watch her, awe in my eyes that this little female has turned my life completely around. I am no longer a lone male. I live on a farm now. I have a female. A mate. I have a life now. "Thank you so much for stepping in on the farm when we couldn't. You really didn't have to go through the trouble. I'm so sorry we had to burden you so."

Arnak's gaze shifts to me for a split click before he grins more naturally, displaying both his fangs. "It was no trouble, kahlesta. I will always be at your service."

Donna chuckles before turning toward the lodge. "Yeah, until you find your mate, I'm sure."

Arnak blinks so many times I think something is caught in his eyes. "My mate..."

Donna pauses and smiles, her gaze shifting to him once more. "You seem like a man with a good heart. I have a good feeling about this."

As she walks into the lodge Arnak turns his confused gaze to me. I shrug. "Believe her," I say. "My mate is wise."

He still has that stunned look on his face as I head in after my mate.

We're there for maybe half a sol when the others arrive.

Donna's friends—Catherine, Xarion, Varek, Eleanor, and Zynar all crowd into the small lodge. Their relief at seeing Donna safe and happy is palpable even though I remain tense. When Zynar and Varek Korruk pull me into a brotherly embrace, it feels like the world shifts once more on its axis.

In all my orbits, I cannot remember ever having a family such as this.

Arnak comes in and Donna serves everyone bluebread and "froot tee". Soon, the air fills with laughter and light-hearted conversation.

"Right, Tovan," the Saffion, Xarion, says, his ear tips twitching in humor, "I hope you're prepared for a lifetime of Donna's stubbornness and terrible jokes."

Donna feigns offense with an audible gasp, but her eyes sparkle with mirth. "My jokes are delightful, thank you very much."

I chuckle, my arm tightening around Donna's waist. "I find everything about Donna delightful."

The humans make sounds in their throats, with Catherine and Eleanor's pigments becoming increasingly red. I stare at them in alarm, but their mates don't seem anxious.

Arnak is the one who speaks. "I have never, once in my existence, heard Tovan speak like that." That makes the others laugh, but I don't care.

"I will say it again and again," I nuzzle Donna's ear. "My mate is delightful. I would savor her now if—"

Arnak, Xarion, and I'm sure some of the others groan before the whole room explodes with laughter.

But as the visit winds down, I notice a slight furrow in

Donna's brow. When her friends are preparing to leave, after Eleanor mentions something about her harvest coming in, Donna mentions, almost offhandedly, "I'm still trying to figure it all out, too, you know. Getting the farm to work, making ends meet."

There's a moment of concerned silence before Catherine speaks up. "You know we're here if you need anything, right?"

Donna nods. "Of course. Thank you."

After her companions and Arnak leave, I take a deep breath. It's time for a conversation I've been both anticipating and dreading. "Donna, there's something I need to tell you."

She stiffens almost immediately and I can't help but pull her into my arms. Walking backward with her against me, I settle onto a seat.

I take her claws in mine, marveling at how small and delicate they seem compared to mine. "I...I have enough credits. More than enough. I can take care of everything—the farm, our future, whatever you need or want."

Even with her back pressed into me, I can see that her expression becomes unreadable, and I feel a twinge of anxiety. Have I offended her? Overstepped?

"That's...that's very generous," she says slowly, but her voice is uncharacteristically neutral. "But I don't need much to—"

"It doesn't matter how much you need. I have more than enough. More than *I* need."

She frowns now, tilting her head so she can meet my gaze. "Just how much are we talking here."

I grimace. But she is my mate. No use hiding this, even if it makes me embarrassed. "Enough to purchase as far as your eyes can see on these plains."

Her eyes bug out. "What? How?"

I look away. This has always made me uncomfortable. It's why I live in the nestkans. To feel more normal. It's why Arnak and I live in the town. Not many beings…not many beings have the assets we do.

"Prospecting is good when you know what you're looking for." I give her a tight grin and Donna spins in my arms. Her soft claws come up to frame my face.

"You're meaning to tell me that I thought you were a hobo when you're really a prince?"

"Hm? Hoh-no?" It must be my reaction that makes her snort and before I know it, she's laughing. Must have gotten it wrong. That reminds me. I have to contact that male about upgrading my translator.

"Hobo," Donna says, a smile still on her lips. "What on earth were you doing working on my farm when you don't have to work at all?"

I look deep into her eyes, because she already knows the answer to that, but if she needs, I will tell her again. "I couldn't be away from you."

She softens, leaning into me. But then she sobers a bit, too. "That's great and all." She becomes thoughtful. "But I've spent so long being independent. It feels strange to rely solely on you. I still need my own thing, too, you know."

I shake my head. "You don't have to rely solely on me, lira'an. And you don't need to worry about the farm, either. There's something else I discovered while working here—there is ore on your land."

Her eyes widen. "You're joking."

"I speak truth. You have valuable ore. But even without that, you have another incredible thing, my sweet." My voice dips as does my gaze to her lips. "Your voice."

Donna blushes, I can feel the warmth go through her a moment before she tries to pull away. My arms tighten around her. "It's the truth," I say.

"Oh, Tovan, you're just biased because you love me."

"No," I insist. "Your singing is truly extraordinary. It would draw crowds, I'm certain of it. If you want, I know just the person to contact. Someone I've been meaning to reach out to anyway—a bounty hunter who can fix my translator chip and get your voice broadcasted through the servers."

Donna stops trying to get out of my grasp. "A bounty hunter? Tovan—"

"He's a good being. Honorable."

"Mmmmhm," she intones, but she's studying me. For a moment, she says nothing. And then. "You really think people would want to hear me sing?"

I cup her face gently in my claws. "I know they would. When you sing, it's like the stars themself pause to listen."

She leans into my touch, her eyes glistening. "Nobody's ever...you're the first person..."

"Then those others were fools."

We sit there for a moment, just breathing each other in. Then Donna pulls back slightly, a determined look in her eyes. "I think...I think I'd like to try. The singing, I mean. To share my music with others. But I want to do it alongside working on the farm, at least for now. This place...it's more than just land to me. It's where I found myself. Where I found you."

I feel a surge of pride. "Whatever you decide, I support."

"And the ore...leave it." Then she chuckles. "It's not like I have kids or anything to pass it down to, but—"

I growl, my claws shifting to grip her behind as I pull her into me. "You want young?" I dip my lips to her ear. "I'd be very happy to oblige."

Donna slaps me, a playful tap that doesn't even sting. "Now you stop that. I'm too old for such talking."

"You are not," I dip my face into her hair, inhaling her. Rearing younglings would simply be a bonus, not a necessity.

"My time has passed." The way her voice drops, the way her whole body seems to sag with those words makes me draw back so I can see her properly.

"You know…" I hedge. "We can fix that."

Donna's brow furrows. "Fix what?"

"If you want young, there are many options we can take."

She stares at me for a long moment. "I never…I stopped considering that for myself a long time ago."

I tug her toward me. "This isn't your homeworld, lira'an. If you want young, we will make it so." Then I blow a breath through my nostrils. "You will have a long time to think about it. We Kari age very slowly."

"Xarion mentioned something about that," she whispers into my shoulder, and I can tell she's thinking about everything I've said.

I nod, dipping my face into her hair. "I am ready to give you young whenever you want."

That makes a laugh rumble through her. "You're always ready."

"Mm," I growl. "I'm ready now, too."

My shaft jerks, making her aware of its presence, and Donna jumps. With a chuckle, she distances herself, eyes wild with mirth. "No."

But she shouldn't have run. Because now I'm going to catch her.

She must see the change in my eyes because she squeals and heads toward the one place where she will definitely be claimed. The bedroom.

Whether she knows it or not, her body and her core-beat have already decided that I will take her this cycle. And as I rise and head after my mate, I know I will take her over and over and over again, until she cries my name, until the stars align, until she knows without a doubt that she will always be mine.

EPILOGUE ONE

DONNA

"I just need an upgrade," I hear Tovan say on his comm as I head into the kitchen. He's been trying to get in contact with this bounty hunter guy all day and finally, the ping's gone through. I can't help but feel nervous though. A bounty hunter? Tovan's a good guy. How does he even know someone like that?

"Why don't you go through the usual route, Kamesh?" The voice is rough, guttural, and when I pass by again, I'm sure I catch a glimpse of a metal mask, only the dude's green eyes visible.

Now, what in God's good name…? I want to tell Tovan to forget it, but he's adamant that his translator requires renewal and this is the best source to get it through. Something about the guy being the one to upload English on Hudo's servers in the first place. How or why a bounty hunter would do that, I don't know.

What if it was because he was hunting a human and needed better coverage of the language?

"You know as well as I do that you're the best source for this sort of tech. The council's language implants take forever to update."

The bounty hunter grunts.

"I'll pay you double."

Silence on the other line.

"Triple," Tovan presses. "And there is something else. My mate…she sings beautiful melodies—"

There's a low growl. "Not interested, Kamesh. Find someone else."

Even from where I am in the kitchen, I can tell that the bounty hunter is about to hang up and I hear Tovan's exasperated breath. The fact he's trying to get the guy to help me, too, with broadcasting my songs, melts my heart. After having no one believe in my voice to having such support touches something deep. The fact that he's being turned down actually makes me ache because he's trying so hard.

Dropping the kitchen towel, I wipe my hands on my skirt as I walk out to Tovan.

"It's alright dear," I say, my voice making him look over his shoulder. "It's alright. We'll find another way." I smile at Tovan before my gaze shifts to his comm, only to find intense green eyes staring back at me from beneath a metal mask. The bounty hunter is staring into my soul.

I can't look away. It isn't fear. I don't know what it is. Awareness?

Tovan releases a breath. "Urgmental…I suppose we shall do business some other time. When you're more…agreeable."

Tovan shifts his claw to end the transmission when the bounty hunter speaks.

"Who is that?"

We both stiffen. Tovan's brow tightens slightly as he sits up straighter. "My mate." The way he speaks, his voice has changed completely, and I catch a glimpse of that male who fought to protect me, fought to get to me.

"You didn't say she was human."

My hand slides to Tovan's shoulder, squeezing slightly.

Now what does this stranger mean by that? Obviously, he has an interest in humans. If what Tovan said is true about him uploading English on the servers, perhaps we should have tried to discover exactly why *before* we contacted him.

I'm suddenly feeling unsure and I squeeze Tovan's shoulder again. He stands from where he was sitting, blocking me from view of the bounty hunter's piercing gaze.

"What does it matter, Urgmental?"

I can hear the male grunt, almost as if he's laughing. "You know, you're one of the few that call me by that name."

Tovan is still stiff. "It is your name, is it not."

The bounty hunter grunts again before a beat of silence passes. I strain my ears to hear, wondering if he's still on the line when he suddenly speaks again.

"I'll be at your lodge in the next sol. I'll bring your translator upgrade. And don't worry, no charge."

My frown increases when a second later there's an audible click. Ping ended.

Tovan is standing staring at the device in his claw when I walk around to face him.

"Tovan?"

His gaze shifts to mine.

"Who is this male?"

His gaze shifts back to the comm as if he can't quite believe what just happened.

"He is...complicated. He's known for being unpredictable, but he's not inherently dangerous. At least, not to those he doesn't consider a threat."

I swallow hard, my mind racing. "And us? Does he consider us a threat?"

Tovan shakes his head. "No, I don't believe so. If anything, I think we've piqued his curiosity."

A shiver runs down my spine at his words. Curiosity from a bounty hunter doesn't sound particularly comforting. But then a thought occurs to me, and I feel a small wave of relief wash over me.

"Well," I say, trying to inject some optimism into my tone, "at least he doesn't know where we live, right? So maybe it'll be alright. We don't have to meet him if we don't want to."

Tovan's expression grows somber. "He'll find us."

Because he's a frickin' bounty hunter. Oh shit. I feel my heart rate quicken, but as I look at Tovan, I see determination in his eyes and some of the anxiety seeps away. This is Tovan. He won't let anything happen to me, and I won't let anything happen to him.

The next day dawns bright and clear, and after a night of thinking through the possibilities, I wake with a determination myself. We have a gun now, a 'blaster' as Tovan calls it. After that stranger's visit and what he almost did, we thought it best to get some protection. I've never fired a gun in my life, but Tovan has. If this bounty hunter wants to find us and start trouble, then he will be surprised when we won't make it easy for him.

As I'm sweeping the floor in the front room, movement outside the window catches my eye. My heart nearly stops as I see three vehicles pulling up to the farm. They're sleek and look fast. Definitely not Xarion, Arnak, or any of my other friends.

When the first vehicles stop and a tall figure hops out, my heart does a big wallop in my chest. Even from this distance, I can see the glint of the metal mask, those piercing green eyes scanning the surroundings. Urgmental. He's found us, just as Tovan said he would.

And he's brought friends?

My first instinct is to run and get Tovan, but before I can move, I see him striding out to meet the bounty hunter. They stand facing each other in silence, an unspoken tension crackling in the air between them.

Grabbing the gun from where it's strapped up, hidden underneath the table, I hide it in my skirt as I step out behind him.

There's a slight cool breeze, one that only highlights the tension but doesn't give me any idea as to what's about to happen. I step outside to stand beside Tovan when the bounty hunter's eyes meet mine. I feel a chill. I'm about to tell Tovan we should head back inside when movement from the vehicle catches my eye again.

This time, I freeze. Because a young Black woman hops out after Urgmental. She's human, unmistakably so, and in her arms is a small, wiggling blue child. As blue as the alien in the metal mask. After the woman comes another child of a different species with little antennae atop her head.

The bounty hunter. He brought...he brought his family?

Before I can process this unexpected sight, the doors of the other vehicles open. From one emerges another couple—a blonde woman holding another blue baby, accompanied by a tall, scowling alien. From the last vehicle, a redheaded woman steps out, her hand clasped tightly in that of yet another big, blue dude.

My mind reels, trying to make sense of what I'm seeing. Humans. Aliens. Babies that look like a blend of both. It's like something out of a dream—or perhaps a vision of a future I never dared to imagine.

I step forward without even realizing. All my attention is focused on the gathering in front of my home. Tovan steps up beside me, his arm sliding around my waist with a touch that grounds me.

The Black woman smiles at me, bouncing the infant in her arms before her smile freezes on her lips when she takes me and Tovan in. Her gaze slides to the bounty hunter. "Ka'Cit, I told you not to scare them!" Her whisper is low but loud enough that we hear anyway.

The bounty hunter tilts his head her way. "I didn't. I promise. I was quite friendly."

She laughs and steps forward. "Hi, you probably didn't expect to see so many of us, but after Ka'Cit told us there are other humans out here, we had to come visit. I'm Nia." She grins, still bouncing the infant who takes that moment to coo. He's a big boy, well-fed, strong, with his momma's face and his father's green eyes. He stretches for me with a coo and I have no choice but to release the gun in my skirt as I reach for him.

The weapon drops and they don't even flinch.

"Oh hello!" I say to the baby, my mind still struggling to catch up with all this.

He clutches my cheeks in his little palms and coos.

Behind Nia, the bounty hunter, Ka'Cit, comes closer. Crouching, he lifts the other child, who smiles at me, too.

"So," he says, his voice just as gravelly as it was over the comm, "you're the one with the beautiful melodies."

My mouth falls open. Damn, Donna Johnson is speechless. "How did you…"

I glance over at Tovan. "Did you send him…"

Tovan is glaring at the bounty hunter. "He hacked my comm."

Nia grimaces before she jams an elbow into the bounty hunter's side. "Ka'Citttt."

"I had to be sure it was safe to bring you here," he says to her before he shrugs, unapologetic. "I heard the melody he recorded." His gaze meets mine. "It will be well received. There are already orders for more of your recordings."

"Wh…what?"

My eyebrows are high on my forehead as the other two couples come closer.

"Hi, nice to meet you. I'm Lauren."

I nod, not trusting my voice just yet.

Lauren gestures to the male at her back. "This is Riv. Don't mind him," she says, jerking her thumb towards the male. "He's always grumpy at first."

As if to stop himself from scowling, Riv gives me a smile that looks like a grimace.

The blue child in her arms gurgles happily, reaching out towards me with tiny hands, too. I can't resist and soon I have two bouncing babies in my arms and a heart that is swelling so much it's becoming overfull.

"And this is Cleo and Sohut," Lauren gestures to the other couple, who also come closer, the female waving and the male dipping his head in greeting.

As introductions and lighthearted greetings are made, I can't believe what's happening.

"This is a delightful surprise. Why don't we all go inside?" I suggest, finding my voice at last. "I've got some fresh bluebread, and I'm sure we have a lot to talk about."

"Bluebread?" Nia grins. "Sounds yum."

As we make our way into the house, I can almost feel the intensity of Tovan's gaze as he watches me balance the babies. I talk to them and laugh, marveling at their little alien-human traits, and soon my little cottage is packed full again with strangers that might actually become family.

It's a tight fit with all of us, but I make it work. As I serve the food and drinks, Nia, Lauren, and Cleo tell me how they found their mates. They live half a day's travel away and mentioned that there was a rumor of more humans arriving on Hudo.

However, they'd thought the new humans were slaves and had been searching the underground networks to no avail. I tell them about New Horizons and how this is all voluntary, much to everyone's relief.

"So, Kamesh," the bounty hunter says, addressing Tovan,

"you wanted an upgrade for your translator?" He slides a device across the table to Tovan. "Here you go."

Tovan meets his gaze. "Appreciate it. How many credits do I owe you?"

I can't see the bounty hunter's face but I can hear his growl. "I don't charge family."

The word drops like a weight in the entire room, a moment before my heart gets light. Family. Something I never thought I'd ever have again.

"Family," Tovan repeats.

"You are mated to a human, Kamesh." The bounty hunter says. "We're all connected now."

Nia and the other women nod, a hint of approval in their eyes.

Tovan's gaze shifts to mine and I can tell he's wondering if I want this. I nod and he visibly relaxes, his shoulders releasing some of the tension I didn't realize was there.

"Good." Nia takes the lead. "We'll start with upgrading Tovan's translator. Then we'll work on getting your voice out there. Small steps, but important ones."

My gaze shoots to her. "My voice...you mentioned something about orders."

Nia nods, a gentle smile playing on her lips. "Ka'Cit's got some contacts that are willing to pay a lot of credits to hear you sing."

"What?" I almost can't believe it.

Nia nods and Lauren pipes in. "It's not just them, us too. What I wouldn't give to have some tracks of songs from Earth. And your *voice!*" She does a chef's kiss that makes me chuckle even as I'm blushing inside.

Cleo chimes in too. "Your songs can help others see the value in humans. To show that we're not just some primitive species to be exploited or ignored."

I didn't even consider that. Heck, I didn't consider anyone except Tovan ever hearing me sing.

A mix of excitement and trepidation swirls in my chest.

"No pressure," Nia says. "I know how hard it is just getting settled in this new life." She grins at her children who are currently climbing her mate like he's a jungle gym. "Especially while raising a family."

As the evening winds down, our guests start preparing to leave. The bounty hunter—Ka'Cit, I remind myself—helps Riv gather their children, who have fallen asleep. Cleo and Lauren collect their things, exchanging warm smiles with us.

Nia approaches me as the others are heading out. She pulls me into a gentle hug, surprising me with the gesture. "Thank you for welcoming us into your home," she says as she pulls back.

I smile, feeling a warmth spread through my chest. "Thank you for coming. You all have such beautiful families," I say, glancing at the others as they make their way outside.

Nia's eyes soften, a hint of moisture gathering at the corners. "I never thought it would happen, you know," she confides. "When we adopted our daughter, I thought that was all we'd have. But life has a way of surprising you."

My curiosity piques at the mention of adoption. "You adopted?"

Of course, they did. The child doesn't exactly look like either of them, but apart from the appearance, one would never know. They love that girl just as they love their biological son. That just tells me they're good people.

Nia nods, a fond smile playing on her lips. "It's a long story. I'll tell you more about it next time we visit, if you'd like."

"I'd love that."

As their vehicles drive away, Tovan pulls me into his arms. "That was…a lot, my kahl. I am sorry."

I lean back into him, smiling. "I liked it. Back on Earth, I grew up with a big family. The house was always full. Family. Friends. Neighbors. Cousins playing. Gramps sitting on the porch talking about music. Ma in the kitchen cooking. My brother sneaking bites of food from the pot…" I trail off, letting the memories wash over me.

We stand in comfortable silence for a moment, watching the sun go down. Finally, Tovan speaks, his voice soft and filled with emotion.

"Lira'an," he pauses.

"Mm?"

"Seeing all of them today, with their families…it made me think."

I tighten his arms around me. "About what?"

"About us. About our future." He pauses again. "I know we've talked about younglings before, and I understand…I understand your concern. But I want you to know that there are other options. We could adopt, too."

My breath catches in my throat. The idea of adoption hadn't really occurred to me until I saw Nia. Seeing her daughter, a spark of possibility ignited within me. Maybe that dream isn't dead and maybe…

I swallow hard, turning in Tovan's arms to face him.

"Is it that *you* want a child?" I whisper.

He shakes his head. "I am content to be selfish and have your complete attention for the rest of my sols. But I saw the way you held those younglings. I've never seen that sort of warmth in your eyes before. It is a different warmth from the one you offer me."

I blink, forcing away whatever emotion is threatening to rise. He can see through me so easily.

"I want to build a life with you," he continues. "Whatever that looks like. If that means adopting a youngling, then I will do it ."

Tears prick at my eyes as I lean into his touch. "I love you too," I murmur. Because all those words, that's what he's saying. That he loves me. Truly loves me. "And I...I think I'd like that. To explore the possibility, at least."

Tovan's face breaks into a wide grin.

Closing my eyes, I lean into my mate, my *kahl*, eager to see what tomorrow will bring.

EPILOGUE TWO

THE YOUNGLING CENTER

DONNA

The morning dawns with a peculiar stillness, the kind that settles over momentous days. I stand at our bedroom window, watching the first hints of orange streak across Hudo's sky, my heart thrumming with anticipation. Today is the day. After three months of preparation, paperwork, and proving our worthiness to the adoption council, we're finally heading to the Youngling Center.

"Lira'an?" Tovan's voice, still rough with sleep, draws my attention from the window. He's propped up on one elbow, golden eyes searching my face. "You're up early."

I try for a smile, but my nerves make it wobble. "Couldn't sleep anymore." Moving away from the window, I perch on the edge of the bed. "What if none of them like us, Tovan?"

His large claw finds mine, engulfing it completely. The familiar warmth of his touch grounds me, as it always does.

"That is not possible," he says, gaze moving through mine.

"You have enough warmth in your life-organ to fill this entire farm."

"But what if—" I start, but he sits up fully, pulling me against his chest.

"No more what-ifs, my kahl. Today, we go where the fates are leading us."

The journey to the Youngling Center takes nearly three hours by hover-transport. I spend most of it with my gaze out the window, watching the landscape change from our rural farmlands to the bustling outskirts of a city. Tovan uses one claw to steer, the other resting on my thigh. Now and then, he squeezes gently, his eyes flicking to the side, to where I sit with my hands clenched in my lap.

"Tell me again what Nia said."

Tovan squeezes my thigh again, sending reassurance my way. "She said that when they went to adopt their youngling, they too, were nervous. But the moment they saw her, everything else faded away. The core-beat will know."

I nod, twisting my hands in my lap. God, I've never been more nervous. "And the bounty hunter's contact at the Center? They're expecting us?"

"Yes, lira'an. Everything is arranged."

The Youngling Center rises before us, a sprawling complex of interconnected domes. Unlike the stark government buildings we've become familiar with in this process, this place is painted in soft colors—blues and greens that remind me of the ocean. Gardens surround the building, and I can see small figures darting between the plants, their laughter carried away by the wind.

My throat tightens as Tovan lands the transport. Children. So many children, all shapes, sizes, and colors. Some purple and pink like Tovan, others with different hues entirely. Some with extra limbs, others with fewer than expected. All of them precious. All of them waiting for someone to choose them.

"Ready?" Tovan asks, his claw finding mine again.

I squeeze his fingers as I look at him. I've never been more sure about the person I want to share this with. Through the entire process, Tovan's made me feel like I will be the best mother. But after giving up on that idea so long, it's now the scariest thing I will face. "Ready."

The entrance hall is bright and welcoming, with murals depicting various species living in harmony. A tall, willowy being with iridescent skin greets us, their movements fluid like water. "Welcome to the Youngling Center. I am Caretaker Zyl'a. You must be the Kamesh unit?"

"Yes," Tovan confirms, his professional tone barely masking his own nervousness. "We have an appointment."

Zyl'a's face ripples with what might be a smile. "Of course. Ka'Cit Urgmental spoke highly of you both. Please, follow me."

We're led through corridors that echo with distant chatter and laughter. Everywhere I look, there are signs of life and love—artwork pinned to walls, tiny handprints in rainbow colors, toys tucked into corners. This isn't an institution; it's a home.

For a moment, I wonder if the child will even like it on my farm out in the middle of nowhere.

"We have thirty-seven younglings in our care," Zyl'a explains as we walk. "Ages range from infancy to twelve orbit cycles. Some are here temporarily while their families navigate difficult circumstances. Others..." They pause, something sad flickering across their features. "Others are waiting to find a new family unit."

We stop at a large window overlooking an indoor play area. My breath catches. Below us, children of various species play together, their differences forgotten in the universal language of childhood joy. A small blue girl helps a younger child with tentacles build a tower. Two identical furry children chase each other around climbing frames. A tiny being that seems to be made entirely of glass reads a book to a group of what looks like mesmerized toddlers.

I swallow hard and Tovan pulls me into his side in that way he always does. Reminding me he's there. Grounding me. Reminding me I'm no longer alone. On my chest, the kahl sigils thrum with his proximity and I release some of the tension with a smooth breath.

"Would you like to meet some of them?" Zyl'a asks gently.

It's only then that I realize I'm pressed against the glass like an eager child myself. Stepping back, I smooth my dress. "Yes. Yes, please."

The playroom is warm and filled with the kind of controlled chaos only children can create. As we enter, several little ones look up. A few of the older children whisper among themselves, pointing at me—probably because they've never seen a human before.

"Younglings," Zyl'a calls out, their voice carrying easily across the room. "We have visitors today. This is Tovan and Donna Kamesh."

A chorus of greetings rings out, some in Standard, others in languages my translator doesn't quite catch. I lift my hand in a nervous wave, my heart already melting at their eager faces. Glancing at Tovan, his warm eyes are on me. They crinkle the moment I look back at him.

"Let's go find our chid," he whispers.

My heart warms and swells so much it feels like I might combust.

As we enter the play area, several children rush over. It catches me by surprise. I thought they'd be cautious, distrustful, shy—or maybe that's just my own experiences on Earth coloring my outlook. These children are different. They're full of questions about who I am and where I'm from. I try to answer as nicely as possible, leaving out the whole abduction and hardship part. I tell them about my farm instead. They're beautiful, all of them, with their different colors and forms and ways of moving.

We spend the next half hour walking among them, watching them play. A group of green willowy children invite us to see their art project—splashes of color that catch and reflect light. The two furry siblings show off their climbing abilities on the play structure. A small aquatic child demonstrates how she can create bubble shapes in her water tank.

But as time passes, something begins to gnaw at me. These children are wonderful, creative, full of life and joy. I smile and nod and participate, but with each interaction, the feeling grows stronger. That spark, that instant connection I was so sure would happen…it…it isn't there.

My steps slow as I watch a caretaker help a young one with their meal. Shouldn't I feel something more? That overwhelming sense of rightness I felt when I first met Tovan? These children deserve someone who feels that way about them. Someone who knows, deep in their soul, that this is their child.

I glance at Tovan, who's letting a tiny reptilian child examine his claws with scientific curiosity. What if I don't connect with any of them? What if this whole idea was a mistake? The thought sits heavy in my chest, making it hard to breathe.

Zyl'a must notice something in my expression because she touches my arm gently. "Would you like to see another part of the center?" she asks softly.

I nod, not trusting my voice. If I open my mouth, I'm afraid some other sound than words will come out. A whine, maybe, or even a choked sob.

As we walk away from the playroom, I try to push down the growing heaviness in my chest. I should be grateful, still, shouldn't I? How many humans get to experience what I have? Freedom among the stars. Peace after so much chaos. A mate who loves me completely, unconditionally. I have more than I ever dreamed possible back on Earth. Maybe this is asking too much of the universe.

"Lira'an?" Tovan's hand finds mine, and I force a smile, brightening my features. His concerned frown doesn't shift. It sometimes still surprises me how well he's gotten to know me. "We can do this another time, if you like."

My heart heaves. He's giving me an out. A reason to leave this place and never return, if I want to. Always if I want to. But what about what he wants? And me...I *do* want this. I've wanted this more than anything for as long as I can remember. I just...

I want it to feel right.

Zyl'a leads us down a quieter hallway where the sounds of play fade into a gentle hush. The air here is different—warmer, softer somehow. She pauses at a doorway, her expression gentle but unreadable.

"Take your time," she says, and steps back.

I hesitate for just a moment, then step forward, the doors sliding open to reveal a...nursery. The room is bathed in soft, golden light. Several small curved vessels float gently above the floor. Cots. They line the walls, each surrounded by quietly humming monitors. But I barely notice any of it because my eyes are drawn immediately to one cot near the window.

I move toward it without conscious thought, pulled by something I can't explain. My feet carry me forward until I'm looking down at a tiny infant wrapped in pale, silvery fabric. Her skin is the color of twilight, delicate ridges along her temples catching the light. She's...perfect. Completely, utterly perfect.

And suddenly I can't breathe for an entirely different reason.

The baby's eyes flutter open, revealing irises the deep purple of evening stars. She looks right at me, and in that moment, everything else falls away. All my doubts, all my fears—they dissolve like morning mist in sunlight.

"Can I…?" My voice is a choked sound as I whisper, looking back at Zyl'a, who nods with a knowing smile.

My hands tremble slightly as I reach down, remembering everything I know about supporting a baby's head. She's so small, so delicate, but as I lift her, she feels solid and real in my arms. Warm. Present. She makes a soft cooing sound that brings tears to my eyes.

Tovan moves closer, his presence warm against my back, and I feel his breath catch as the baby turns those twilight eyes to study him. She reaches up with one tiny hand, fingers splayed as if trying to touch his face. Without hesitation, he lowers his head, letting her tiny fingers brush against his cheek.

"Hello, little one," he rumbles softly, and she makes another happy sound that seems to vibrate through my entire being.

I begin to hum without thinking—Rock-a-bye Baby. The baby watches me intently, and I feel Tovan's arms wrap around us both, creating a perfect circle of warmth and belonging.

"She doesn't have a name yet," Zyl'a says quietly from the doorway. "She came to us two cycles ago."

"Mira," I whisper almost immediately. My gaze shifts to Tovan and his eyes crinkle again.

"Mira," he nods.

"Mira," I whisper again. It feels right on my tongue, like it was waiting there all along.

The baby—Mira—reaches up again, this time catching one of Tovan's claws in her tiny fist. She holds on tight, making those soft, happy sounds, and I watch as my mate's expression melts into something I've never seen before. Something tender and fierce all at once.

When our eyes meet again, I know he feels it too. This rightness. This certainty. Like the universe has been guiding us here all along, from that first moment out in the fields where we first met, through all the moments between then and now, to this perfect instance.

"There are data tabs to complete," Zyl'a says gently. "And processes we'll need to follow…"

"Whatever it takes," Tovan says, his voice firm but gentle. "She's ours."

Mira falls asleep in my arms, one hand still gripping Tovan's claw, the other curled against my chest right over my heart. Looking down at her perfect face, I understand now why none of the other children sparked that connection. They weren't her. They weren't our daughter.

Everything we've been through, every step of this journey— it was all leading us here, to this moment, to her. To our family becoming complete.

"Yes," I whisper, leaning back against Tovan as tears of joy slip down my cheeks. "She's ours."

AFTERWORD

❀☆❀☆❀

Dear Reader,

Thank you for joining Donna and Tovan on their journey to finding each other. When I first started writing their story, I had no idea how deeply it would touch me, or how these characters would become so real in my heart. What began as a tale about stubborn human and a besotted alien male grew into something more—a story about finding family in unexpected places, about healing, and about the kind of love that transcends boundaries.

Inspiration came from my own journey from fear to trust, from isolation to belonging. Of finding love in unexpected places, of building a family that doesn't fit conventional molds, of learning to trust again after—and even during—hardship.

For those wondering about Donna, Tovan, and little Mira's future adventures—yes, there are more stories to tell. Their journey is far from over. But for now, thank you for letting me share this story with you. Thank you for opening your heart to a human woman, a Kari warrior, and their perfect purple baby. Most of all, thank you for believing in the kind of love that can bridge the distance between stars.

Until next time, happy reading and may your life be filled with love – alien or otherwise!

🖤 AG

P.S. For those curious about the inspiration behind Mira's name —in several Earth languages, it means "wonder" or "peace." In Kari, it means "beloved star." Sometimes the perfect name finds its own way home.

ALSO BY AG WILDE

Xul

Series Title: Captured by Aliens

Athena wakes up in hell.

Well…it's an alien slave ship, but it might as well be hell because she only has three choices.

Mate. Become a sex slave. Or be killed.

Great options.

Desperate for freedom, a chance for survival is presented in the handsome rogue alien called Xul.

But Xul is caught up in problems of his own and a mission he cannot afford to let fail—one that could be easily compromised if he dared open his heart.

That doesn't leave her with many options and it doesn't help that she finds him utterly frustrating...

...and strong, hot, irresistible…

She shouldn't really be thinking about him like that. Should she?

Other books in the series: Crex, Yce, Kyris, Kyro

Ajos

Series Title: The Restitution [Spinoff from Captured by Aliens]

She didn't move to the big city just to be kidnapped by aliens.

That wasn't even possible...

Right?

WRONG.

When Kerena wakes up, she's not on Earth anymore.

Heck, she's not even in the same galaxy, and the face hovering so close she can make out every detail? That face is definitely...not...human.

But before she can really figure out what's going on, Kerena realizes she's caught in the middle of a war—one she was thrust into as soon as she was ripped from Earth.

She's surrounded by aliens in a rebellion, but there's one—the one with the strange golden eyes, minty-teal skin, and rippling muscles—that holds her attention.

His presence is magnetic and his heated gaze makes something stir deep within her.

He's battling something that has nothing to do with the war and his warning that she should stay away does not go unheeded.

He's a dangerous rebel fighter. She gets that. So...why is he still hovering so close? And why is he growling at everyone that so much as looks in her direction?

Most of all, why does he keep looking at her like she belongs to ... HIM?

Other books in the series: V'Alen

Riv's Sanctuary
Series Title: Riv's Sanctuary

Abducted from Earth over a year ago, Lauren spent most of that time getting accustomed to her new life as one of the "animals" in an alien zoo.

When she's sold by the zookeeper, her life takes a turn she wasn't expecting. She has no idea where she'll end up till she's brought to a sanctuary owned by a tall blue hunk of an alien called Riv.

Riv's life is quiet and peaceful in a place as far away from civilization as he can manage. So when an annoying chatterbox of a human ends up on his doorstep, he's less than pleased. The human disrupts his life and his solitude and he can't wait to get rid of her.

He's not interested in helping her, and he's definitely not interested in love.

Except…she's managed to wheedle her way in and suddenly those barriers around his heart don't seem so strong anymore.

He has two options: Let her go.

Or let her in.

Other books in the series: Sohut's Protection, Ka'Cit's Haven

Arrival

Series Title: Captured Earth

Adira

The machines came, and they trampled us all.

I have nothing left. No family. No friends. No home.

They harvest us. They breed us. They feed from us…

There is no hope…Not until one fateful moment when my eyes open and I see something streaking across the skies.

What appears is like a demon before my eyes…

But can they be worse than the evil already upon us?

I will just have to wait and see.

Fer'ro

Sailing across the stars for what feels like eons…we have followed our enemy to a little blue planet.

We had wanted to arrive before them…now I think we may be too late.

But when we kill the first Scrit and I see the being drowning within its depths, I know I have to save it.

And *it*…turns out to be a *her*. **A female.**

This planet has hope yet. I will save her and her kind.

…Little do I know…she's the one who ends up saving me instead.

Dark. Steamy. Gritty. A thrilling romance intertwined in a plot that will give you chills.

Other books in the series: Base Zero, Cataclysm, War

Claiming His Mate
Series Title: Fated Mates of the Atari

When I get a once-in-a-lifetime chance to go on a luxury space cruise, I jump at it.

This cruise is the beginning of something amazing, and nothing is going to stop me from going.

But when things go wrong shortly after departure, it's clear I have made a mistake.

Suddenly thrown into a world where I have no way of defending myself, the last thing I expect is an Atari warrior coming to my rescue.

This cruise has been full of surprises…but the Atari is the biggest one of all.

He's tall, growly, possessive, and he sends my pulse into overdrive with just the slightest look.

Why the heck is my body reacting this way to this stranger?

And did he just declare that I am his mate?

Other books in the series: Craving His Mate, Fighting for His Mate, Guarding His Mate

Outlaw

Series Title: The Midnight Seven

Our colony is dying.
We're out of time. Out of hope. Out of options—*unless I risk everything on him.*
The outlaw.
One not bound by rules or mercy.
With lives at stake, I offer him a deal he can't refuse. And one I can't go back on.
Bargaining with a demon to save my people, only time will tell if I've sealed their fate, or found their salvation.
And mine.
Find on Amazon

An Alien for the Farm

Series Title: A New Home

Eleanor
I thought starting over on this quiet farm would finally give me a chance to heal. But the moment that towering alien walks through my door, I know real trouble has found me. Zynar is all corded muscle and raw masculinity—nothing like the weak men who've used me. Worse, this alien hunk stirs feelings in me

I swore were long dead. Each time his intense yellow gaze locks onto mine, my resolve weakens. I tell myself to keep my distance, that this attraction can only lead to heartbreak. But as Zynar proves himself gentle yet strong, passionate yet restrained, I start to crave the pleasure his touch promises to unlock in me once more.

Zynar
From the moment I lay eyes on the delicate creature named Eleanor, my core-beat quickens in a way I hadn't thought possible. This fragile flower survived abduction and abuse, yet her spirit remains unbroken. I want nothing more than to make her feel safe and cherished. But this female threatens to expose vulnerabilities I've long tried to bury. As a displaced Kari without a homeworld, getting close means entertaining the thought of something I never thought possible. But keeping my distance is torture. How can I resist a female who awakens feelings I swore were dead?

Other books in the series: An Alien for Her Heart, An Alien for the Future

***

Scan the QR code to view all books

ABOUT THE AUTHOR

A. G. Wilde is an avid reader, a gamer, a lover of all things space, alien, and sci-fi.

She is addicted to intense romance, irresistible heroes, and deliciously naughty things.

❉☆❉☆❉

facebook.com/agwilde

instagram.com/authoragwilde

tiktok.com/@authoragwilde

x.com/authoragwilde

bookbub.com/profile/a-g-wilde

amazon.com/author/agwilde